"A thrilling and satisfying read…highly recommend."

~K.C. Finn for Readers' Favorite

FOOL'S GOLD

ALSO AVAILABLE BY BRENDA LYNE

NOVELS

Charlie's Mirror

Sister Lost

The Thirteenth Cabin: A Raegan O'Rourke Mystery

Angel Baby: A Raegan O'Rourke Mystery

SHORT STORY COLLECTIONS

Bourbon & Burlap

FOOL'S GOLD

A Raegan O'Rourke Mystery

BRENDA LYNE

Cover design by Susan@yuneepix.com
Book design by Jennifer DeVries

Published in the United States by Brenda Lyne Books

Printed in the United States

ISBN: 978-1-7376133-9-8

First edition: September 2024

brendalyne.com

For my cousin Mark. I'm sorry you had to leave us so soon.
You are – and always will be – deeply loved.

PART 1:
RAEGAN & JESSE

Tuesday, July 20, 2021

CHAPTER 1

The aroma of fresh-brewed coffee drew me grudgingly out of unconsciousness. I breathed deep, yawned, and untangled myself from my blankets without opening my eyes. I wasn't ready to face the day just yet. I'd been having the most wonderful dream.

I dreamt that my mother was home and my family was whole for the first time in over thirty years. Love and joy enveloped us, and it was like not a single day had passed. I'd been waiting for this moment for most of my life – and if I woke up, I feared it would be gone forever.

Reality is a jealous lover, however, and eventually her persistence won out. I opened my eyes and sighed. *Fine.* I would get up. A nice hot cup of Mimi's coffee would help take the sting out of reality's bite.

I dressed in a pair of capri-length leggings and a faded green t-shirt that said KISS ME I'M IRISH, threw my copper curls up in a messy bun, then left my room and beelined for the kitchen. There I poured myself a big cup of joe, then went looking for Mimi and whoever else might be up.

I heard voices and followed them to the front living room. There I found Mimi, my brother Kieran, my dad…and my mom. They all held mugs of steaming coffee and were talking and laughing like this was any normal Tuesday morning. Like my mom hadn't been gone for thirty years. For a second I thought I was still dreaming.

Kieran finally noticed me standing in the door. "Good morning, sunshine."

My mother sat on the couch next to my dad; the morning sun illuminated her platinum curls and she gazed at me with the sweetest smile on her softly lined face. She looked like an angel. Then she patted the cushion next to her. "Come. Sit."

Still a bit dumbfounded, it took me a few beats to get my feet moving. Finally I crossed the room and sat, placing my mug on the coffee table. My mother wrapped an arm around my shoulders; I leaned into her like a child and sighed. She smelled like sunflowers.

"Are you all right, love?" Mimi asked from her perch on a plush chair across from us, her short white hair spiky from sleep and a grin playing at the wrinkled corners of her mouth.

I blinked. "I–I thought it was a dream," I said, referring to the previous day. I'd come home after solving a huge case expecting to see my dad, who'd been gone for a few days. I got the shock of a lifetime when I discovered he'd brought my mom back from the secluded cabin deep in the woods north of Duluth where she'd been living – and hiding from the Fausts – for over thirty years. I didn't remember anything after that.

"I suppose you've had quite a shock," Mimi said.

"We all have," Kieran said. He occupied the chair next to Mimi. He wore basketball shorts and a yellow t-shirt with DUCKS emblazoned on it in green block letters. His hair, the same copper color as mine, also had a bad case of bedhead. "All night I kept wanting to get up and check on Mom, make sure she was really here." He sipped his coffee. "It was a little like waiting for Santa Claus on Christmas Eve."

"How are you feeling, Dani?" Mimi asked.

My mother's reply was swift. "A bit overwhelmed."

My dad, who looked comfy in a pair of black athletic pants and a faded blue t-shirt, picked up my mom's slender hand, encased in a thin leather glove, and held it in both of his. "I must admit, I can't help but wonder if we've done the right thing."

"We have, Liam. We have." My mother's voice was firm.

"I know," he acquiesced. "I just struggle with the idea that you're now within spitting range of Edison Faust."

"The Fausts were about to find me anyway," she said. "This is what we have to do."

"They're going to be so pissed when they get all the way to Uncle Carl's cabin and find out you're gone," I said. I snuggled a little closer to my mother, and the world around me started to feel a little more solid.

Mimi smiled. "Kieran said the same thing yesterday."

Did he? I picked up my mug and sipped my coffee, trying to remember. A heavy gray fog shrouded everything after the moment I first laid eyes on my mother yesterday. *What is wrong with me?* I wondered. "What else did we talk about after I got home?"

"You told us why Edison is so motivated to get his hands on Mom right now," Kieran said. "You tried to, anyway. Something about some mythical stash of gold I didn't quite follow. And you filled Mom and Dad in on your relationship with Nicholas Faust."

"Boy, I must have been a wreck," I said. I didn't remember any of this. Had I been drinking? I didn't think so, but that's what this felt like: an alcoholic blackout.

"You seemed fine," my dad said. "Really."

"You were all over the place with the part about the gold, though." Kieran tipped his head back to dump the last of his coffee down his throat.

"Maybe we should run through it again," my dad suggested. "Just so we're all on the same page."

Everyone nodded and looked at me. I sat up, leaving the warm cocoon of my mother's arm, and took a deep breath. "Okay. Jack Hughes was a reclusive widower who was killed in his home in River Junction in nineteen ninety-seven. Jack was famous for not trusting banks and conducting all his business with cash. After he died a rumor spread around town that he'd left behind a substantial stash of gold. Nobody's ever found this gold, and Nicholas says there's never been any evidence that it actually exists."

Saying Nicholas' name hurt my heart a little. Until recently he'd been the love of my life, the one I'd risked everything to be with and had been prepared to wait forever for. Then Edison Faust, the man who had been terrorizing my family for decades and also happened to be Nicholas' grandfather, turned him against me. He'd nearly killed me two days ago; the bruising on my neck and my broken heart still ached.

"But Edison is completely convinced that the gold exists and there's a lot of it. That's why he wants Mom so badly. He thinks her touch will guide him to the gold and the wealth it will bring." I was referring to the psychic ability that my grandmother Emily

("Mimi" to me and Kieran), my mother Danielle, and I all had: we could touch things and see visions of past events. This ability afflicted every woman in my family for generations. Sometimes the touch was a helpful thing; usually it was more of a curse than a gift. We all wore thin lambskin gloves to blunt its unintended effects and help preserve our sanity.

My mother's touch was different from Mimi's and mine. She could also see the future. And this made her extra attractive to the psychopath Edison Faust; he'd been trying to get his hands on her since she was born, but he'd really stepped up his efforts recently.

"Who killed Jack? Was it Edison?" my mother asked.

"Jesse says Jack's murder is officially still unsolved, but the general consensus is that Edison probably had something to do with it. Edison and Jack had a long history."

"Who's Jesse?" My mom asked.

"Jesse Hendricks is with the River Junction Police Department," I explained. "He and I worked together to solve an old kidnapping case there, and he is intimately familiar with the Fausts."

"He's good people," Kieran chimed in. I couldn't stop a smile from spreading across my face.

"So to sum it all up," he continued, his tone derisive. "Everyone thinks there's this stash of gold, but nobody's ever seen it, but Edison Faust is convinced and he wants Mom to help him find it, so we have to be even more on our guard than ever."

I nodded. "Pretty much." Hearing this crazy business summed up like that made me want a crisp, cold glass of chardonnay, even this early in the morning. I picked up my coffee and drank that instead.

Kieran shifted in his chair. "This sucks," he muttered.

"Yeah. But I think this is our chance to get the Fausts out of our lives for good," I said. "Jesse thinks there might be some truth to the rumors. If we can find the gold before Edison does, we'll have the advantage. And if we can prove he killed Jack, he's done. They're all done."

"I for one would love to see that happen." Mimi's hazel eyes snapped. "That bastard has been trying to get his hands on me and my family my entire life. I'm nearly eighty years old now. I'd truly like to know what a normal life is like before I die."

"I lost thirty years with my family because of that crazy old man." Danielle's eyes looked exactly like Mimi's at that moment. "Oh, Mom, could you imagine a life without the Fausts always lurking in the shadows?"

Mimi shook her head. "No. They've always been there, trying to eradicate all Ainsleys from existence."

"And all because Grace Ainsley rejected Benedict Faust back in the nineteen-thirties. Talk about holding a grudge," I said morosely. *I wonder what Jesse's doing,* I thought, staring into the obsidian well of Mimi's hot, strong coffee in my mug. Its warmth was no substitute for the comforting solidness of his body. I felt anxious and uneasy.

The long-running and violent feud between the Ainsleys and the Fausts would be coming to a head soon. I could feel it in my bones. I took a deep breath and wished again that my cup was full of chardonnay rather than coffee. "So what do you guys think? Should we see if we can't take that old bastard down?"

"Yes." Kieran's deep voice was firm. "And let's find that gold before he does."

We spent the next hour debating the best way to do that. We all agreed right away that Jesse and I would leverage the resources of the River Junction Police Department to investigate Jack Hughes' murder. "It's like any other cold case," I said. "I can't imagine Captain Bailey wouldn't be on board with putting the homegrown terrorists behind bars."

"Low-hanging fruit," my dad murmured, nodding.

Then the conversation turned to how we might track down Jack Hughes' gold. "Did Jack have any family?" Kieran asked. "Seems like a good place to start."

"I'll ask Jesse," I said. "He grew up in River Junction, he would know." I picked up my phone and sent a quick text. The reply came in less than two minutes: **Yes. His brother Paul Hughes. Remember I mentioned the elderly couple that was badly beaten? That was him and his wife Jeannette.**

"Ohhhh," I breathed.

"What did he say?" Kieran asked.

I told my family what Hendricks told me.

My mother forced her next words out through tightly gritted teeth. She was absolutely furious. "Let him take me."

We all turned toward her. "What?" I asked, unsure I'd heard her correctly.

"No. Absolutely not," Kieran said. "You're kidding, right?"

"Out of the question." My dad's voice nearly matched my mom's in intensity.

"Dani." Mimi's voice was reproachful.

"If we want to take Edison Faust down, we'll have to do it from the inside." My mom's fiery hazel eyes landed on Mimi. "I think you know that better than anybody, Mom."

Mimi's gaze dropped to the floor.

"Dani," my dad interjected.

My mom held up a gloved hand. "Liam, Edison Faust has not managed to avoid accountability all these years by being a damn fool. He's got a network in River Junction protecting him. I guarantee it."

I remembered something Hendricks had said when I first met him: *The Fausts have a long history of wiggling their way out of criminal charges in Greenhaven County. Edison has an absolute chokehold on this town. Everyone is afraid of him and his son. So nothing ever sticks.*

"I have to go in," my mom said. "It's the only way."

"He could kill you, Dani." My dad's voice broke.

"He won't kill her until he gets the gold," I said. "He needs her for that." I couldn't help but wonder: would Nicholas protect my mother like he'd done for more than a decade before his grandfather turned him against me? I didn't know. I rubbed my still-sore neck with my left hand, trying not to remember the absolute evil in Nicholas' black eyes as he slowly squeezed the life out of me.

All I could do was hope.

We sat in heavy silence for a minute or two, pondering the wisdom of allowing Edison Faust to get his hands on my mother. Well…*they* pondered. *My* thoughts centered on how nice a glass of crisp chardonnay would taste right about now.

Mimi finally spoke. "We'll need a way to communicate with Dani while she's inside the Fortress." This was the name of the

Fausts' hulking family home in River Junction, on the banks of the Bourbon River.

"Mimi." My brother shifted in his chair, panic rising on his face. "You can't be serious."

"Your mother is right, Kieran. It's the only way."

Kieran looked around the room, inspecting each face to see who agreed with him and who agreed with Mom. Then, clearly not liking what he saw, he scowled and crossed his arms over his chest like a pouting schoolboy. Pink streaks glowed on his pale, freckle-covered cheekbones.

"I wonder." Mimi held a finger in the air, then dipped it in an *aha* gesture. "I'll be right back." She disappeared.

The rest of us sat in silence, not looking at each other. I didn't think any of us were truly convinced that sending my mother into the Fortress was such a great idea. We had, after all, worked so hard to keep her out of there. But it was also increasingly obvious that if we truly wanted to end the Fausts' reign of terror, we had to burrow in and dismantle Edison's machine from the inside. Only my mother was positioned to do that. I sighed, tempted to head to the kitchen and replace my coffee with wine. The stress was unbearable.

Mimi came back before I could, holding something in a gloved fist. She shooed me off the couch and sat next to my mother, then laid the objects on the coffee table. Kieran and I knelt on the floor and leaned in close.

They were rings: a thin gold engagement ring with a small princess cut diamond, a simple gold band, and another, wider band made of white gold. Embedded in that band were two gemstones: a blue topaz and a green emerald. They were all pretty tarnished and seemed made to fit impossibly small, delicate fingers.

"This was my mother Grace Ainsley's wedding set." Mimi slid the diamond engagement ring and the gold band together. "And this was her mother's ring." She touched the white gold band and ran a fingertip lovingly over hers and Aunt Pearl's birthstones. I knew topaz was the birthstone for November, Mimi's birth month. Pearl's birth month must have been May.

"What are you thinking, Emily?" My dad's eyes were bright.

Mimi shrugged. "What if Grace's rings can help the three of us" – she pointed to herself, my mother, and me – "connect to each other?"

The idea felt brilliant and impossible at the same time. "Mimi, Grace has been gone a lot of years," I said.

"Sixty-three years," she replied matter-of-factly.

I nodded. "So…how can these rings help connect us? Do you think there's enough psychic energy left in them after all that time?"

"Have you ever tried anything like this before?" Kieran chimed in. It seemed he'd gotten past his little tantrum and now was as bright-eyed and curious as our father.

"I haven't, and I'll admit this idea seems a bit far-fetched. But. My mother was the first Ainsley woman with the touch. She never took these rings off. They were on her fingers until – until the day she died." That moment's hesitation made me think she was about to say something different: *Until the day she was murdered by Benedict Faust.* "Maybe her psychic energy can amplify our abilities, even after all these years. Don't you think there could be a chance?"

"I'm willing to give it a try," my mom said, scooting closer to the table.

"Whatever it takes," I said. There was something exciting about the idea that maybe we could control our touch, rather than *it* control *us*. After a lifetime of feeling like a slave to my ability and struggling to cope, this was exciting. Empowering, even. All thoughts of wine dissipated. "So who wears which ring?"

Mimi pondered for a moment, then shrugged. "I don't think it really matters."

Danielle carefully picked up the mother's ring and handed it to Mimi. "You wear this one, Mom. I can see it means a lot to you."

Mimi nodded somberly and pulled the glove from her left hand. The ring slipped onto her gnarled finger like it was made for her. Chills ran the length of my spine.

Danielle pinched the wedding band between her gloved thumb and forefinger and held it out toward me. It was still shiny enough to reflect a tiny beam of light. "You wear this one, Raegan." She set it on my outstretched palm.

I let the simple gold ring sit there for a few seconds. It looked impossibly small, meant for a hand much more petite than mine. "I don't think it'll fit me, Mom," I said doubtfully.

"Try it, love," Mimi said. She was smiling, but her eyes were brimming with tears. I took a deep breath, removed my glove, and slid the ring onto my own finger. I fully expected it to jam up at the knuckle. To my surprise it slid on smoothly, as if it had always been mine.

"There you go," Danielle said triumphantly. She picked up the diamond engagement ring and turned to my father with a smile. "Liam, would you do the honors?"

"It would be my pleasure," he said. He positively beamed as he placed the ring on her finger, next to the simple band he'd put there forty-three years before.

Suddenly I was seeing my father's smiling face full-on, rather than from my perch on the opposite side of the coffee table. "What the?" I blurted, and my view swiveled away from my dad's careworn face to my own; that's when I realized I was seeing through my mother's eyes. My outburst had prompted her to turn toward me.

I realized with mild shock that time and stress had caught up with me over the last few weeks; I looked every day of my thirty-nine years, and then some. Dark circles had taken up residence under my pale blue eyes, and my copper curls, usually vibrant and now dull, were piled on top of my head. I could even see the bruises that Nicholas had left on my slender neck. I watched myself bring my hands up to cover them.

"Whoa," my mom breathed.

"Oh my." Mimi sounded surprised. "I…I think it worked."

"What can you see?" my dad asked, intrigued.

My mom's head followed my dad's voice; the sensation of moving while my own body was still made my stomach turn. Much like long car rides in the backseat did when I was a kid. I yanked my great-grandmother's gold band off my finger and my own view immediately returned.

"What a trip," my mother murmured.

"I–I was seeing through Mom's eyes," I said tentatively, not convinced I wasn't completely insane.

My mother pointed at my grandmother. "I saw through your eyes. Does that mean you saw through Raegan's?"

Mimi nodded. "And as soon as Raegan took her ring off, everything went back to normal."

"Is that how it would always be?" Kieran asked. "Or could one of you see through either of the other's eyes?"

With Kieran and my dad watching and offering suggestions, Mimi, my mom and I spent the next hour or so experimenting with Grace Ainsley's rings to figure out how this newfound ability worked. We learned how to turn it on and off while still wearing the rings so we wouldn't have to take them off. We traded the rings between us to see what might change. We touched things with bare fingers. Each of us went to different rooms in the house. I even got in my SUV and drove to a park down the street.

As I stood in the shade of a giant oak tree, seeing my dad's kitchen through my Mimi's eyes and half-convinced a glass of wine would help keep my motion sickness in check, I decided to see if I could transmit as well as receive. *This psychic connection doesn't mean much if we can't let each other know when there's something to see,* I reasoned. I closed my eyes and laser-focused my attention on Mimi. She must have sensed something, because she stopped moving and brought her hand up to her forehead. *Sweet, it works.*

I went back to my dad's house and we reconvened in the living room. We exchanged rings again, back to the ones we started with. Mimi seemed relieved to have Grace's mother's ring back on her finger; she gingerly ran a fingertip over the vibrant blue and green gemstones. She was thinking about her sister Pearl. I would have bet money on it.

"Short answer: Grace's rings create a psychic connection between us," my mother said. "We can't hear anything or see each other's touch visions, we can't read each other's minds. But we've figured out how to connect, see through each other's eyes, disconnect, and send mental signals when we want the others to see something."

"I didn't know what was happening when you did that, Rae. My vision suddenly turned blue. I thought I might be going a bit mad." Mimi said.

"A very handy feature indeed," my father chuckled.

"This is so great," I said. "We can leave these rings on all the time and we'll be able to connect whenever we want, and —" My phone buzzed, interrupting my train of thought. I picked it up and glanced at the screen, and my heart plummeted.

We're coming for her. Give her up and nobody gets hurt.

"Rae? You okay?" Kieran sounded concerned.

I looked at my family with wide eyes. "It's a text. From Nicholas.

"They're coming."

CHAPTER 2

Kieran shot out of his chair and snatched my phone from my shaking fingers. He read it, made a noise of disgust and handed it back to me. I promptly used it to dial Jesse Hendricks' number and fill him in.

"How far out are they?" Hendricks' deep voice soothed my rattled nerves.

"I don't know," I said. "They could be any–" Something occurred to me. "Hang on."

I pulled the phone away from my ear and scrolled through its apps until I found the one I was looking for: a chat app that also had a location feature. Nicholas and I had used the chat app to communicate the last few years because it had another feature that we both found useful: messages disappear after a certain amount of time. Carrying on a clandestine relationship forbidden by both families meant we had to cover our tracks.

I tapped the location map, and there was Nicholas' avatar, steadily making its way south on I-35 from Duluth. My heart thumped so hard I went lightheaded for a few seconds. I took a deep breath to reground myself and returned to Hendricks. "They're at North Branch. They'll be here within the hour."

"I'm on my way," he said, and ended the call. He had to leave River Junction now to have any hope of beating the Fausts to my dad's south Minneapolis home.

"Jesse is on his way," I said. I sat in a chair, pulled Nicholas' text back up, and read it again. *How far we've fallen.* Less than a month ago I'd thought Nicholas hung the moon. Two days ago he nearly killed me. Now this text.

I had questions.

"Why in the hell would Nicholas warn you they're coming?" Kieran asked as he sat in the chair next to me. "Don't the Fausts prefer a sneak attack on unsuspecting prey?"

"You read my mind," I said and read the text message again. "I can't make it make sense in my head."

"I guess we should be glad," Kieran said. "Whether he meant to or not, Nicholas gave us a chance to finalize our plan before they get here."

"I would have liked more time to perfect our psychic connection," Mimi said with a sigh. "It seems we'll have to figure it out as we go."

"One thing I do know, I'm not sending Dani in blind," Liam declared. "I will be keeping an eye on the Fausts and the Fortress." His bushy eyebrows, once the same copper color as mine and now snow white, drew together. "I wonder where I put my binoculars."

"Those old things?" I remembered my dad's ancient field glasses and knew he would need something much more powerful. "Forget it. I'll ask Jesse if he has a pair of high-tech ones you can borrow." The possibilities – taking down Edison, of course, but also working with Jesse Hendricks on another case – made my heart flutter.

"Mimi, how about you and I see if we can't track down that gold?" Kieran proposed. Mimi smiled and nodded in agreement.

We talked a bit more, but mostly small talk. All we could do now was wait for the Fausts to arrive, and the collective anxiety level rose with each passing minute. *Where the hell is Jesse?* I wondered. As if on cue, a soft knock on the front door made us all jump. Kieran hopped up and went to the door, and I was hot on his heels.

Hendricks, wearing jeans and a gray RJPD polo, started talking before he was completely inside. "I saw them gassing up their Suburban down the road," he said as he came to me and wrapped an arm around my shoulders. "They'll be here any second." Introductions would have to wait. "I parked around the corner so they wouldn't see my squad."

Everyone stood, and the waterworks started. We took turns hugging my mom. My heart hammered against my ribs and a pit yawed open in my gut. *Damn it, she just got here. This isn't fair.* I felt like I was losing her all over again. I glanced at my brother and knew he felt the same way. He was usually pretty stoic, but tears fell from his pale blue eyes and cascaded down his freckled cheeks like they did the day she left us the first time.

After giving my mom a long hug and struggling to hold back tears, I surrendered her to Kieran and went back to Hendricks. He wrapped an arm around me again. "I'm going to stand around the corner, out of sight," he murmured into my ear. "I will have my gun in hand just in case, okay?"

I leaned my head against his chest. "Okay." His strong heartbeat was reassuring.

"Hey." He turned so he could hold my upper arms and look me directly in the eye. His green eyes were fierce. "I got you, okay? Nobody's going to get hurt."

I couldn't stop a small sob. "I-I know. I just…I'm having a hard time letting my mom go. Again."

"Oh." Hendricks' voice was pure empathy. He pulled me in for a real hug. "I'm sorry, Rae. I can't imagine how hard this must be for you. But you know what?"

"W-what?" I said into his chest.

"We're gonna get him. He won't be able to hurt anyone else."

"A-and I'll g-g-get my m-m-mom back?" It was becoming increasingly difficult to keep my emotions in check. My tears soaked his gray RJPD polo shirt.

"Of course you will. Whatever it takes."

I swallowed hard, forcing the lump in my throat back, then inhaled deeply. "Okay. Okay."

Hendricks nudged me toward my family and slipped into the hallway. We formed a Red Rover chain in the middle of the living room, facing the door. My mother was in the middle with my dad and Mimi on each side of her, holding hands. I held my dad's other hand and Kieran held Mimi's.

The silence in the room was deafening until several businesslike clicks made us all jump a little. Hendricks' gun was ready to fire if needed. My dad squeezed my hand hard.

Nicholas was nearby. I could feel him.

My stomach churned and my heart thudded. I thought I might throw up. I leaned forward and looked down the line at my family; they all looked as nervous as I felt.

Seconds later the door flew open with a crash and there stood Morgan Faust – tall, skinny, clad in black jeans and t-shirt with heavy black boots, long salt and pepper hair straggling to his shoulderblades. A deep scar ran vertically down the right side of his grizzled face, giving him a particularly sinister look. He'd kicked the door so hard that the doorknob pierced the wall and stuck it open. His motorhuckle boot had left a perfect print on the wood surface.

Edison shoved Morgan to the side and stomped into the house where we waited, calm and defiant. "Get out of my way, you idiot," he snapped. He was nearly as tall as and skinnier than his son, with wild white hair and a humped back. I was struck again by how grandfatherly he looked – except for the evil glint in his sunken black eyes. Nicholas followed him wordlessly. He looked like he'd aged since our last encounter just a few days ago;

his black hair, usually so carefully coiffed, stood in unkempt clumps. The circles under his eyes were big and black. He would not meet my gaze.

Edison turned to see us standing shoulder-to-shoulder in the middle of the living room and stopped short. Uncertainty clouded his deeply wrinkled, hawkish face for a moment, and then he turned to Nicholas. "Did you warn them we were coming?" His reedy old-man voice was tight with anger. With that, I no longer had to wonder if Edison knew about Nicholas and me. A month ago this knowledge would have sent me into a panic. Now I hoped Edison was making Nicholas' life good and miserable.

Nicholas shook his head and threw me a quick black glance before looking away again.

"I knew you were coming before you did, Edison," my mother said. I blinked in surprise but kept my face still. *She did? Why didn't she say anything?*

"Danielle." Edison crossed his liver-spotted arms over his bony pigeon chest and gave my mother a thorough up-and-down. "You've been a rather difficult person to track down. A test of my patience, really. I must admit, you look…" A devil's grin. "Old."

My mother's only reaction was a slight raise of her chin, but Mimi cackled. "Oh, Edison. Are there no mirrors in that rock pile you're living in?"

Edison shot Mimi a look that could have killed something slightly weaker than my grandmother, like a grizzly bear. "Always a feisty one, aren't you, Emily?"

"Oh, you're just bitter because you haven't managed to catch or kill any of us." She chuckled. "Lord knows you've tried enough times. And failed."

I bit my lip hard to stop my smart mouth from chiming in with *Worst criminals ever* and making a bad situation ever so much worse.

Edison's eyes narrowed and his nostrils flared. "I don't intend to fail today." He surveyed each of us in turn. Gooseflesh ran up my spine when his evil eyes landed on me. They triggered an unwanted memory I'd locked tight behind a door in my mind many years ago.

I saw those eyes when I was fifteen years old and opened the front door – the very door Morgan had just kicked in – to find Edison Faust standing on the front step instead of the pizza delivery guy I'd been expecting. He grabbed my arm and yanked before I could react, nearly pulling me out the front door. Kieran, who'd heard the doorbell and come to investigate, grabbed my other arm and pulled me back in. I was the rope in a life-or-death game of tug of war until sirens sounded in the distance; Mimi had called 911. Edison let go and disappeared before the police arrived. I shuddered and pushed the memory back behind the mental door, making sure it was locked tight.

I rarely had an appetite for pizza after that, and I never again opened a door without first checking to see who was on the other side of it.

Edison's putrid gaze lingered on me for a few beats, and I thought he might say something about my relationship with his grandson. Instead he turned to Morgan and nodded. Morgan loped across the room and took up a position behind my mother. He smelled like stale beer, sour sweat, and body odor, and it took everything I had not to gag.

"Now. We can do this the easy way or the hard way," Edison said. "Come with us, Danielle, and nobody in your family gets hurt. Resist and I'm sorry to say I can't guarantee their safety."

I heard a faint rustle from the hallway behind me and knew Hendricks was getting ready to join our little party if things started to go south. I felt a little better knowing he was there – and armed.

"Leave my family out of this," my mother said. I marveled at how she could keep her voice so steady. "You've hurt them enough. I'm the one you want."

"Oh, Danielle. All those years of pain could have been avoided if you'd been this cooperative at Pearl's funeral all those years ago."

I had no idea what Edison was talking about, but I wanted to march over and slap that smirk right off his pruney face.

"You leave my sister's name out of your stinking lying mouth, you son of a bitch." Mimi, all ninety pounds of her, tried to lunge at Edison. My mother and Kieran held her firmly in place. I'd never seen her so angry.

My mother smiled sweetly. "It happened like I said it would. Didn't it, Edison?"

The old man glowered.

"The bank manager died, didn't he?"

"Shut up," he said. Then he turned to Morgan and Nicholas. "Take her."

My dad's hand crushed my fingers. It hurt, but I held on. *Keep your eye on the prize,* I told myself. *We'll take them down and get her back.*

My mom stepped forward. "That won't be necessary, Edison. I'll go with you."

Morgan took my mom's upper arms and guided her out the front door. Edison followed without a word. I tried to bore a hole in the back of Nicholas' head with my eyes as he went after his grandfather, but he didn't turn around.

They disappeared into the bright July sunshine.

CHAPTER 3

Kieran and I raced to the open front door and stuck our heads outside just in time to see my mother climb into the backseat of the Fausts' big black Suburban, followed by Nicholas. With Edison in the passenger seat and Morgan behind the wheel, the SUV pulled away from the curb and roared down my dad's quiet residential street. We watched until we couldn't see them anymore, then I closed the heavy wooden door. Morgan had broken the latch with his kick, so I had to turn the deadbolt to make the door stay closed. I leaned against it and sighed. "Suddenly I'm not so sure we've done the right thing," I said, echoing my dad. An electric ball of anxiety hummed in my chest, making my voice shake.

Hendricks stepped into the room from his post in the hallway, sidearm safely back in its holster, and offered me his elbow. "Come on, let's sit."

I grasped his arm and let him guide me back to the living room couch. Everyone ended up more or less in the same spots as before, but the energy in the room had darkened. She was our light.

We sat in stunned silence for a few minutes, none of us quite sure what to do next. I tried to remember if I had an open bottle of wine in the fridge. Mimi finally broke the silence. "Raegan? Are you going to introduce us to your friend?"

I shook my head and the craving for alcohol dissipated. "Oh. Um, yes. This is Jesse Hendricks, he's with the River Junction Police Department. He helped us after the Fausts kidnapped Dad." I gestured toward my family. "Jesse, you've met my dad Liam and my brother Kieran." All three men nodded and gave each other a half-assed wave. I pointed at Mimi. "And that is my grandmother, Emily Lownsdale. Kieran and I call her Mimi."

Hendricks stood and offered his hand to Mimi. She smiled and took it. "It's nice to meet you, Jesse. We're so grateful you've been taking such good care of our Raegan."

Hendricks grinned and looked at me. "Thank you ma'am, but really, *she's* been taking care of *me*."

Mimi waved this away. "And we thank you for being here to protect us, Jesse."

Hendricks nodded and sat back down. "Of course."

With that out of the way, we resumed staring blankly at each other.

"Now what?" I asked, jonesing for a glass of wine again. I'd started to stand and make my way to the kitchen when Kieran spoke up.

"Should we put those rings to the test?" he asked.

Damn it. The wine would have to wait. I sat down again, stomach churning, then pulled the glove off my left hand. Grace Ainsley's gold wedding band still sat on my ring finger as if it belonged there. I shifted my eyes to Mimi. "Should I?"

Mimi fiddled with the ring on her own finger and nodded.

"What? What's going on?" Hendricks asked.

I ignored him and closed my eyes, focusing tightly on my mother. I imagined that I was sending her signals like radar pulses. Almost immediately, as if she'd heard a telephone ring and picked up the receiver, a picture appeared against the darkness behind my eyelids. It was much brighter and clearer than my touch visions typically were. That was because what I saw through her eyes was happening in real time, not an old and faded memory. I swallowed hard to block the nausea as I peered through my mother's eyes.

∞

My mother was in the backseat of the Fausts' Suburban as it hauled ass north along Interstate 35W. The downtown Minneapolis skyline, along with the enormous, sharply-angled football stadium, whizzed by to my left. Her hands were not restrained, and I could see the bulge formed by Grace's diamond engagement ring under the left glove. Nicholas sat to her right, mute, his face carefully neutral.

Edison Faust occupied the front passenger seat. His untamed white hair was terribly thin, with patches of shiny bare scalp showing in some places. Morgan, who was driving, exhibited some of the same tendency toward male pattern baldness.

I couldn't see Edison's face very well, but he was talking animatedly, his thin arms waving in the air. He occasionally pointed at Morgan or Nicholas as if emphasizing a point. Once he even pointed at my mother.

This went on until the Suburban crossed the Mississippi River into River Junction and finally pulled into the driveway of the Fortress, the Fausts' longtime home. Constructed of gray granite, it sort of looked like a medieval castle. My mother got out of the truck and Nicholas led her inside.

I was a little shocked that the interior of the Fortress did not have cold stone floors, torches hanging on the walls, or heavy wood furniture. It looked like any regular house: drywall and paint, carpet and tile, and electric light fixtures. Nicholas led my mother up the stairs and down a long second floor hallway. He stopped at the last door on the right, opened it, said something, and gestured for her to go in. She obliged, and turned around just in time to see the door shut firmly behind her.

The first thing she did was test the doorknob. It didn't budge. Then she turned and surveyed the room. It was a good-sized guest room with its own bathroom. The queen-sized bed was covered with a pilly old electric blanket. A rocking chair stood next to the window. A television sat on a low dresser. The walls were painted white and completely bare. The window was covered by cheap aluminum miniblinds — I could almost hear the metallic ziiiip sound they made as she pulled the cord to open them and let the sunshine in.

My mother sat on the bed and covered her face with her gloved hands.

∞

I disconnected from my mother and blinked until my dad's living room reappeared. Mimi was the only one left, and she had taken Hendricks' spot next to me.

"Where is everyone?" I asked, then yawned. I was so *tired.*

"Your dad is taking a call in his office, and Jesse went out to his car to check in with his sergeant. Kieran is on the phone with Annie."

"How long was I gone?"

"A little less than an hour." Mimi patted my knee. "At first you described everything you were seeing, but that didn't last very long."

"God, why do I feel like I just went ten rounds with Mohammed Ali?" I could have curled up right where I sat and slept for days.

"I suppose these psychic connections are real time and require considerably more energy to maintain than a quick snippet of a memory vision," Mimi mused. "You were connected to Dani for almost an hour. That's a long time."

I yawned again. "That makes sense, but how useful are these rings going to be if connecting drains us of energy?"

"We'll just have to be prudent about when we use them," Mimi said.

Well, damn, I wish we'd known this before we sent Mom with the Fausts, I thought bitterly. The constant, on-demand access I had envisioned simply wasn't possible. Not if I wanted to be awake and alert and helpful to our cause. I sighed.

"Is Dani okay?" Mimi's eyes were anxious.

"She's fine. She has a decent room and doesn't seem to be in any danger."

She sighed, relieved. "Okay."

I covered her gloved hand with mine and gently squeezed it.

Kieran entered the room from the kitchen and took one of the chairs. "Annie says hello." His wife was at their home in Eugene, Oregon, no doubt anxiously awaiting his return. Their trip back to Minnesota for a baby shower was unexpectedly extended after my dad was abducted and assaulted by the Fausts nearly ten days ago. He looked at me. "Is Mom all right?"

Mimi and I both nodded.

My dad appeared from the hallway that led to his office. He was a bit more stooped than usual and his brow was furrowed.

Mimi immediately sensed that something was amiss. "Liam? What's wrong?"

My dad sighed and shuffled into the room. "That was Carl."

Carl Engelman, the former husband of my dad's sister Deirdre, owned the remote northwoods cabin where my mother had spent the last thirty-two years living in isolation and had done more than his fair share of making sure she was well taken care of.

"The cabin in Isabella burned to the ground today."

Thunderstruck silence filled the room.

"That son of a bitch," Mimi whispered.

"It's his calling card," my dad sat in the chair next to Kieran.

The locked door in my memory cracked open, and despite my efforts to contain them, two memories from my college years barreled out like overexcited dogs.

During my sophomore year at the University of Minnesota, Murphy Hall, home of the journalism program, burned down in a spectacular midday fire. The fire was attributed to construction work that was going on as part of a multimillion-dollar renovation, but I knew better. I was a journalism major, and under normal circumstances probably would have been in the building that day. Luckily classes had been moved to a different location due to the construction – but the Fausts clearly didn't realize that.

Just a few months later, my dad and Mimi awoke to smoke alarms in the middle of the night and discovered a fire taking hold in the sunroom. The Minneapolis Fire Department would extinguish it, but not before significant damage was done. A Molotov cocktail was determined to be the cause, and despite our pleas to look into the Fausts, no suspects were ever officially identified.

I herded those memories back behind the mental door and closed it tight. The less time I spent with them, the better. A girl could only drink so much wine.

The front door swung open and Hendricks stepped inside. He saw me and smiled. "Hey, you're back. Everything go okay for your mom?"

"Seems so," I said.

He sat on the other side of me. "I imagine you all would like to be closer to Danielle while she is a guest at the Fortress."

We nodded in unison.

"The house next door to mine happens to be between renters for a couple of weeks. The owner is a friend, he said you can stay there while you have business in River Junction. All he asks is that you cover the cost of any utilities you use. And best of all, it's fully furnished."

"Thank you, Jesse. That's very kind," my dad said, gratitude written all over his face.

Kieran stood. "Let's pack our bags."

CHAPTER 4

Hendricks offered to give me a lift back to River Junction in his RJPD squad, but I politely declined. "I'd prefer to have my car there with me, but thanks for the offer."

He nodded, pulled me close, and kissed my head. "All right. I'll see you in a bit then."

I couldn't tell him the real reason I wanted to drive separately. I felt guilty about it, but not guilty enough to stop myself from swinging by River Junction's municipal liquor store on my way to his house and buying a couple bottles of chardonnay. I slipped them into my overnight bag and reminded myself to stash them in my family's refrigerator next door. They wouldn't be surprised to see them. Hendricks probably would, and he would have questions for me that I didn't want to answer.

I pulled up to the curb in front of Hendricks' house just as he was letting my family into the house next door. I slung my bag over my shoulder and walked across the lawn to meet them.

While Hendricks gave them the ten-cent tour, I went to the kitchen and surreptitiously stuck one of the wine bottles in the fridge. The other I left in my bag for later.

The house was laid out exactly like Hendricks', but was decorated and furnished in the basic utilitarian rental motif. There were only three bedrooms, so when Hendricks offered up his guest room, I immediately volunteered – knowing full well the guest bed would never be slept in. Nobody in my family seemed surprised.

Once my family's belongings had been stashed in bedrooms, we all met back in the kitchen. Early afternoon sunshine poured in through the window above the sink. I glanced at my phone and was mildly shocked to find it was only a little after one o'clock. The last few hours felt like a full day in themselves.

"I have to get back to the station," Hendricks said and slipped an arm around my shoulders.

Perfect, I thought but did not say. I would be able to enjoy my wine in peace.

"I need a nap," Mimi said. "And then I want to go to the supermarket for some provisions."

We all agreed a nap sounded like a great idea after such an eventful morning. I hugged my family and promised I would see them later. Then I followed Hendricks out the door and over to his house.

"I should be back around five," he said as he wrapped his arms around me.

I leaned against him and breathed deeply of his beachy scent. "Okay." Then I tipped my face up, asking for a kiss.

He obliged, then left. My stomach twisted as I watched the squad drive away. *Be careful, O'Rourke*, I warned myself as I pulled the still-cold bottle of wine out of my bag. *Don't get carried away. A couple glasses is all you need.*

I poured a glass and went to Hendricks' living room, where I curled up on the end of the couch and pulled my legs under me.

The first cold and tart sip exploded in my mouth and went down smooth. When did I last have a drink?

I took another sip while I wracked my memory. *Saturday. After our fight.* It was scarcely my favorite memory. I had put the Mia Masterson case in jeopardy by continuing to communicate with Nicholas after he'd been identified as a suspect in her disappearance. Hendricks did not react well when he found out. Even though we made up the following day, after I'd tried to make things right and nearly died, I was still more than a little mortified by my own behavior that day.

Three whole days without a drink. I'd been so good. I deserved this little reward.

Each sip blunted my sheer terror over sending my mom with the Fausts. It dulled the raw pain from the hole in my gut that had torn open when she left us. Would I ever see her again? I'd tried to be brave for my family, but deep down I wasn't so sure. I thought maybe we'd just made the biggest mistake of our lives. Edison Faust was no fool, and he was powerful here in River Junction. Nobody else had been able to stop him…what in the hell made us think we could? And on his home turf?

As usual, I started drinking with the best of intentions, but as the effects of the alcohol took hold, I lost all inhibitions. One glass turned into two, and then I just started drinking straight from the bottle so I wouldn't have to keep getting up and going into the kitchen.

The buzzing in my head grew louder and my eyelids grew heavier with every gulp. Soon the bottle was empty and I was no longer confident in my ability to stand and walk without falling down. I blearily wondered if I could connect with my mother, just to see how she was doing. I closed my eyes and tried to focus, and that's when the room started spinning. My stomach angrily flipped and my mouth started watering. I lurched off the couch and stumbled to Hendricks' bathroom, nearly falling twice along the way. I landed on my knees in front of the toilet just as my gut heaved, sending a frothy mixture of hot wine and acid bile out of my mouth and into the bowl. I retched until nothing was left, then retched some more. Sweat poured down my face, snot ran from my nose, and I actually thought I might die.

The dry heaves and the spins finally subsided, but I was still inebriated. And so, so tired. The chill of the ceramic floor tile felt nice against my hot skin. *Maybe I can just rest here for a few minutes,* I thought dully. I curled up on the floor between the toilet and the bathtub.

I was unconscious within seconds.

∞

"Rae."

I opened my eyes, and an arrow of bright hot pain shot through my head. My tongue was stuck to the roof of my mouth.

"Raegan."

I blinked and turned my head in the direction my name had come from. "Wha?" I croaked. Everything was blurry and I didn't recognize where I was; all I knew was that the room was bright and my bed was very hard. And cold.

"Can you sit up?"

I finally recognized the voice: it was Hendricks. Then it all came back: I was a guest in his house and I'd gotten wasted as soon as he'd left to go back to work. My heart fell. *What the fuck is the matter with you, O'Rourke?*

"Uh, I think so," I said, and, eyes closed, slowly began pushing myself up to sitting. I realized I was in the bathroom, of all places. The arrow of pain pierced my head again, and I groaned.

"Come on." Hendricks' big, warm hands gently hooked under my armpits and lifted me up. My stomach rolled again, but there wasn't anything left to throw up. He set me on my feet. "Look at me, Raegan."

I didn't want to. My shame was too great. But I forced myself to open my gritty eyes and look at his kind and concerned face.

"Are you okay?" he asked.

I shook my head miserably. I thought I might cry, but tears wouldn't come. *Too dehydrated,* I thought.

"Come on." He wrapped an arm around my shoulders and guided me out of the bathroom. "Let's go sit down."

My wine glass and bottle were no longer sitting on the coffee table. They'd been replaced with a giant glass of ice water. I sat on the couch, grabbed it greedily, and drank. It tasted like nirvana.

Hendricks sat next to me. "We need to talk about this."

I wiped my wet lips with my hand and nodded. Pain pulsed through my head again. "I know. I'm sorry, Jesse."

"You're upset about your mom. I get it. But this is not a healthy way to cope."

"It's all I know," I said. I stared at my water, unable to meet his gaze. I'd struggled most of my life with an alcohol problem; it was the only way I really knew to cope with my psychic ability. And, if I were being honest with myself, with life.

"You need help, Rae."

This time the tears came. "I know," I sobbed.

He let me cry it out. Once I calmed down, he said, "So what are you going to do about this?"

I wiped the tears from my cheeks and took a deep breath. "I don't know."

"The correct answer is, 'I'm going to check myself into rehab, Jesse,'" Hendricks said.

I stared at him with wide eyes. "Now?"

He shrugged. "There's no time like the present."

"Are you kidding me? No. Not now. No way." My heart pounded in my chest and I fiddled anxiously with Grace's ring on my left hand. "My mom needs me."

"You won't be much help to her if you're drunk all the time," he pointed out.

The fact that he was right only pissed me off. "I'm not drunk all the time," I snapped, scowling.

"True," Hendricks acknowledged. "But if you really want to help her, you have to stay sober until we get her back. Can you do that?"

I frowned and stared at my water glass. I could do anything for my mom. "Yes," I whispered.

Hendricks used a finger to lift my chin and held my gaze. "I know you can. And then, after that, we'll get you some help."

I nodded and blinked back tears. "Okay."

He pulled me in for a hug, and we sat like that, wrapped in each other's arms, for a long time. When he finally let me go he stood and took my water glass back to the kitchen. He returned with a full glass and two aspirin.

I felt a little better with every sip of water, although my eyesockets felt like they were stuffed with cotton. It didn't take long for true fatigue – rather than alcohol-fueled unconsciousness – to crash over me, and I nodded off with my head against Hendricks' shoulder. I woke up just enough to realize he was carrying me to bed.

I slept soundly the rest of the night.

Wednesday, July 21, 2021

CHAPTER 5

I awoke at four-thirty in the morning. The room was dark and Hendricks slept soundly beside me. Desperate to brush the fur off my teeth, I decided to get up. I was still tired, but felt pretty good, all things considered. *I guess the water really helped,* I thought. I cleaned up and swallowed a couple aspirin to knock out a nagging hangover headache, then padded to the kitchen and started a pot of coffee. I peeked through the kitchen window and decided an early morning walk might help clear my head. I drank some more water, then strapped my walking shoes on and slipped out the front door. The sky was clear, the stars were bright, and the eastern sky was starting to illuminate.

I should do this more often, I thought as I walked. *More walks, less wine.* All of the houses, postwar Cape Cods just like Hendricks', were dark and quiet. A black cat darted across the sidewalk in front of me, then stopped and turned to look deep into my soul with its unsettling yellow eyes before sauntering away. *Can it see the turmoil inside me?* I wondered. Lord knew there was plenty of it.

I hated to admit it, but our plan for taking Edison Faust down still troubled me. I hoped with everything I had that we hadn't put my mother in danger. I couldn't abide the thought of losing her again, forever this time.

I thought about how this all started: Nicholas withheld a key piece of information from me, sparking an avalanche of events that brought us to yesterday's tense confrontation – and my mother being taken from me. Again.

Nicholas.

It had only been three days since he tried to strangle me to death inside the Ainsley Mansion, my own family's ancestral home. The bruises he'd left on my neck were just now starting to turn yellow on the edges. But he'd walked into my dad's house yesterday looking like a different man. His usual easy confidence and quick smile were gone. The deep anger and madness were also gone. They'd been replaced with an uncharacteristic pallor and downcast eyes. He'd so quickly gone from the love of my life to a haunted shell of himself, I just had to wonder: did he regret turning against me and aligning with his grandfather?

Was the Nicholas I knew and loved still in there somewhere?

Ultimately it didn't matter. He was a Faust. I now knew he was capable of their brand of evil, and nothing he could ever say or do would convince me to come back. Besides, I thought something special might be happening between Hendricks and me. What started as a mutually beneficial partnership to investigate a River Junction cold case had deepened into something that very well might turn out to be real. My tall, blond, flat-topped, green-eyed, logical, introspective aspiring detective had something that Nicholas never did: the freedom and ability to accept everything about me – including who my family was. And they had accepted him without reservation. That alone made me feel like my judgment was sound.

I wondered if he felt the same way.

The sun was peeking over the horizon by the time I got back. I stood on the sidewalk outside the house next door, where my family was staying, and watched for signs of life inside. Seeing none, I walked toward Hendricks' house and the coffee within it.

He was sitting at the kitchen table dressed in a white t-shirt and gray athletic shorts, hunched over his phone. Two steaming mugs sat in front of him.

"Morning." I picked up one of the mugs and inhaled the fragrant steam. He'd bought fresh beans from Beananza, the local coffee shop. My mouth watered a little before I took my first life-affirming sip.

He glanced up from his phone. "Hey."

"What do you have there?"

He set his phone facedown on the table and picked up his own coffee mug. "Oh, nothing. How are you this morning? Feeling better?"

"Much," I said and dropped into a chair. "Thanks to you." I sipped my coffee. "What time is it?"

"A little after six," he said. "How long were you gone?"

"An hour or so, I guess." Another sip. "I went for a walk to clear my head." My phone lit up; it was a text from my brother, trying to entice me over to their place with an offer of hot cinnamon rolls. My favorite, and he knew it. "They're awake next door. And they have breakfast."

We went next door. As promised, Mimi had set a pan of fresh-baked cinnamon rolls on the kitchen counter. They were the kind you could get in a vacuum-sealed roll at the grocery store and bake yourself. We each grabbed a warm, gooey roll and went into the living room and sat on a loveseat that looked as if it could withstand a nuclear blast. Everyone ate in silence for a few minutes.

"So." Kieran chewed a few more times, then swallowed. "Are we sticking with the plan?"

"I for one am going to keep an eye on the Fortress," Liam said firmly; he seemed worried we would challenge him. "I can't bear the thought of leaving Dani there all alone."

I nudged Hendricks. "Do you have a set of binoculars my dad can borrow? The ones he has may have been previously owned by Fred Flintstone."

"As a matter of fact, I do." Hendricks tipped my dad a wink.

Relief washed over my dad's worried face. "Thank you, Jesse."

"Mimi, still want to go see Paul Hughes?" Kieran set his plate, scraped clean of all cream cheese frosting, on the scarred side table next to his armchair.

Mimi nodded.

I looked at Hendricks. "That leaves you and me."

He smiled. "Captain Bailey is expecting us at eight o'clock sharp."

So that's what he'd been doing with his phone when I returned from my walk. "Do you think she'll have any objections?"

"After we brought Mia and Isabel home? Nope, I don't think so." He wiped his mouth with a napkin, stood, and gathered everyone's plates. "I'll be right back." The dishes clinked as he set them in the sink, and the side door creaked open and then closed.

A tired, uneasy silence that was becoming entirely too familiar settled over me and my family. Nobody spoke. Nobody needed to. We knew what had to be done and what was at stake.

Hendricks returned within a few minutes bearing gifts. He handed my dad a pair of high-tech binoculars in a black case. "Here you go, Liam. I bought these binocs from RJPD when they upgraded last year. When the sun is at just the right angle, you might be able to watch one of the gorillas at the Como Zoo take a dump."

That made everyone chuckle; we were at least twenty-five miles from the Como Zoo in St. Paul.

Hendricks also gave my dad a walkie talkie about the size of a cellphone. "This is on the same frequency as my radio, and it has a range of about thirty miles. As long as we're all in River Junction, we should have no trouble communicating."

My dad nodded, his eyes misty. "Thank you." He cleared his throat. "Well, I suppose I should head over there."

We all stood to hug him. "Be careful, Dad," Kieran said and patted his back.

"I'll report back when I see you all tonight." And with that, my dad and all his new tech were gone.

"Having him keeping an eye on things at the Fortress could turn out to be pretty useful," I said. "Especially with that walkie."

"Great minds think alike," Hendricks said. "I'm going to go get ready, and then we gotta head over to the station."

I nodded. "Right behind you."

After the door creaked shut behind him again, it was just me, Mimi, and Kieran. We looked at each other, and then Kieran said, "You guys ready for this?"

"It's now or never," Mimi said fiercely.

I agreed. Reluctantly.

CHAPTER 6

The captain sat behind her desk waiting for us when Hendricks and I strolled into her office promptly at eight o'clock, fresh Beananza coffees in hand. Hendricks handed her one. Her almond-shaped eyes snapped as she pointed to the chairs in front of her desk. "Sit."

We sat.

Sarah Bailey stood maybe five feet tall, but what she lacked in height, she made up for in chutzpah. She oversaw the entire patrol division of the River Junction Police Department and entertained exactly zero bullshit from anyone. I sort of wanted to be more like her when I grew up.

She leaned back in her chair and brushed her blunt black bangs away from her gorgeous eyes. "So. You two solved one cold case, and now you want to solve them all?" She spoke with the slightly clipped diction of a native Korean who learned English as her second language.

"Come on, Captain. Wouldn't it be great if RJPD had no cold cases on its books?" Hendricks replied with a grin.

She smirked and pointed a perfectly manicured fingernail at him. "Don't push it, my friend. Your investigation damn near crashed and burned just a few days ago."

But then we brought Mia and Isabel Masterson home, restoring Hendricks' reputation and putting him solidly on the detective track. The banter was fun, but I was ready to get down to business. "So what do you think, Captain? Can we give the Jack Hughes case a shot?"

Bailey picked a pen up from her desk and fiddled with it. "Of course. Although if you thought Mia Masterson's case was difficult, Jack Hughes' will drive you crazy."

"Why's that?" Hendricks asked.

"Because there's really no question who killed him. We just don't have a shred of evidence to prove it."

Hendricks and I pondered this for a second or two. Just yesterday my mom had said *He's got a network in River Junction protecting him. I guarantee it.* I wondered if that network included someone within RJPD, but I didn't dare ask.

Hendricks had no such reservations. "Inside job?"

"You mean, is someone in this department making it so nobody can prove Edison Faust killed Jack Hughes?" Bailey narrowed her eyes and I braced myself for an outburst.

Hendricks shrugged. "Don't you think it's possible?"

"Of course I think it's possible," Bailey said, and I gave her props for being realistic. In my experience, many in law enforcement would shrug off the possibility that they had a crooked cop among them. That's how Brett Henke stayed chief of the Minneapolis Police Department for as long as he did, before I exposed his corruption and he was sent packing. I wondered if a replacement had been named yet. *I should call Todd Waterman,* I thought.

"But…who that might be is an even bigger mystery," Bailey said.

"Maybe that's the real mystery," I said.

She nodded. "Maybe. Now you two get out of here and go solve Jack Hughes' murder."

We stood.

"Be careful," she said. "Edison Faust casts a long shadow in this town."

Hendricks and I thanked her and headed for the empty office we called our war room. We stood and gazed at the mess of papers and boxes from our last case. The whiteboard was covered with jotted notes, photos, and a veritable web of witnesses and suspects in the eleven-year-old disappearance of local waitress Mia Masterson and her newborn daughter Isabel.

"I still can't believe we found her," Hendricks said somberly.

"Yeah," I said, and reached for his hand. His strong fingers intertwined with mine. I could feel his warmth through my thin sheepskin glove.

"But." He raised my hand to his lips and kissed the back of my glove. "It's time to move on. Let's put all the Mia files away. Then I'll run to the vault and swap them out for the Jack Hughes case files."

We worked mostly in silence, carefully gathering up documents and photos, taking snapshots of the whiteboard before cleaning it, and placing everything back into banker's boxes. Hendricks found a large black marker in a drawer and wrote CLOSED on each box above the case number. Then he gathered up all the boxes and headed out into the hallway. "I'll be right back."

I sat in the rolling desk chair and pulled my phone out of my purse, settling in for a wait. Then I decided to try checking in on my mother.

I closed my eyes and concentrated, sending psychic signals to let her know I wanted to connect. She accepted my pings right away and a bright vision appeared like someone had just turned on a TV.

∞

The bedroom window overlooked the Bourbon River, and this side of the house was shaded by enormous oak and maple trees with rustling green leaves. Sunlight sparkled like diamonds on the water's surface.

My view suddenly shifted from the window to the bedroom door. Edison Faust shuffled in, a perma-scowl taking up most of his wrinkled face. He wore a blue polo shirt that hung on his bony frame and a pair of stained and frayed khaki shorts. His arms and legs were covered in liver spots. He held something in his right hand and his razor-thin lips moved over crooked yellow teeth. I wished I could hear what he was saying.

Then he held out his hand and I could see what was in it: a tarnished old belt buckle. He shoved it close to my mother's face and shook it, prompting her to lean back and raise her gloved hands protectively.

My view swiveled back to the door, and there was Nicholas. He was fresh out of the shower and looked a little more rested than yesterday. He took tentative steps into the room and gestured with his hands, trying to calm his grandfather down. I lowered my hands and watched the exchange.

Nicholas said something, and Edison visibly took a deep breath to calm himself. Then he held the belt buckle out to me again.

I hesitated, and reached for it.

∞

With a series of thumps and swishes, Hendricks reentered the war room carrying four yellowing banker's boxes marked with JACK HUGHES and a 1997 case number. I disconnected from my mother and blinked to focus on his face.

"You all right?" he asked as he distributed the boxes across the desk.

"A little tired, maybe. Just checked in on my mom and it turns out making those connections is pretty draining." I yawned. "I think I need a nap."

"Being hung over doesn't help much, I'm sure," Hendricks remarked. "How's your mom? Is she all right?" Hendricks removed the lids from the boxes and stashed them under the desk.

"Seems to be. Edison wanted her to touch an old belt buckle." I pulled a box closer to me.

We spent the next half hour or so poring through case documents. Then Hendricks picked up a dry-erase marker. "Okay, let's —"

He was interrupted by the crackle of his radio, followed by my dad's tinny voice. "Hello? Can you hear me, Jesse?"

Hendricks pressed the button on his own radio. "Hey Liam, I can hear you. What's up? Over."

"Oh, right, I should say 'over.'" My dad released his button, then immediately pressed it again. "Uh, thought I should tell you that Edison, Morgan, and Nicholas have left the Fortress. Uh, over."

Hendricks glanced at me with equal parts confusion and concern. "Is Dani with them? Over."

Crackle. "No, it appears they left her behind. I believe she is safe, so I'm following them."

I winced.

"Be careful, Liam. You don't want them to see you. Over."

Crackle. "They haven't spotted me." A pause, then: "They're turning into Greenhaven Grotto Park."

I caught Hendricks' eye and raised my brows. He gave me the briefest of nods, then keyed back into his radio. "Got it. Can you hang there and keep an eye on them? Over."

Crackle. "Yes. I'll find a spot out of their view and watch them with these newfangled binoculars."

That made us both chuckle. "Keep us updated, okay?" Over."

"Over and out." There was a note of childlike excitement in my dad's voice. *Walkie talkies: fun for all ages,* I thought.

"What is Greenhaven Grotto Park?" I asked.

"It's a large county park on the river, and it is full of sandstone caves. Dozens of them."

"I bet that's where my mom told them to go when she touched that belt buckle."

Hendricks pondered this for a few seconds. "It just…it seems so *obvious.* I thought Jack would have been more creative in finding a hiding place for his gold."

"Should we go out there?" I didn't like the thought of the Fausts finding the gold before we could. That would decimate our plan and put my mother's life in immediate danger. But then something occurred to me. "Hold on. She's not going to tell the Fausts where the gold *really* is. She's going to send them on a wild goose chase so we can get to it first." I knew I was right as soon as the words left my lips, and I felt immensely better.

Hendricks nodded and uncapped his marker. "Then how about we go back to Jack Hughes' case?"

∞

Nearly three hours later, Hendricks had sketched a basic murder board outlining what we knew about the Jack Hughes murder based on the case files we had. In the middle was Jack's driver's license photo from 1996; he was a friendly-looking man with a lined face, a long nose, a crooked coffee-stained grin and basically no hair left. Around this photo Hendricks had jotted a few of the more salient facts from the case:

FOUND 6/24/97, BEATEN: Jack's badly beaten body was discovered in his home on June 24, 1997 after Rusty Griffith, the neighborhood's mail carrier, noticed mail still in his mailbox and newspapers on the front step. This was so completely out of character for Jack that Rusty immediately called the police. When RJPD officers arrived, they noted the front door had been kicked in and discovered a mess of overturned furniture and massive amounts of blood. Clearly Jack had fought hard for his life.

DOG FOUND ALIVE: A small brown and white dog was found curled up next to Jack's body. He became aggressive and wouldn't let police near Jack. Animal Control had to be called.

TOD 6/22/97, HOMICIDE: Winston Steele, Greenhaven County medical examiner, noted extensive injuries on Jack's body, including broken ribs, a lacerated liver, a lacerated spleen, broken forearm and hand bones, and a six-inch fracture to the back of the skull. This caused his death, and Steele ruled it a homicide. He estimated Jack's time of death at about 11:00 the morning of June 22, 1997.

"Did they find a murder weapon?" I asked. The documents I reviewed didn't say.

Hendricks stopped writing on the board and paged through a report on the desk. "Doesn't look like it."

CAMPBELLS ELIMINATED: Investigators interviewed the sister of Jack's wife Arlene and her husband, Colleen and Teddy Campbell. Both had solid alibis for the day Jack died, and investigators couldn't land on a decent motive for them to kill Jack.

"Whoa. Teddy mentioned Jack's gold in his interview," Hendricks said, capping the marker and sitting in his chair to read.

"Wouldn't that be a potential motive?" I asked, intrigued. "What did he say?"

"He just asked what would happen to it now that Jack's gone." He turned a couple pages. "Yeah. Roy Shaw, lead detective on this case, wrote that he didn't consider either Colleen or Teddy to be a viable suspect. He also wrote 'Conducted additional search of house, no evidence of gold found.' So he probably dismissed it as a possible motive." He paused. "But word leaked and the town rumor mill went crazy anyway." He turned to the whiteboard and wrote **NO GOLD FOUND**.

I pulled a large yellow envelope marked CRIME SCENE PHOTOS out of a box and started looking through its contents. It was a violent and messy scene indeed. Jack's living room was quite literally covered in blood. It was splashed and streaked across every surface, and there was a large pool on the floor where Jack had lain for two days before he was found. I wasn't a blood spatter expert, but I knew enough to realize that blood on the ceilings and walls was probably castoff from a blunt instrument as it was being swung again and again, splitting flesh and breaking bone. My stomach turned at the thought of how terrified poor Jack must have been. It was an awful way to die.

Toward the bottom of the stack I found one photo that caught my interest. It showed what appeared to be an unfinished basement or crawlspace that was being used for storage. A large wooden chest, possibly a steamer trunk of some sort, sat under the stairs. I handed the photo to Hendricks. "Did anyone look in there?"

He examined the photo and then consulted a police report. "The trunk is on a list of items found at the scene. Roy wrote 'EMPTY' next to it."

I sighed. "Would have been too easy, I suppose."

Hendricks chuckled. "Who doesn't love the idea of an actual treasure chest full of gold?"

Just then various shades of red in various levels of intensity began to pulse behind my eyes, obliterating Hendricks and everything else within view. It reminded me a bit of the one time I caught a glimpse of the northern lights dancing across the sky.

"Rae? You all right?"

Instead of answering him, I closed my eyes and concentrated on my mother, thinking she might be trying to ping me. Nothing happened, so I shifted my focus to Mimi. A picture appeared behind my eyelids.

∞

I was standing in the living room of what appeared to be an older home. Or, more accurately, a home inhabited by older people. Heavy floral drapes, carpet the color of a pink carnation, brass lamps with yellowed accordion shades, and shelves packed with ceramic angel figurines made the room feel almost claustrophobic. A brick fireplace with a heavy wooden mantel was built into one wall. The mantel was packed with framed photographs; Kieran pointed at one in particular, a black-and-white photo in a gaudy brass frame sitting right in the middle, and I knew that was the one I should be most interested in.

Mimi moved forward for a closer look, leaning back and tipping her chin up to see better. An elderly man with two bruised eyes and a bandage taped to his forehead stepped into view, lifted the photo from the crowded mantel, and handed it to her. This was Jack Hughes' brother Paul. The resemblance was remarkable.

The photo showed a grinning young man wearing dungarees, a long-sleeved plaid flannel shirt with the sleeves rolled up to his elbows, work boots, and a soft cap with a visor cocked to one side of his head. His arms were crossed over his chest and he leaned against what appeared to be an enormous vertical water wheel. The camera flash glinted off the surface of a water-filled canal behind him.

∞

The crackling of Hendricks' radio brought me back. *Any more of those and I really will need a nap,* I thought. "Hello? Jesse? Can you hear me?" My dad's voice was still uncertain, making us both grin.

"We can hear you, Liam. Got an update for us? Over."

"They spent the day poking around in a series of caves along the river. I found a nice spot in the trees on the opposite bank and watched them. I must say, I didn't miss much with these binoculars. I could see just about everything over there."

"I'm glad to hear that, Liam," Hendricks said, smiling. "Did the Fausts find anything? Over."

Crackle. "No, it appears they left empty-handed. I'm going to follow them, and as soon as I'm sure Dani is all right, I'll head back to the house." He keyed out and then in again. "Over."

Hendricks chuckled. "See you in a bit then, Liam. Over and out." He looked at me, his amazing green eyes crinkled at the corners with genuine amusement, and laughed again. "I see where you get your adorable awkwardness."

I pretended to clutch my pearls in shock and indignation. "Excuse me, sir, I'm sure I have no idea what you mean. I am a lady, and as dignified as they come."

Hendricks cast a quick glance over his shoulder to ensure the office door was closed, then half-stood and grabbed my hand, pulling me toward him over the desk. I had to support my body weight with my other hand to keep from toppling over sideways. He met me in the middle with a deep kiss that sent lightning bolts and glitter straight down to my toes. The fact that we were inside a police station and probably on camera only added to the excitement.

He disengaged and, the tip of his nose barely touching mine, stared right into my soul. "I've been wanting to do that all day," he whispered.

I batted my eyelashes. "What took you so long?"

He growled and soul-kissed me again. He held my hand against his chest, and I could feel his heartbeat quicken. Mine was running like a jackrabbit.

He pulled away and let go of my hand so we could both stand up straight. "I'm sure Captain Bailey would disapprove of such wanton behavior in her department," he remarked, but he didn't look one bit intimidated. He was, in fact, still smiling. "Come on. Let's go home and see how the family did."

CHAPTER 7

I had just climbed into Hendricks' truck and buckled my seat belt for the ride back to his house when the colors took over again. Not red, though. This time it was varying shades of green that danced behind my eyes. *Red means Mimi, green must mean Mom,* I thought as I closed my eyes and accepted the pings.

∞

I recognized the cluttered room I stood in. I'd seen photos of Edison, Morgan and Nicholas in this very room, huddled around the computer monitor that sat on the oversized mahogany desk. Nearly every horizontal surface was littered with stacks of newspapers, documents, pens, and yellow legal pads. An old avocado green electric typewriter sat on a rolling cart in the far corner, coated in a thick layer of dust. A battered couch sat perpendicular to the desk to the right, and on the wall to the left hung a massive painted portrait of a clean-shaven young man in an Edwardian-era black suit with a high white collar, black buttoned waistcoat, and a black tie. He held a straw boater hat with both hands below his waist, and his black hair, longer than was customary for the time, was slicked back. His face was carefully neutral, probably because he had to stand still for so long that a smile would have been impossible — but the artist had captured a chilling intensity in his deep black eyes that was unmistakably Faust.

My mother approached the painting and felt around the edges between the gaudy frame and the wall until her fingers hooked into something. She gently pulled and the portrait swung away from the wall, revealing a safe with an intimidating-looking combination dial. She removed her glove and placed her fingertips on the dial for a moment. Then, having clearly gotten the safe's combination from a touch vision, her fingers twirled the dial back and forth a few times before turning the handle and pulling the safe door open.

I peered inside the dark recess and was just beginning to make out the shapes of the objects inside when headlights flashed through the window. My mother slammed the safe shut, closed the portrait back over it, and booked it out of Edison's office. She ran up the stairs and down the hall, slipped into her bedroom, and fumbled with the lock for a brief panicky moment before finally twisting the button to the locked position. She went to the chair next to the window and pulled a blanket over her lap in an effort to look like she'd been sitting there admiring the view the whole time the Fausts were gone.

My view shifted to the door just as Edison stormed into the room, spiderwebby hair floating around his head. He shook the belt buckle in my mother's face again as he shouted, his face turning scarlet with anger.

She wasn't backing down, though. Whatever she said, it was enough to placate Edison. He stalked out of her room, closing the door behind him.

She covered her face with her hands for just a moment, then let them fall to her lap.

∞

I came back just as Hendricks was pulling into his driveway. He gave me a sideways glance and smiled. "Welcome back."

I yawned and told him what I'd seen through my mom's eyes.

"The guy in the portrait was probably Stefan Faust," Hendricks said. "Edison's grandfather, founder of Faust Lumber, and pillar of the River Junction business community. In the privacy of his own home he was a raging drunk who brutally abused his wife Katherine and son Benedict – until Katherine put an end to Stefan's reign of terror with a bullet to his head in nineteen forty-two. She disappeared after that, leaving River Junction and her family in her dust."

A family defined by trauma, I thought.

"It also sounds like your dad was right, they went home empty-handed," Hendricks mused.

"And Edison is pissed. He yelled, but he didn't get aggressive with my mom." Another yawn. "Makes me think she convinced him to keep trying in the caves."

"Do you think he realizes your mom is sending him to the wrong place on purpose?"

"I don't think so. Yet. I'm sure he'll figure it out eventually, and that worries me." Edison Faust was a lot of things, but he wasn't a fool.

"We'll just have to either find the gold or arrest him for Jack's murder – or both – before that happens."

A deep sigh escaped me, as if I'd been holding my breath. "No pressure."

We made our way next door, where we found Mimi and Kieran in the living room. Mimi sat in a chair reading a beat up bodice-ripper romance novel she'd found on a side table, and Kieran sat on the couch with his phone, scrolling through his social media. They both looked up when the door closed behind us.

"Hey." Kieran set his phone on the coffee table and scooted to make room for Hendricks and me.

I plopped down next to him with another deep sigh and laid my head on his shoulder. "Hey."

Hendricks sat on the other side of me in a much less dramatic fashion. "How'd it go with Paul and Jeannette today?"

Mimi marked her page and closed her book. "That poor man."

Before I could ask a clarifying question, the front door opened and my dad walked in carrying several large fast food bags. "Dinner's here!"

Kieran and Hendricks hopped up and each took a bag to lighten his load a bit. They carried the bags into the kitchen and set a veritable feast out on the kitchen counter: two buckets of fried chicken, mashed potatoes and gravy, corn, mac and cheese, and biscuits with butter and honey. I hadn't realized how hungry I was until food was right in front of me.

We all loaded our plates and sat around the slightly wobbly dining room table. The room was silent for a few minutes while we ate, and then the debrief began.

"Mimi, what did you mean when you said 'That poor man'?" I asked before taking a bite of a buttery biscuit. I felt better – less hung over – with food in my system, and I only briefly wished I had a glass of wine in front of me. The craving flitted away with another taste of honey-drenched biscuit.

She wiped her mouth with a napkin. "Well, I was mostly referring to his injuries. Jeannette's too."

At first I didn't know what she was talking about, and then I remembered Paul's bandage and blackened eyes, and the text message Hendricks had sent me the previous day: *Remember I mentioned the elderly couple that was badly beaten? That was him and his wife Jeannette.*

"How are they doing?" Hendricks asked.

Kieran shrugged. "Jeannette is still dealing with concussion symptoms and the big gash on Paul's forehead is starting to heal. But they're both still pretty terrified."

"They didn't want to talk to us," Mimi said. "Wouldn't open the door more than a crack."

"Yeah, it took some convincing. We thought we were going to have to call you, Jesse." Kieran mixed corn into his mashed potatoes and shoveled a forkful into his mouth.

"They finally decided we were safe when we told them we're working with the River Junction Police Department to investigate Jack's murder," Mimi said, stifling a yawn.

"And what really convinced them was finding out we're victims of Edison Faust too." Kieran tossed his napkin onto his empty plate.

Mimi chuckled. "After that we couldn't shut them up."

Mimi and Kieran went on to tell us what they learned during their conversation with Jack Hughes' brother and sister-in-law.

Paul and Jeannette Hughes had just returned home from dinner at local eatery The Rummery with their son and grandkids the evening of July 7 when they were ambushed by Edison and Morgan Faust on the walk between their driveway and back door. Morgan implied that he had a weapon and forced the elderly couple to let them inside the house. Edison demanded that Paul hand over everything that had belonged to Jack; any hint of argument or hesitation earned both him and Jeannette a punch to the head.

My blood boiled as I listened. "What the fuck," I muttered, thoroughly disgusted. And more than a little pissed at myself for believing that Nicholas could be better than his father and grandfather. He was a Faust. I should have seen him for who — and what – he really was much sooner than I did.

Paul eventually acquiesced and, under Morgan's watchful eye, retrieved a dusty old shoe box from a storage closet. The box contained the last of Jack Hughes' possessions: a tarnished silver belt buckle he received as a twenty-fifth anniversary gift from Ainsley Mill, several glossy photos of Jack and his wife Arlene smiling in front Mount Rushmore, a tattered paperback copy of a Louis L'Amour novel, and a wrinkled old flour sack.

"Edison had Morgan give Paul two black eyes for his effort." Kieran said bitterly. "I guess he was looking for something more personal of Jack's, like his wedding ring."

"Why?" Hendricks asked.

"Because he wanted something that would tell Dani where the gold was," Mimi said. "A wedding ring would have been the perfect thing because it was made of metal and probably never left Jack's finger while he was married." She fiddled with her own rings.

"That explains the belt buckle," I said and waved away all the questioning looks. "I'll explain when you're done." I pushed my empty plate toward the center of the table. Was there anything quite as delicious as fried chicken with all the fixings? I didn't think so.

"Jack worked at Ainsley Mill for a really long time." Hendricks stood and started gathering everyone's plates. "Decades. I think it was the only company he ever worked for."

I stepped around the peninsula and into the kitchen to start cleaning up. If anyone was hoping for leftovers, they'd be disappointed.

"Thirty-seven years," Mimi said. "According to Paul, Jack was hired in the summer of nineteen-sixty by Bernard Ainsley himself." A wistful look crossed her soft face as she uttered her grandfather's name.

"That photo on Paul's mantel was Jack, wasn't it?" I had deposited the empty containers in the garbage and was wiping down the counter with a wet washcloth while Hendricks loaded the dishwasher.

Kieran nodded. "Paul said he never once considered working anywhere else. He felt he owed Bernard a debt."

"Why's that?" my dad asked.

Mimi leveled her gaze on Hendricks. "Did you know that Jack Hughes and Edison Faust went to high school together?"

Hendricks opened his mouth to answer, but I beat him to it. "I knew that. Nicholas mentioned it when he told me about Jack's gold. He said Jack and Edison were best buddies in high school." I paused, remembering the midnight conversation with Nicholas outside my dad's house. "Until Edison's girlfriend broke up with him and started dating Jack."

Mimi nodded. "Arlene. She became his wife."

"You won't be shocked to hear that Edison made life pretty difficult for Jack and Arlene after that," Kieran said. "He freaked out at school when he saw Arlene wearing Jack's letter jacket, injured both of them and got suspended. Damn near didn't graduate."

"Dead animals started showing up in their lockers," Mimi added. "He'd follow them around town in his car and just sit there watching them." A shiver visibly wracked her frail body.

"Jack's first job in high school was working as an attendant at Purmort's service station. He lasted two whole days there, until the manager got a mysterious phone call. Jack was promptly fired without explanation," Kieran said.

"I don't know exactly how, but Jack caught my grandfather's attention, and he made sure Jack had a job after he graduated from high school." Mimi sighed. "Edison couldn't touch him after that. I guess I understand why Jack was so loyal to Bernard and the Ainsley Mill."

I remembered something I'd read in Jack's case files. "Arlene passed away a few years before Jack did, right?"

Mimi and Kieran nodded in unison. "Paul said her death devastated Jack. He was never the same." Mimi's voice wavered ever so slightly.

"Did you ask Paul about the gold?" my dad asked.

"We did, and Paul said Jack absolutely did not trust banks and conducted all his business with cash. But if he was hoarding gold, Paul never saw it." Kieran shrugged.

Mimi and Kieran didn't have much else of substance to discuss from their visit with Paul and Jeannette Hughes. We took advantage of the lull in conversation to move from the dining room to much more comfortable seating options in the living room. As soon as we were settled, Kieran brought us back to my earlier comment. "What did you mean when you said 'That explains the belt buckle?'"

I described seeing Edison hand Jack's belt buckle to my mother. The expressions on my family's faces changed from fascination to worry to relief to terror and back to relief as I spoke.

"He's using the belt buckle as the touch object for Dani," Mimi said.

"Seems so," I said.

"Could you tell what she said to Edison?" Kieran asked.

I shook my head.

"But we do know they went to Greenhaven Grotto Park." We all turned to look at my dad, who had sat quietly though most of the conversation. Exhaustion and worry deepened the lines around his eyes. "I watched them put on rubber boots and poke around in sandstone caves for several hours today."

"Did they find anything?" Kieran wanted to know.

"Not that I could see. Watching them interact was quite eye-opening, however."

"Did they argue?" A ghost of a smile played around Mimi's lips.

"Constantly." My dad grinned. "They're like a bunch of nattering old ladies."

Everyone chuckled.

"Nicholas in particular seemed especially frustrated. I got the sense that he's maybe not so enchanted with his grandfather."

I thought of the haunted shell of a man who showed up at my dad's house yesterday and wondered if there might not be a kernel of good still left in Nicholas after all. I'd been angry at him while listening to what Edison and Morgan had done to Paul and Jeannette Hughes. Now I just felt sorry for him.

Mimi asked Hendricks and me what we'd learned about Jack's murder. We sketched out the basics without going too far into the gory details. We did, however, mention one detail that I thought could prove helpful.

"The crime scene inventory showed that Jack had a big wooden chest or trunk stashed in his basement," I said.

"Ooo, do you think he hid his gold there?" Kieran asked.

"I had the same thought, but the report noted that it was empty."

Mimi understood my thought process immediately. "Might still be able to get visions from it, though."

I pointed at her. "Exactly."

Kieran was doubtful. "How likely is it that the trunk is still in his house after all these years?"

I shrugged. "Probably not great, but don't you think it's worth a try?"

Kieran looked at Mimi, who dipped her head in agreement.

My dad stood and stretched. "I'm sorry, all. I know it's early, but I am beat. I'm going to bed."

We all thought that sounded like a great idea.

Thursday, July 22, 2021

CHAPTER 8

A distant beeping sound seared through perfect tranquility.

No. I burrowed deeper into the warm covers.

The beeps grew progressively louder. More insistent. Imploring me to get up and start my day.

No.

"Rae." Even Hendricks' deep, sexy voice wasn't enough. I clung to sleep like a child with its blankie.

"Fine." Footsteps moved away from me, and silence settled once again. I allowed myself to sink back into unconsciousness. Until the bed itself shifted, jarring me awake. I groaned. "No."

"I made you some coffee, but you can't have it until you get up."

I could smell the deep, bitter aroma of fresh Beananza dark roast. "You bastard," I mumbled.

He chuckled, and I finally gave up the fight. I wrangled myself to a sitting position and carefully took the steaming mug from his hands.

"Now get up. They're waiting for us next door."

I sighed and set my mug on the bedside table. "Ugh. Fine."

After a quick shower and a couple of aspirin for a lingering headache, I followed Hendricks through dew-covered grass to meet up with my family. *Ugh. I hate wet toes.*

We found Mimi and Kieran sitting in the living room, dressed and ready to discuss the day's plans.

"Where's Dad?" I asked.

"He left for the Fortress an hour ago, coffee and binoculars in hand," Kieran said.

"You guys still want to visit Jack Hughes' old house?" Hendricks asked. Mimi and Kieran nodded, and Hendricks gave them the address from memory. "The current owners bought the house from Jack's estate; their names are Duke and Blanche Gatlin. One word of caution: they have had numerous break-ins and Fausts trespassing on their property over the years. And they are bitter about it."

"Why do they stay?" I wondered.

Hendricks shrugged. "Got me."

"We will tread carefully," Kieran promised.

Hendricks stood and held his hand out to me. "Come on, Rae. We've got more case files to read through."

"Let's do it." I took his hand and he pulled me up.

∞

Of course we needed to swing through the Beananza drive-thru on our way to the station. My dad radioed with an update just as we were pulling away from the window.

"Edison, Morgan, and Nicholas are headed back to Grotto Park," he reported. "I'll follow and watch them like I did yesterday. Uh, over."

"You're getting pretty good at doing stakeouts, Liam," Hendricks said, smiling.

"I guess I missed my calling." My dad chuckled. "Over and out."

Hendricks parked and we made our way across the parking lot toward the station. "I'm going to go back to the vault and grab more case files."

"For what?"

"I think it might be worth looking to see what other cases we have with Edison's name on them."

I smacked his chest with the back of my right hand. "Oh! That's a great idea!"

"Ow! Dude, your knuckles are sharp," he said and laughed.

"Sorry. Sometimes my enthusiasm gets the best of me."

"Clearly you don't know your own strength." He stopped me just outside the door, looked around to make sure nobody was watching, and kissed me.

We disengaged and I asked, "You do realize this place is lousy with cameras, right?"

His shoulders touched his earlobes and a goofy smile took over his handsome face. "Can't help it." He opened the door and we went inside.

I went to the war room to wait while Hendricks went to the vault to pull more case files. I stared at the beginnings of Jack Hughes' murder board for a minute. It was becoming more and more apparent that Jack Hughes' murder might just be scratching the surface of the wrongs Edison Faust had done over the years. The potential for this case to explode in scope scared and overwhelmed me. I suddenly began to doubt that we could ever destroy the machine he'd spent a lifetime building.

Thinking about that made me want to leave the police station and head directly to the Majestic Saloon for the biggest glass of wine the bartender could pour. I took a deep breath and decided to check in on my mother instead. Seeing that she was okay would make me feel better – and wouldn't leave me with a hangover the next morning.

∞

My mother had headed straight for Edison's office as soon as they left; the garish portrait of Stefan Faust hung ajar and the wall safe was open, exposing a deep, dark recess. She sat on the couch and rifled through the safe's contents.

Numerous manila folders had been meticulously labeled with the name of the documents inside them: Faust Lumber Property Deed. 102 River Street Deed. 2015 Chev Suburban Title. Simone Will & Testament.

I knew that 102 River Street was the address of the Fortress, but I'd never heard the name Simone. Who was that?

One folder was cryptically labeled Nicholas, but it was empty.

She set the manila folders aside and picked up a large wad of cash held together with a thick rubber band. After a quick flip through one end of the stack I estimated she was holding at least twenty thousand dollars in her hands.

She set that on top of the manila folders and pulled a beaten-up old shoebox toward her. She didn't spend a lot of time digging around in it, but I could see that it was stuffed full with a random assortment of notes and papers, as well as photographs taken in different eras – from square black-and-whites with white borders to four-by-six color glossies printed at the local Ritz Camera. Also inside the box: newspaper clippings of varying age and crispiness; notes written in a jerky, uneven script and torn from legal pads, napkins, envelopes — whatever bits of paper someone, presumably Edison, could find; typed memos; printed emails and online news articles. There must have been years worth of stuff in this box. She didn't spend any time reading them, though. Not yet.

She went back to the safe and found an old pocket watch. She held it up by its chain, letting it dangle and spin in front of her face. It was silver, slightly tarnished, and intricately engraved with a leaf-and-vine pattern on the back and front. She set it carefully in the palm of her left hand, examined it closely, then flipped the watch cover open. There was nothing remarkable about the clock face, but something was written on the inside of the cover. She brought the watch close to her face and squinted. Engraved in delicate, worn, nearly unreadable cursive writing was the name Stefan Alexander Faust and the year 1910.

I did some quick math in my head; Edison's grandfather received this watch when he was around fifteen years old. My mother leaned back a bit so I could see Stefan's portrait, and there it was: a silver chain hung between a buttonhole and a lower pocket of his suit vest, where he'd tucked his watch.

Her gloved hands carefully set the watch aside and picked up the last artifact from Edison's safe: a gold circle pin with multicolored carved gemstones set in it. It too was fairly tarnished, but it was still beautiful. Sunlight from the front window gave each stone a mellow glow. I'd never seen anything like it. My mother removed her glove and grasped the pin with bare fingertips.

∞

The familiar bumps and swishes brought me back just in time to see Hendricks nearly go ass over teakettle under the weight of six banker's boxes as he struggled to carry them through the office door. I jumped up and relieved him of the top two just in time.

We set them on the desk, and then Hendricks turned to leave again.

"I have a few more boxes to grab. Sit tight, I'll be right back."

I drank my coffee, hoping the caffeine would offset the fatigue, and thought about the items my mother had found in Edison's safe while I sat tight for Hendricks. *How gorgeous is that pin?* I thought. *Kind of old-fashioned, but it would look so pretty on a nice dress or a sweater. And that watch…it looked like it's seen a lot of use over the last hundred-plus years. If Stefan and Benedict and Edison all carried it, it could be very useful to us. And I'm dying to dig into that shoebox and see what's really in there.* It was pretty obvious that Danielle had found a treasure trove in Edison's safe; I just didn't know quite yet how valuable those items would be.

Hendricks returned carrying more boxes and a thick accordion folder. He set them on the desk with the rest of the boxes and sat in his chair with a dramatic sigh.

"Think you got everything?" I asked, forcing myself to suppress an incredulous laugh. It would take us days to get through all of this. Maybe weeks. Time we didn't have.

Hendricks swiveled his chair to face me. "Oh, I'm positive I missed some." He ran a hand over his blond crewcut. "I grew up here and I'm shocked at how many criminal case files have the Faust name on them. They go back *decades.*"

There had to be a dozen boxes here. Maybe more. All I could do was stare.

"I caught Phelps at his desk and asked if I could borrow his files on the Paul and Jeannette Hughes case while I was at it. That's the only active case, in that folder. Everything else is either cold or closed and in the boxes."

I reached out and turned one of the boxes until I could see the label. C LANGE was written in black marker with a 1981 case number on it. Another one was marked ROBERT MARTIN with a 1987 case number. One box was considerably yellower than the others; this was the M CONLEY case, and it was nearly sixty years old. "Wow, you weren't kidding," I said. "This one is from nineteen sixty-four."

We debated how to organize these case files so we could start to get our arms around them, and decided to start by listing them all in chronological order. Hendricks dragged a huge portable whiteboard on wheels into our increasingly cluttered office so we could keep the broader Faust work separate from the Jack Hughes murder board. He wrote on the board with a black marker while I read police reports and called out pertinent facts. It took us a couple of hours just to get through four of the cases.

M CONLEY was Myrtle Conley, of River Junction. She was found dead in her home in February 1964 at the age of 37. Edison's name was all over the reports as an "acquaintance" of Myrtle's, although the detective, a man named Bill Dodge, seemed to have his doubts about that. His belief was that young Edison Faust had wormed his way into the life of a lonely widow and scammed her out of her life savings. Along the way he'd also convinced her to make him a beneficiary on her $20,000 life insurance policy.

Dodge was able to track down some of Myrtle's family, who told him she'd become estranged from them in early 1963, after she'd met a man who'd claimed to be an operative with the Central Intelligence Agency. They didn't know much more than that; she'd been secretive about it. Then Dodge called Myrtle's bank and mortgage company and discovered she'd died penniless. Her bank account had been drained and she was on the verge of losing her house.

Maybe there was something to the detective's theory after all.

And then something strange happened: the coroner abruptly changed the manner of Myrtle's death from homicide of undetermined means to suicide by drug poisoning, and that ended Dodge's investigation. He went on to other cases, and Myrtle's case went into the vault.

Edison probably laughed all the way to the bank.

I closed up the M CONLEY box and pushed it aside to make room for another box – this one labeled L PORTER II.

Lewis Porter, Junior was a chronic alcoholic who was found lying next to a trash bin behind the Majestic Saloon in July 1965 with a hole in his chest. Detective Bill Dodge was back on the case. Bar patrons spoke of an "investment opportunity" that Edison Faust had been pitching for months: a futuristic flying car that was supposedly in development by a secret new automobile manufacturer. He offered Porter and other bar patrons the exclusive opportunity to "invest in the future" for only $1,000 and promised a guaranteed 40% return.

Porter, a fan of the animated TV show *The Jetsons*, had promptly written Edison a check. It was money he couldn't really afford to spend, but his drinking buddies said he was over the moon excited to be in on what he called "the wave of the future."

And then…nothing happened. Edison strung Porter and the rest of his "investors" along for over a year.

Two days before Porter was shot and killed, Majestic Saloon patrons ganged up on Edison, demanding to see the 40% return he'd promised them on their investments. It got physical, and he ended up tossed out on the street with a broken nose and a black eye.

Edison returned to the bar the following day with his Colt Trooper revolver in hand, drunkenly shouting at fellow patrons to back off or they would find out for themselves what he was capable of.

The next day Porter was dead – and Edison was inexplicably never questioned. Porter ended up in the vault with Myrtle Conley, their cases ice cold.

It seemed to me that someone was actively intervening in these cases to stop or prevent detectives from investigating them. *I wonder who it was*, I thought as I moved L PORTER II out of the way and opened the box labeled E R FAUST.

I was shocked to discover that this was Elaine Reese Faust, Edison's first wife.

"Holy shit, that fucker was *married?*" Hendricks stared at me with wide eyes.

Elaine's body was found floating in the Bourbon River in late April 1972. Detective Loren Watson found that Elaine had suffered a terrible personal loss six months earlier when her beloved aunt, Catherine Parkay, died under mysterious circumstances on her expansive ranch in Watford City, North Dakota. Elaine fell into a deep depression and never recovered. Her death was declared a suicide and Edison inherited her estate. Watson did not document how much it was worth before the case was closed and sent to the vault.

The box marked AHLQUIST involved an armed carjacking in downtown River Junction in October 1978. Peter Ahlquist and his young daughter Stacy were on their way to Levendal's on Third Avenue for an ice cream. When Peter stopped at the four-way intersection with Hughes Street, two masked men with guns materialized, forced them out of their 1975 Chevy Monte Carlo, and drove away, tires squealing. The car was found submerged in the Mississippi River the next day. Watson strongly suspected the traumatic carjacking was related to the robbery of the First State Bank of River Junction that same day, but could never prove it.

The case files on the bank robbery were rather sparse, but that was not surprising. Bank robbery was a federal crime, so the FBI would have immediately supplanted RJPD as the primary investigative agency. However, Watson did note that two masked men with guns escaped with over $50,000 in cash. He also noted that bank manager Frank Barnale was pistol-whipped during the course of the robbery and died three weeks later without regaining consciousness.

Watson clearly suspected Edison Faust in the carjacking, the bank robbery, and the death of Frank Barnale — but somehow neither the RJPD nor the FBI could ever establish a tie.

"How?" I asked, incredulous. "How does Edison Faust escape the F-B-fricking-I?"

Hendricks shook his head. "There's only so much law enforcement, even the FBI, can do when nobody's willing to talk," he said.

I sighed. "I have to stop." Completely overwhelmed by the sheer volume of case documentation surrounding us, I sat back in my chair and pulled my hair up in a messy bun. We had so many cases to look through. I pulled my hair out of the messy bun, then promptly tied it back up again. "Holy shit, Jesse. We're never going to get through all of this."

Hendricks nodded, but didn't say anything. He just let me process.

"I mean, holy *shit*." I gestured at the case list on the portable board, and then at all the boxes, just in case he didn't yet grasp the size and scope of what we were taking on. "How in the fuck do the Fausts leave such a trail of destruction for so long and get away with it?"

He shook his head and stuck his marker between his teeth as he contemplated the list. "And like I said, I probably didn't even grab them all."

I stared at Frank Barnale's name for a few seconds; something about his case seemed familiar. I couldn't place it, so instead I said, "This is how Edison has been bankrolling his entire life."

Hendricks thought about that for a few seconds, then shrugged. "Probably. Fraud, life insurance payouts, inheritances, bank robberies…"

"…making a living from a life of crime," I finished. "And he's got government cronies sweeping it all under the rug for him."

"It does make a morbid sort of sense."

The locked door in my memory cracked open, and a lone memory, one I had already wrangled back inside, sneaked out: the killing of school resource officer Ray Schuster outside my high school the fall of my sophomore year. My breath caught in my throat. "Jesse.

"There's more."

CHAPTER 9

He frowned. "More what? More Faust cases?"

I nodded. "We haven't even considered cases outside River Junction."

Hendrick's hands flew to the top of his head, as if to keep his skull from exploding. "Holy crap, you're right."

"Kieran watched Morgan shoot Ray Schuster dead in the street outside Washburn High School in Minneapolis. Mimi's sister Pearl died in Minneapolis."

Hendricks scooted his chair closer to the desk and picked up the phone. He dialed an extension and only had to wait a second or two for the RJPD records tech to answer her phone.

"Laura, can you get me a phone number for Detective Matt Starr in Minneapolis?" A brief pause, then a chuckle. "We used to bowl together, but I haven't talked to him in a long time. I don't know if the number I have for him is current." Another pause. "Thanks a ton, Laura. I owe you one." He hung up and looked at me, his green eyes on fire.

I was stuck on something he'd said. "Did you…" I tried to hold in a giggle and only succeeded in snorting a little. "Did you say you used to bowl?" The mental image of the handsome, physically fit cop in front of me wearing a bowling shirt and shoes was so delightful, I laughed out loud.

Hendricks' face reddened, but he smiled. "I was Twin Cities Police League champ in twenty-twelve and twenty-thirteen. I was also captain of the bowling team in high school. Go River Junction Cyclones!"

"Shut. Up," I gasped between howls of laughter. "I would have pegged you for captain of the football team, not the bowling team."

His smile widened. "I was that too. Football in the fall, bowling in the winter, baseball in the spring. And I played guitar in a band with three of my buddies."

I took off my gloves and wiped my eyes, my laughing fit trailing into occasional hiccupy giggles. "A more talented fellow I've never met."

The desk phone rang and Hendricks picked it up. He grabbed a pen and scribbled on a piece of scratch paper as Laura read a number to him. "Got it. Thanks again." He disconnected from her and reopened the line, then dialed Matt Starr's number.

"Rock Star! Is that you?" His voice reverberated in our little office. "It's me, Hambone!"

Hambone? The insane urge to giggle again bubbled up into my throat. I bit my lip hard to suppress it and started spinning Grace Ainsley's ring around and around on my left ring finger.

"I know, it's been a long time. How've you been, my man?" Hendricks seemed genuinely glad to be speaking to his old friend. He listened for a minute or two, then: "Congratulations, that is fantastic news! I always knew you and Sunshine would end up together." He chuckled, then listened. "I get it. Sometimes the path to our true love is longer than we'd like it to be." Hendricks looked straight at me and held my gaze for two or three intense seconds, igniting a fireball in my gut. Then he looked back down at the desk. "So listen, the reason I called…"

I tuned out and stared at Grace's ring as I fiddled with it, completely hung up on the look he'd just given me. I didn't want to read anything into that look, but it sort of felt like he was trying to tell me I was his true love. My heart skipped a beat at the thought. We'd known each other not quite two weeks, but in that short time he'd enriched my life in more ways than I ever thought possible. He offered a level of stability and kindness that I'd never experienced outside my family. My life felt more complete with him in it.

The crazy thing was, not so long ago I'd thought Nicholas Faust was my true love. I'd waited a dozen years for him and for the life I thought he could give me. As much as I hated to admit it, I'd been wrong. Even on his best day Nicholas couldn't hold a candle to Jesse Hendricks.

Hendricks brought me back. "Raegan."

I blinked. "Yeah?"

"What was Pearl's last name?"

"Oh. Uh, it was Christensen." I spelled it for him.

He nodded and returned to his call. "I'm interested in any case files, hot or cold, open or closed, that MPD might have related to Danielle and Liam O'Rourke, Emily Lownsdale, Pearl Christensen, and Edison and Morgan Faust." He spelled each last name as he said it. "Right. And you'll want to go pretty far back. I know Pearl died in the nineteen-seventies." He paused, listening. "Awesome. Appreciate it, Matt. Tell Sunshine I say hello."

Smiling, he hung up and looked at me. "He's going to check and get back to me."

We sat and stared at each other for what felt like an eternity. Then I realized we had one more call to make. I stood up, put my gloves back on, and opened Elaine Faust's case file box. I dug around inside until I found the coroner's report.

"What are you doing?" Hendricks asked, intrigued.

I sat back down. "I'm just spitballing here, but what if Edison had something to do with Elaine's aunt's untimely passing?"

The frown deepened. "You think Edison Faust is going to travel all the way to –" he snatched the typed report from my fingers and consulted it " – Watford City, North Dakota to take out his wife's aunt?"

I sat back in my chair and grinned. "I bet he would if said aunt had money. That part of North Dakota is lousy with oil."

Understanding dawned on Hendricks' face.

"And what if the aunt planned to leave that money to her favorite niece Elaine?"

"Elaine's husband might be tempted to make that happen sooner than nature intended," Hendricks mused.

"Right. And once the money is Elaine's, all he has to do is get rid of her. They have no kids, so he's the sole beneficiary of his wife's estate."

Hendricks leaned forward and propped his elbows on the desk and his head in his hands. "Bankrolling his life. Holy shit."

"I have no idea if that's what happened, but I think it's worth looking into."

Hendricks pulled the desk phone toward him, picked up the receiver, and dialed a number. "Hey Laura, It's your fav–" He grinned. "Just one more, pretty please?" He pumped a fist. "Awesome, thank you. I need to get in touch with law enforcement in Watford City, North Dakota." Another pause, another grin. "You heard correctly. I'm not sure if it would be city or county out there, I'm hoping you can dig up a name and number for me." Pause. "Thank you, Laura. I owe you a big piggy Beananza drink for this." He hung up. "She's getting tired of hearing from me." He stood and stretched. "I don't know about you, but I could use a break."

"Me too." Watching him stretch made me yawn. I could not wait to get out of this cluttered and claustrophobic room. The air felt heavy. And sad.

"What do you say we go see what your dad's up to at Grotto Park?"

I grinned and grabbed my purse. "Speaking of Beananza…"

CHAPTER 10

A cardboard drink carrier holding three fresh coffees sat precariously on my lap as Hendricks navigated his truck through the woods across the Bourbon River from Grotto Park. We slowly rounded a curve and I spied my dad's SUV parked way off to the side. "There."

Hendricks nodded and pulled up behind it, then grabbed his RJPD-issued field glasses. We got out of the truck and tried not to make too much noise as we made our way through the trees, toward the river. It reminded me of the time I spent up in the northwoods, investigating the cause of a cabin fire that claimed the life of my neighbors' dog and uncovering a local cold case while I was at it. That was just a few weeks ago. It felt like forever ago.

"Oh, here's a deer trail," Hendricks murmured. I fell in behind him and we marched along in single file like a couple of schoolchildren. The trail ended at a small clearing that looked out on the river.

I heard my dad before I saw him. "Over here, kids."

Hendricks and I veered right and there he was. He'd set up a folding camp chair in the woods just next to the clearing. He had a great view of the caves across the river, but nobody over there could see him among the trees on this side.

"How's it going?" I handed him a still-warm coffee.

He accepted it gratefully. "Oh, entertaining as ever. They've been inside one of the bigger caves for fifteen minutes. I expect they'll emerge anytime now." He took a sip. "Have you connected with your mother today?"

I sat cross-legged on the forest floor next to his chair and drank from my own cup. "I did, and she seems fine. She figured out how to get out of her room and has been going through Edison's things while they're away."

My dad chuckled and shook his head. His relief was palpable. "Anything interesting?"

I told him about Edison's safe and its contents.

"Do you think there's anything useful in there?" Hendricks asked. He stood next to a tree and trained his binoculars on the caves across the river.

"Oh, I have no doubt Edison's safe is loaded with clues. I know that's where I would stash incriminating evidence if I were a lifelong criminal," I said.

"Here they come." My dad handed me his binoculars. I raised them to my eyes and adjusted the zoom and the focus a bit – and I could see everything across the river with perfect clarity, like I was standing right there. The quality of the optics was incredible, and I said so.

"Nothing but the best for the River Junction Police Department," Hendricks said in a low voice.

Nicholas emerged from the cave first. He wore green rubber boots, jeans, and a filthy white t-shirt. His jet-black hair hung in his eyes. Right behind him came Edison, also wearing rubber boots and leaning on a tree branch he was using as a walking stick. Morgan brought up the rear, looking as scarred and raggedy as ever. All three held flashlights. They stood in a loose circle on the rocks and immediately started bickering. At first my brain didn't know how to handle the dissonance caused by seeing them up close but hearing them a couple hundred yards out. I adjusted, and if I listened extra closely, I could make out what they were saying.

"She's lying to us," Edison rasped.

"Oh, give it a rest," Nicholas retorted. He looked exhausted; I could count every dark circle under his eyes, if I wanted to. "She didn't know exactly which cave."

"But she *should*." Edison was shouting now, making it much easier to hear him. "With that psychic ability of hers, she should know with pinpoint accuracy where the gold is. She's got us searching hundreds of caves like a bunch of damn fools."

Morgan said something unintelligible, earning himself a smack in the shin with Edison's walking stick. The *thuck* sound the impact made was perfectly clear where I sat, and I winced as Morgan doubled over in pain.

"Asshole," Hendricks muttered.

Nicholas apparently felt the same way. "Enough!" he shouted and lunged at his grandfather. He had no trouble snatching the stick from Edison's bony, liver-spotted hand. He held it like a baseball bat. "You hit either of us with this fucking thing again and I will crush your worthless skull with it."

He could do it, too. Nicholas wasn't tall, but he was very fit and stronger than he looked. The old man wouldn't stand a chance.

"Danielle wants to go home to her family. You're the fool if you think she's going to jeopardize that by lying to us." He tossed the stick on the ground in front of Edison and stalked away, presumably to their car.

"You think I'm going to share this gold with you now? You fucking ingrate." Edison picked up the stick and followed Nicholas, his thick-soled shoes shuffling over the rocks. Nobody offered to help the old man. *I'm sure neither would be heartbroken if Edison fell into the water and drowned,* I thought. Morgan limped after Edison, his head down and stringy salt and pepper hair hanging in his face. They all disappeared from view.

So Nicholas was telling the truth when he said Edison had offered to cut him in on the gold, I thought. It was cold comfort as I touched the fading but still tender bruises on my neck. I lowered my binoculars and looked at my dad. "Was he…protecting Mom?"

Liam shrugged and unfolded himself from his chair. "That certainly isn't the response I was expecting."

Hendricks helped me up. "I thought that was weird too."

"Come on, let's head home," my dad said. "See how Emily and Kieran did with the Gatlins today. We can grab a pizza on the way."

"Gino's is the best pie in town," Hendricks said. "My treat."

The Fausts had the benefit of a several minute head start and a short commute from Grotto Park, so I figured they were back at the Fortress by the time Hendricks and I climbed into his truck. "I'm going to check on my mom," I told him, bracing myself for the inevitable exhaustion I would have afterward. He nodded and I closed my eyes.

∞

She was sitting in the chair by the window again, looking out at the sparkling river and the glorious summer afternoon. My view shifted toward the door, and there was Nicholas. He'd changed into his usual black athletic shorts and t-shirt, and he looked even more exhausted up close; the dark circles under his eyes had dark circles of their own. He held a black metal tray with a floral pattern on it, upon which sat a TV dinner and a large glass of milk. His lips moved as he set the tray on the bedside table.

I gazed at the TV dinner — fried chicken — for a moment, then my mother's eyes shifted back to Nicholas' face as he spoke. My mother nodded, and Nicholas held my gaze as she replied. They were having an entire conversation. Judging by the fairly relaxed, almost friendly look in Nicholas' eyes, it was going well and she wasn't in danger.

I wished I could hear what was being said.

After a minute or two, Nicholas dipped his head, signaling that the conversation had ended, and made his way back toward the door. When he got there he turned and glanced at me briefly, his eyes unreadable, then ducked through the door and closed it behind him.

My mother picked up the tray and brought it to her bed, where she sat and began to eat.

∞

Hendricks followed me into the house carrying two large pizza boxes and a foil-lined bag containing aromatic garlic bread. He set them on the counter while I rummaged through the kitchen for plates and silverware.

"What is that deliciousness I smell?" Kieran called from the living room.

"Dinner," I replied. "Jesse says it's the best in town."

Kieran appeared, followed closely by Mimi. My dad emerged from the hallway a few minutes later, fresh from the shower. While my family and Hendricks loaded their plates with gooey thin-crust pizza and warm garlic bread, I remembered the bottle of wine I'd stashed in the fridge yesterday. *Boy, that would sure taste good with pizza,* I thought. I decided to pour myself a glass. *Just one.*

I went to the fridge and retrieved the bottle, then opened the cupboard that housed the cups and glasses. I was so focused on having a drink that I didn't even consider the fact that Hendricks was right there in the kitchen, watching my every move.

"Raegan." I heard the warning in his voice loud and clear, and ignored it. I set a drinking glass on the counter and twisted the cap on the wine bottle.

"We talked about this." His tone was wracked with disappointment.

I decided right then that I was not having any of Hendricks' sanctimonious bullshit. "You know what, Jesse?" I stared defiantly at him as the wine gurgled into the glass. "I'm having one glass. With dinner. There's nothing wrong with having just one." I gave Hendricks a look that dared him to challenge me.

He set his plate on the counter and crossed his arms over his toned chest. His green eyes snapped. "Since when have you been able to stop at just one?"

That was a low blow, but he was absolutely right – and that enraged me. I slammed the bottle down on the counter. "Fuck you, Jesse. I will have a drink if I want one. End. Of. Discussion." I took a provocatively long drink from my glass.

Hendricks shook his head, picked up his plate, and sat at the table. We all followed suit and spent a few tense minutes stuffing our faces with delicious Gino's pizza.

My dad finally broke the silence. "Emily, Kieran, did you visit the Gatlins today?"

"They wanted nothing to do with us," Kieran said. "Opened the door angry. Told us they call the cops on trespassers and invited us to leave their goddamn property immediately."

Hendricks sighed and nodded. "I thought that might happen. They've been pretty well terrorized."

"Mimi was able to get something, though."

"How?" I asked.

Mimi delicately wiped her lips with her napkin. "Well, I happened to notice that there's a cast iron handrail on their front steps. I may have removed a glove and touched it."

"What did you see?"

"I had to sift through a couple decades' worth of visions, and more birds, squirrels, and mail carriers than I could count, but I finally found what I was looking for. The vision was quite faded, but I saw a much younger Edison and Morgan Faust running out of the house. They were both covered in blood. Morgan had a length of wood under one arm, and it also was covered in blood."

My mind reeled. Mimi had just confirmed what we all knew: that Edison and Morgan did indeed kill Jack Hughes. The challenge now would be to corroborate what she saw with actual, physical proof. And as far as I could tell, there was only one way to do that.

I turned to Hendricks. "Did they find the murder weapon?" I wracked my brain trying to remember if the case files I'd seen mentioned that critically important detail.

"Nope," he said tersely.

"We have to find it," I said. "That'll be the key to tying the Fausts to Jack's murder."

"It could be anywhere. Maybe they buried it, or tossed it in one of the rivers. If that's the case, it might be gone forever."

I thought of Edison's safe. "I think there's a decent chance they still have it. I don't think they throw anything away." My whole head felt warm and fuzzy.

Kieran asked what I meant by that, and I described seeing the contents of Edison's safe while our mother rifled through them, which led to Hendricks and I talking about all we'd learned so far about Edison Faust's criminal past.

"We could have Mom look for that hunk of wood inside the Fortress," I suggested. "She breaks out of her room and snoops around every time the Fausts leave."

"Oh, I hope she's careful," Mimi said.

"I don't think I would throw anything away either, if I lived a life of crime," Kieran said. "I mean, jeez, you never know what could end up being evidence."

I went to the kitchen and searched drawers until I found a notepad and pen. I sat back down at the table and scrawled LOOK AROUND FOR A HEAVY LENGTH OF WOOD. MIGHT HAVE BLOOD ON IT. on a sheet of paper, then closed my eyes and pinged my mom. She connected and I opened my eyes, allowing her to see the note in front of me. I held the connection open for a few more seconds, then let her go. I hoped she'd seen and understood.

Message passed, the conversation shifted to my dad's day, and he described watching the Fausts tromp in and out of the sandstone caves of Grotto Park and not find anything. "Edison is getting frustrated," he finished.

"But Nicholas is trying to keep him in line," I interjected. "He threatened to bash Edison's head in with his own walking stick." I drank the rest of my wine and made a show of setting the empty glass on the table. I looked at Hendricks to see if he noticed I was stopping at one glass, just like I said I would. His face was passive.

Kieran frowned. "Why is he doing that?"

I shrugged. "Maybe Nicholas is frustrated too. Frustrated with how Edison treats people. Could be he's becoming disenchanted with what it takes to get his cut of the gold." Hendricks' lack of reaction was starting to piss me off all over again.

"You think he still has a good side, don't you?" Kieran asked.

I shrugged again and tried to ignore Hendricks. "I just don't know how someone can pretend to be good for as long as he did, if there isn't good inside him. If that makes any sense."

"His mother was good," Mimi said. "And she raised him."

"I think he's confused and torn and doesn't know what he is or what he wants to be." I touched my glass. That didn't get a reaction out of Hendricks, but what Kieran said next did.

"I bet he still loves you. And with Mom there, he can't help but —"

Hendricks abruptly pushed his chair back and stood. "It's time for me to go home. Raegan, you should stay here tonight."

Surprised, I reached out and tried to grab his arm. This wasn't the reaction I'd been fishing for. "What? Hold on. What's the –" The door closed behind him before I could finish my question.

Shit. I exhaled and leaned back in my chair.

"Nice going, Rae." Kieran stood and picked up his plate.

I glared at Kieran. "Really?"

"You were behaving like a petulant child," Mimi admonished.

"Why are you guys taking his side?" I whined. "I only had one drink."

My dad scooted over to the chair next to me. "If I were a betting man, I'd say you and he had some sort of agreement that you wouldn't drink at all."

I scowled and crossed my arms. "So?"

"So, you blatantly disregarded that agreement, and you treated him terribly while you did it. I can't say I blame him for leaving."

My dad had always had a way of talking sense into me. I realized what I'd done and my defiant facade crumbled. "Oh, god." I covered my face with my hands.

Kieran came back to the table and sat again. "It's like you're actively trying to fuck things up with Jesse," he said. "Why would you do that?"

It was like he was reading my mind. "I don't know." My throat was tight with the effort of holding back tears.

"Are you going to go after him?" Mimi asked.

I sighed deeply and shook my head. "No, I think I'll let him be alone tonight and sleep on your couch."

"I'll go get you a pillow and some blankets." Mimi disappeared down the hallway.

A wave of exhaustion crashed over me, and I glanced at the time on my phone: 6:30. Just about bedtime.

I would fix things with Hendricks in the morning.

Friday, July 23, 2021

CHAPTER 11

Sleeping on the sturdy, utilitarian sofa felt much like sleeping on a concrete floor, but I did manage to get a few hours of sleep. My dreams were haunted by images of Hendricks and the hurt in his eyes as he'd shrugged me off and left the house.

I awoke at 4:30 in the morning with one clear thought bouncing around my brain: *I should have gone after him.* Had I put the Jack Hughes case at risk by not doing so? Did I ruin my own chances with him? I rubbed my eyes and rolled off the couch, dying for a long, hot shower.

My bag, and all of the clothes within it, was at Hendricks' house, so I re-dressed in the clothes I'd worn the day before and just slept in. I cringed and hoped I'd have a chance to change before going to the RJPD.

I made myself a cup of coffee and took it to the living room. I sat in the spot where I had slept on the couch, bunching the pillow under one arm and covering my legs with the well-worn knit blanket. It was rather chilly in the house. My dad had always preferred to keep the thermostat set low, even in the doldrums of winter. A glance at the moisture-covered front window confirmed that the day promised to be hot and excruciatingly humid. Another messy bun day, for sure.

I sipped my coffee, expecting the robust flavor of Beananza's dark roast and instead getting the charred firewood taste of a mass-produced brand. I grimaced and smacked my lips. "Yuck," I muttered, then set the cup on the coffee table and pushed it as far away from me as I could.

I scrolled through the news on my phone, trying to achieve mindlessness and divert my thoughts away from Hendricks. My guilt over my asshole behavior the previous evening was a little too strong, however, and I eventually had to give up and set my phone down.

I thought that might not be the only reason Hendricks left so abruptly. We'd been talking about Nicholas when he decided to leave, and it seemed likely that played a part too.

Hendricks and I were currently occupying that ever-confusing space between like and love. We liked each other a whole lot, but hadn't had any discussions about what was next. We hadn't talked about Nicholas really at all since we wrapped up the Mia Masterson case, and I hadn't had (or, more accurately, hadn't *taken*) the opportunity to clarify that I was done with Nicholas. That he, Hendricks, was the one I was falling in love with. In the absence of that clarification, I supposed it might look to Hendricks like I wasn't totally over Nicholas, even though he'd tried to kill me. As a cop, he probably saw the effects of battered woman syndrome often enough to know that some abused women live in denial and stay with their abuser. It wouldn't be a stretch for him to think that might be happening to me.

Why is it so hard for me to communicate when it comes to matters of the heart? I sighed and debated giving that sorry watered-down excuse for coffee on the table another try; I badly needed a shot of caffeine.

And then there was this business with my drinking. Even more than Nicholas, that had real potential to destroy everything between me and Hendricks. *Get a grip, O'Rourke,* I thought bitterly. *Keep that shit up and the wine will be the only friend you have left.*

I shuddered. I'd lived that life. It sucked. I did not want to go back.

I returned my attention to my phone and called up the messaging app, preparing to text Hendricks a long, heartfelt apology. That was when a soft knock on the side door startled me. I stood up and tiptoed through the kitchen with bare feet. I peeked through the sidelight to find Hendricks standing there, freshly showered and holding two Beananza coffees in his hands. He held them up and smiled.

I opened the door and relieved him of one of the lidded paper cups as he stepped inside. "Good morning. I, uh, I wasn't sure I would see you today." I kept my voice low.

"Come on, let's sit down. We need to talk." The volume of his voice matched mine.

I nodded and closed the door, then followed him. We sat shoulder-to-shoulder on the couch, and I shared my blanket. My first sip of Beananza dark roast was like heaven on my tongue. "Thanks for this. I just couldn't choke down the crap they have here." I gestured toward the abandoned mug on the far side of the coffee table.

Hendricks set his coffee on the near side of the table, then carefully lifted mine from my gloved hands and placed it next to his. Our knees touched, and he held both of my hands. His gaze was direct and intense, and those clear green eyes sent a white hot spark through my belly. "Look, Raegan, I'm sorry."

"You don't —"

He shook his head, and I bit my lip. *Let the man talk, O'Rourke.*

"I do. I shouldn't have stormed out like that. I should have stayed and talked this out with you like an adult."

"To be fair, it's not like I was behaving like an adult," I admitted.

"Look. You're a big girl. If you want to drink, there's nothing I can do to stop you." He sighed heavily. "I just...I don't like what the alcohol does to you. You're better than that."

I couldn't make my lips and tongue form words.

"But you know what? This really isn't about me. This is about your family. You are critically important to this mission, Raegan. We cannot take the Fausts down without you. Your mother needs you. Your family needs you." He squeezed my hands. "If you need a reason to stay sober, I can't think of a better one."

My chin dropped to my chest. *I am a selfish, despicable human being,* I thought as hot shame leaked out from behind my closed eyelids. *No more, O'Rourke.* I would not take another drink until my mom was home safe. Maybe I never would. "I'm sorry, Jesse."

Hendricks pulled me close and we sat like that for a long time. Eventually he released me and looked closely at my face. "Are we good?"

I nodded. "Yes, but there's one more thing I want to say."

"All right, let's hear it."

"I just want you to know that I'm truly done with Nicholas."

It was Hendricks' turn to look down at his lap. He *wanted* to believe me.

"I'd started having doubts about him and about our relationship before I met you, and during the Mia Masterson case he–he just stopped giving me reasons to believe him when he said he loved me. Then he went all Faust on me and tried to kill me. So, yeah, that was the end of that." I picked up my cooling coffee and drank. "I'm more than a little pissed at myself for wasting all those years."

"You have a kind heart, Raegan. You tried to see the best in him. Nobody can blame you for that."

I chuckled softly, then nudged him a bit with a shoulder. "Besides, you're here now." That made him smile, and before I quite realized what was happening, he was cradling my face in his warm, strong hands. Upon contact a vision bloomed behind my eyelids: Hendricks had tossed and turned and sat up all night.

"I am," he whispered, then leaned in and gently kissed me. He smelled like the ocean and tasted like Beananza dark roast. A spark ignited in my belly, and I kissed him back with increasing urgency.

He responded in kind and gently pushed me backward until my head lay on the pillow and he lay on top of me. I was completely lost in his warmth, and forgot about everything else until the kitchen light popped on. We scrambled to sitting like a couple of busted teenagers and grabbed our coffees just as Mimi rounded the corner wearing her pink terrycloth robe.

"Good morning, kids," she yawned. I supposed she would always think of me as a kid, even at thirty-nine years old. And she didn't seem at all surprised that Hendricks was here.

"Morning, Mimi." I hoped my hair wasn't too mussed.

She sat on one of the industrial-strength easy chairs. "I trust you've worked through whatever issue you had last night?" Her eyes sparkled.

Hendricks and I nodded in unison. "All good," he said.

"I made coffee," I said. "It should still be hot."

She chuckled and pointed at the cup in my hands. "I'd rather have one of those."

I nudged Hendricks. "Help an old lady out, would ya?"

He stood and headed for the door. "Back in a jiff."

I looked back at Mimi and grinned. "Beananza will blow your mind, guaranteed. There's nothing like it in Minneapolis."

She gazed at me for so long that I began to wonder if she was inspecting the deepest recesses of my soul. I dropped my eyes and made a show of rearranging my blanket over my legs. When I looked up again she was still staring at me.

"What?"

A smile softened her eyes. "He's a good man, Rae."

"I know he is."

"The heart wants what it wants. But sometimes the heart is so focused on what it wants that it misses what's right in front of it."

She was under the same impression Hendricks had been: that I was still pining for Nicholas despite everything that had happened. I held a hand up. "Give me a little credit, would you? I'm done with Nicholas."

Mimi nodded and glanced down at her own gloved hands. "I just worry about you, love. You and Nicholas were together for an awfully long time. That's not easy to get over."

"Normally I would agree with you, Mimi, but let's not forget that Nicholas damn near killed me." I touched the fading bruises on my throat. "And, you said it yourself. Jesse is a good man." I shrugged and smiled. "I promise, this heart sees exactly what's in front of it."

She came to me and wrapped her bony arms around my shoulders. "I'm glad to hear it. We all are."

Does everyone think I'm in denial? I wondered, then decided to let it go and lean into Mimi's hug instead. She was only trying to help.

Kieran stumbled in, pulling a black hoodie with OREGON blazed across the front in green and yellow letters over his messy copper curls. "Good morning all," he yawned.

My dad appeared a few minutes later showered, shaved, and dressed in a pair of khaki shorts and a plain gray t-shirt. He looked skinnier to me, somehow. And tired. *This is what stress does to a man.*

Hendricks brought back enough Beananza coffee for everyone, along with a dozen of their famous donut muffins. We sat around the table and hammered out the plan for the day. Hendricks and I would continue digging into old RJPD case files related to Edison Faust. Kieran and Mimi would try again with the Gatlins. And my dad would head back over to the Fortress with his coffee, camp chair, walkie, and binocs and keep an eye on the Fausts.

It would prove to be another eventful day.

CHAPTER 12

The mess of boxes, papers, and whiteboard markers was exactly as we'd left it the previous evening. Still overwhelming, still damn near insurmountable.

"I swear that pile of boxes grew overnight," I remarked as I set my purse and coffee on the desk and collapsed into a chair.

Hendricks inspected the stack. "Nope, nothing new here." He glanced at the phone on the desk. "And no messages, either. Rock Star must still be digging."

I chuckled. "Bowling nicknames are so lame."

He grinned and leaned over me. "You're just jealous that you don't have one." He kissed me. "Especially not one as badass as mine."

"Okay, Hambone." My tone was derisive, but I was genuinely amused. And maybe I *was* a little bit jealous.

The desk phone rang. Hendricks answered. "This is Jesse. Oh, hey Laura. "Wha—" He propped the receiver between his shoulder and his ear, picked up the nearest pen, and started writing. "Okay, okay, slow down a bit. You said his name was what? David?" He nodded and made a note. "David Guilder. Got it. Which agency is he with?" He made another note. "Did you get a number?" Laura spoke, he wrote. Then he set the pen down and stood up straight. "I owe you big time for this, Laura. Tha–" He listened and grinned. "Right. Half caff mochachino with almond milk. It will be on your desk, hot and fresh, first thing in the morning." He hung up.

"She must have found somebody we can talk to about Elaine Faust's aunt," I said.

Hendricks nodded. "I think so. One Detective David Guilder with the McKenzie County Sheriff's Office." He picked up the receiver again and started dialing.

I decided this would be a good time to run to the little girls' room. I took care of business, and on my way back to the war room I noticed Captain Sarah Bailey sitting alone in her office with the door open. A rare occasion. I stopped, stood in the doorway, and knocked softly on the door.

She looked up from whatever report she was reading on her computer. A pair of red half-moon glasses sat awkwardly on her flat nose. "Hey, Raegan. What can I do for you?"

I took a couple tentative steps into the room. "I–ah, I thought you'd like an update."

She removed the glasses from her face and let them fall; they hung from a sparkly beaded chain around her neck. "Sure."

I sat on the very edge of the chair. This small yet powerful Asian woman did something nobody in my twenty years reporting the news had ever done: she intimidated the hell out of me.

"How's it going?" Captain Bailey's brown eyes searched my face.

"It's going all right," I ventured. "There's a lot of information to go through." I realized I had to be careful; she didn't know we were expanding our investigation to include every other crime Edison had committed during his lifetime.

It turned out maybe I didn't have to worry so much about that. "Yes, Jack Hughes' murder was extensively investigated and it's a shame we couldn't find a way to tie it to Edison Faust back then. That happens a lot. We get to a certain point, and then…we hit a roadblock. And then another roadblock. To the point that every case associated with him just *dies*." Bailey folded her hands on the desk in front of her and leaned forward, pinning me with her intense gaze. "It seems to me that there must be some evidence somewhere out there that could bring that son of a bitch down. Not just for Jack's murder, but for *all* the things he's done to hurt this city and its people."

I didn't know what to say, so I just nodded.

"And it seems to me that I have someone working with my team who maybe has the tools to help find that evidence. Tools that nobody else has."

It was like she was reading my mind, and it scared the hell out of me. *Is she…giving me permission?*

"I think until that evidence is uncovered, you and Jesse will just run in the same circles with Jack's case that all the detectives before you did." She perched her glasses back on her nose. "I would hate to see Jack Hughes end up back in the icebox."

At first I couldn't speak. It was like my tongue was paralyzed. I managed a weak "M-me too," and stood up.

"Oh, there's one more thing."

I sat back down, heart pounding.

She pointed at my chest. "I had my doubts about you there for a while, Raegan." And then, incredibly, she smiled, revealing perfect white teeth. "But you've really come through for us. Bringing Mia and Isabel home was huge. I know you want Jesse to have the credit, but you'll never convince me he did that all on his own."

I grinned. "I want Jesse to have the credit so he can become a detective. I'm just a lowly newspaper reporter with a weird ability, like being able to roll your tongue."

Bailey smiled. "We both know that's not true, but I'll let it slide. Get out of here and go solve Jack Hughes' murder."

I did.

∞

When I got back to the war room Hendricks was making notes on the Jack Hughes board. He saw me and smiled. "Hey, where did you go?"

I sat in my chair. "Stopped by Bailey's office."

"How did that go?"

"Fine," I said and left it at that. "Did you get a hold of Detective David what's-his-name in North Dakota?"

"His name is Guilder, and no, I didn't. Left him a long voicemail." He went back to writing on the board. "Murder weapon was a big piece of wood," he muttered, his marker pounding and squeaking against the board.

"I'm still hopeful my mom can find that at the Fortress." I picked up the C LANGE box from 1981 and set it on the desk in front of me. I thought back to the Catclaw Kids case I'd worked up north earlier in July and remembered how sparse Sheriff Chad Overton's case files had been. That made the case difficult to work, but now I was learning there was also such a thing as too much information. I didn't know how Hendricks and I were going to get through all this stuff.

I opened the box and caught a whiff of stale paper and deteriorated rubber bands. It was about two-thirds full of manila folders containing hand- or typewritten police reports, notepads covered in scrawled ballpoint pen, stacks of glossy photos, and several cassette tapes. A review of the paperwork revealed just how quickly and thoroughly veteran River Junction homicide detective Roger Faherty had been stumped by Chester Lange's bizarre death.

Sixty-five-year-old Chester Lange of River Junction was found dead in the parking lot of the Majestic Saloon late in the evening of January 15, 1981 with a gunshot wound to the chest. Blood and markings in the snow across the parking lot indicated that someone else had also been injured, but that person was able to leave the scene. Faherty talked to witnesses and learned that Chester had shown up at the bar drunk, gun in hand, and raving about money Edison Faust had reportedly stolen from him while in a relationship with his daughter Pamela. He challenged Edison to an old-fashioned, and highly illegal, pistol duel.

Edison, who never left home without his Colt Trooper revolver and was equally if not more intoxicated than Chester, relished a good confrontation and accepted. The party spilled into the parking lot, where the men stood back-to-back, counted out fifteen paces, then turned and shot each other. Edison escaped with his life. Chester was not so lucky.

Faherty tracked Edison to the trauma unit at Hennepin County Medical Center in Minneapolis, where he'd been sent by ambulance after staff at River Junction Hospital determined he needed more intensive treatment than they could provide. In fact, the gunshot to Edison's abdomen tore through intestines and nicked his liver, nearly killing him.

"I wish," I muttered.

Edison was awake but heavily medicated, so Faherty wasn't able to interview him right then. But he did note that from the beginning Edison claimed self-defense in Chester Lange's death. *Faust claims Lange came after him, challenged him to the duel, he feared Lange would shoot him anyway if he didn't accept the challenge, said at least this way he had a fighting chance.* Edison's story generally tracked with witness statements, and when Edison was released from the hospital two weeks later he lawyered up and refused to talk to Faherty anymore. Witnesses from the Majestic Saloon clammed up too. Faherty had nothing left to go on, and the case went into the icebox. Where it remained to this day, forty years later.

Chester's daughter Pamela Lange would be found dead a month later, her body trapped under ice on the Bourbon River. The circumstances were suspicious enough to justify opening an investigation. Roger Faherty noted that Pamela met Edison Faust in early 1980 while working as a waitress at the Majestic Saloon, and they started dating soon after. Interviews with bar patrons revealed that Edison had thoroughly convinced Pamela that he was a special agent with the CIA. Everyone else in the bar knew this was complete bullshit, but young Pamela would not be deterred. She was over-the-moon proud to be dating such an important man.

Over the next twelve months, Edison would often disappear for days or weeks at a time, then reappear claiming to be in trouble with some foreign government and needing money. Pamela eventually drained her meager life savings trying to help her man. When she ran out of money, she went to her father. Chester Lange's nest egg also ran dry in early 1981; that was when he took his gun to the Majestic Saloon to collect and ended up dead.

The coroner determined Pamela's death to be a suicide and Faherty's investigation came to an end – although his notes made it clear he suspected Edison Faust had murdered her. He just couldn't prove it.

Roadblock after roadblock, I thought.

There was something else about this case that bothered me: the dates. Edison Faust was sent to Hennepin County Medical Center on January 15, 1981. My brother Kieran was born there the very next day. This connection seemed very important, and I made a mental note to ask Mimi and my dad about it later.

"How's it going over there?" Hendricks asked from behind the 1987 ROBERT MARTIN box.

As I shared what I'd learned with him, he stood and went to the rolling Edison Faust board and added key facts from the Chester and Pamela Lange cases. Then he told me what he'd learned about Robert Martin's suicide.

"So in nineteen eighty-four, Edison bought a suit and started calling himself a financial advisor. He'd go to the Majestic and talk to his drinking buddies about investing in the stock market. Promised them huge returns."

"Sounds like that flying car scam he ran back in the sixties that ended with Lewis Porter's murder," I said.

Hendricks nodded. "They gave him their money, and for a couple of years he delivered. Word spread around town, and before you knew it, everyone was investing with him. It was a classic Ponzi scheme. He put some clients' money into risky stocks and kept the real returns for himself while using new clients' money to pay old clients' returns. He was positively raking in the cash…until the bottom fell out of the market on Black Monday."

October 19, 1987: the day the Dow Jones Industrial Average lost almost 23% of its value. It was still the largest one-day decline ever, and it resulted in nearly two trillion dollars in losses. Every single one of Edison's investors lost the money they'd invested with him. Some, including Robert Martin of River Junction, watched every penny they had disappear before their eyes. Teenagers looking for a secluded spot to smoke weed found Martin's body in Greenhaven Cemetery on Halloween night. He'd sat on his wife's grave with a bottle of whiskey and shot himself in the head.

My stomach turned. "Oh. That poor man."

Hendricks nodded. "He lost his entire life savings."

"If Robert's death was a suicide, why is there a case file on it?"

"Good question. Maybe because it's tied to the Ponzi scheme." Hendricks dug in the box, pulled out a manila folder full of papers, and started paging through them. "Turns out that was a big deal and…yeah, here it is. Edison actually went to federal prison for it."

"What? You mean he was actually held accountable?"

Hendricks was reading another report. "Yes, but only because the FBI took over the case. And even then it was pretty much a slap on the wrist. Says here he was convicted of a single count of wire fraud and sentenced to five years. He spent fifteen months at Leavenworth and was released early for good behavior."

I rolled my eyes.

There was another bank robbery in 1983, this time at the Greenhaven Bank and Trust. It was a pretty run-of-the-mill event where a tall and skinny man in a mask and sunglasses approached the counter, flashed a silver gun, and demanded the tellers empty their drawers. He got away with roughly $15,000 in cash.

"This robber is still on the FBI's wanted list," Hendricks remarked. "Never been identified, and it's been almost forty years."

The last of our case files gave me pause, and I read the reports with a furrowed brow. It was that of Laura Faust – Nicholas' mother. She dropped dead in the middle of a street festival in downtown River Junction in September of 2000, at the age of forty. As far as detective Hope Kroeger could ascertain, Laura had no health concerns save for well-managed Type 1 diabetes; Winston Steele had noted several puncture marks on her body from insulin injections. The medical examiner noted she'd likely suffered a heart arrhythmia; heart problems were common in people with diabetes. Her case was classified a natural death and closed.

Nicholas had chosen to live his life from the age of eighteen believing his mother had died a natural death, but I knew he always wondered deep down if his grandfather had something to do with it. *She passed away ten years ago,* he'd told me the night we met. *Heart attack. Maybe she had something on him, who knows.*

This would gut him.

I shared my findings with Hendricks, who added them to the growing web around Edison's name on the rolling board. We sat back and stared at both boards, then glanced at each other.

"I'm beginning to wonder if we took on more than we can handle," Hendricks said. "Do you think we should ask Bailey for some help?"

My gut twisted. "No. We can do this." Captain Bailey would provide help if we asked, but I felt strangely protective of what Hendricks and I were doing here. I didn't want to share it with anyone.

His gaze lingered on me for a couple beats, as if he were debating whether it was a good idea to argue with me. "Okay," he said. "We'll see how things go."

Before I could tell him he'd made the right choice, shades of green began pulsing around the edges of my vision. "Hang on, Mom's calling," I said instead. He nodded.

I closed my eyes and opened the connection.

CHAPTER 13

The safe was open again and my mother sat on the couch with the shoebox squarely on her lap. The items she'd inspected yesterday — the pocket watch and pin — sat in a neat little pile on the corner of Edison's desk. It was time to see what secrets this box held.

Her fingers deftly dug through the box's contents; I caught glimpses of photographs, napkins, torn scraps of paper, envelopes, matchbooks. Finally she settled on an item and lifted it from the mess. It was a square black and white photo with a white border and scalloped edges. APR 62 was stamped at the bottom in tiny black print. The photo showed two men in what looked like a motel room, and not the high end kind.

One of the men was big and burly and covered in curly black hair, including a thick walrus mustache. He wore mirrored aviator sunglasses, a lacy bra and panties, fishnet stockings, and spiky heels. He stood with his hand on the shoulder of a much younger man, who was seated on the bed. There wasn't a hair to be seen on his underdeveloped body. He stared off in the distance and his eyes were unreadable — but there was little doubt about what was about to happen when the photo was taken. Someone had written "A.F. & boy toy @ Rainbow" along the bottom, to the left of the date the photo was developed.

She set this photo aside and resumed digging. She pulled out another, larger item for inspection. This appeared to be an Instamatic pocket camera with a paper envelope wrapped around it and held in place with an old rubber band. She carefully removed the envelope and closely inspected the camera; S RIDLEY had been crudely scratched into the camera's black plastic case. I set that aside and opened the envelope; inside were about half a dozen photos, some black and white and some color. They showed young girls, ranging in age from maybe five to about twelve years old, in various states of undress and sexually explicit poses. I couldn't determine a time period from any of the photos. Another peek inside the envelope revealed a scrap of paper with "Scotty's Girls" and a series of names and ages of the subjects written on it in fading blue ink.

My mother put the package back together the way she'd found it and set it aside. Her fingers found another envelope, this one much newer. Inside was a typewritten memo on official-looking letterhead:

RIVER JUNCTION POLICE DEPARTMENT
FROM THE DESK OF
CHIEF PATRICK J. ERICKSON

```
To: Chief Martin Alcorn
Minneapolis Police Department
October 15, 1997


Chief Alcorn —
Due to conflicts that are beyond the control of
the RJPD, I regretfully inform you that we are
unable to assist the MPD with its investigation
of Edison or Morgan Faust in relation to the
shooting death of Washburn High School Resource
Officer Raymond Schuster. On behalf of the
entire RJPD, please accept my condolences for
```

the loss of your officer. I have no doubt he was a fine man and a dedicated law enforcement officer.

Regards,
Patrick Erickson

My mother placed the memo back inside its envelope, set it atop the pile of items she'd inspected, and went back to rifling through the contents of the shoebox. She pulled out a wrinkled old white napkin and unfolded it. It was a white cocktail napkin from the Majestic Saloon, with the clear outline of the bottom of a glass beer bottle imprinted on it. "Pleasure doing business with you, Wint" was scrawled across the napkin in black ink.

My view shifted to the clock, and then my mother's gloved hands began gathering up items as if she were about to put them away.

Further exploration would have to wait.

∞

I opened my eyes to find Hendricks standing at the Edison board, furiously writing notes.

"What did I miss?"

"Matt Starr called back," he said without turning around or missing a beat with his marker.

I stood and joined him at the board. "What did he say?"

"Hang on." He finished writing something as if he was afraid he'd lose his train of thought if he stopped too soon. Then he capped his marker and glanced down at me. "Okay. You may want to sit down again for this."

I frowned. "Why?"

"Because one of the cases he called about was your aunt Pearl's death."

I went back to my chair and sat. "I take it there's more to it than I've been told."

He shrugged. "I don't know what you've been told, but I can tell you what MPD has." He went on to explain that Pearl's body was found in the Mississippi River near the Franklin Avenue bridge in near south Minneapolis on September 12, 1978. MPD canvassed the neighborhoods on both sides of the river between the University of Minnesota and the Veterans Administration Hospital, but turned up no witnesses to her death. The Hennepin County medical examiner determined she'd been in the water for about two days and, absent evidence to the contrary, ruled her death a suicide.

None of this was news to me. "Mimi is convinced that Pearl didn't kill herself and Edison Faust had something to do with it," I said.

Hendricks nodded. "MPD never turned up any evidence."

I sighed. "Okay, what was the other case Rock Star called about?"

"Ray Schuster. The resource officer at your high school."

"Right. This one I remember clear as day. School had started just a couple weeks earlier; Kieran was a senior and I was a sophomore. Kieran saw Morgan sitting in his truck outside the school and reported it to the office. They sent Officer Schuster out to talk to him, and Morgan shot him in the face and took off. That was a really hard day…Kieran saw the whole thing and Ray Schuster was beloved at Washburn."

"Starr says MPD tried to investigate, but even with Kieran IDing the shooter, they couldn't make any headway. He said –"

I thought of the typewritten memo my mother pulled from Edison's shoebox. "RJPD stonewalled them. Wouldn't help them get their hands on the Fausts."

Hendricks gazed at me, eyes full of wonder. "That's right. How did you know that?"

I told him about the memo.

"Holy shit." Hendricks' wonder morphed into disbelief.

"I think that memo is the clearest evidence yet that Edison has a network of law enforcement and government officials protecting him," I said.

"And I bet blackmail is his preferred method of bringing them in and keeping them in line."

I agreed and filled him in on the Instamatic camera with its envelope full of photos, the creepy hotel room photo, and the Majestic Saloon napkin.

"Fascinating." Hendricks picked up a pen and started doodling on a piece of scratch paper. "Somebody named Ridley was dabbling in kiddie porn, and who or what the hell is 'Wint?'"

"Good question," I said.

"Maybe it's time to switch to some old-fashioned detective work." Hendricks flipped his paper over to the blank backside. "Get the hell out of this office. Let's make a list of people to talk to. See if we can't verify some of this stuff."

"Good call," I said.

"All right." He pointed at the Jack Hughes board. "I think we definitely need to chat with Arlene Hughes' sister Colleen and her husband Teddy."

"Who?" I'd been so caught up in Edison Faust's dark and murderous world that I'd nearly forgotten about Jack Hughes and his gold. "Oh, right. Yes. That's a good idea."

"Then, I happen to know that Chief Erickson is still alive and living over in Soderton. He's got some explaining to do."

I nodded. "Yes, he sure does. Remind me who the medical examiner was when Jack died?"

Hendricks perused the Jack Hughes board. "Here it is. Uh, Winston Steele."

"Add him to the list."

Hendricks nodded and made a note. "Done. He had his hands in a lot of these River Junction cases."

"I mean, he was the M.E., so it sort of makes sense." I sat back and looked at both of our boards. We'd received and distilled a tremendous amount of information, but it didn't feel like we were making any actual progress on Jack Hughes' cold case. It all still felt completely overwhelming.

Hendricks opened his mouth to say something, but his walkie burred before he could speak. "You there, Jesse? Over."

"Hey Liam, I'm here. What's up? Over."

"The Fausts are finished for the day, it seems. Still haven't found anything, and Edison's madder than ever. I'm starting to worry for Dani's safety."

They're done already? What time is it? I consulted my phone: 5:53. Some people were a drink or two into happy hour at the Rummery by now. I gestured for Hendricks to hand me the walkie. "I just connected with her, Dad, and she seems fine. Over." I released the button and looked at Hendricks while I waited for my dad to respond. He calmly returned my gaze; I winked at him, and the smile he gave me made my stomach do a happy flip.

"My concern is that the longer she's in his house and he's not finding anything, the more likely he is to take it out on her," my dad said.

I couldn't argue with that logic.

He continued. "You said yesterday that it seemed like Nicholas was watching out for her."

I glanced at Hendricks, half-expecting a sour reaction at the mention of Nicholas, even after our talk this morning. His face didn't change at all. "It did seem that way, yes," I said.

"I hate to put my trust in any Faust, but I guess I have to hope that he'll protect her until we can get to her. Over." My dad's voice had grown a bit shakier.

I sighed. "I know it's hard, Dad. It's hard on all of us. We just need to remember our ultimate goal here."

A long pause, then my dad keyed back in and said, "I know you're right, hon. See you back at the house."

I hated how defeated he sounded. But I also couldn't blame him. I handed the walkie back to Hendricks and said, "Maybe it's time for us to head back too. My brain is so full it's overflowing."

"Mine too," he said. "Let's go."

CHAPTER 14

Hendricks didn't say anything else while we gathered our things and made our way to his truck. But as soon as I climbed in and closed the door behind me, he started talking like his mouth was a dam that had been holding back a flood of water and finally failed.

"I have lived in River Junction my entire life. I'm not stupid, and I have eyes; I know the Faust family has been terrorizing this town for generations. But I cannot believe that law enforcement would turn a blind eye. No. They're not just turning a blind eye, they are *helping* him. And innocent people in this city are being hurt and killed."

I tried to get a word in edgewise. "Look, Je–"

"And it can't just be the River Junction PD. Greenhaven County is enabling Edison Faust too. This Winston Steele character? How about the sheriff and his deputies? The county attorney? Where does it stop?"

"We don't know tha–"

"They are, Rae. Of course they're in on it. There's no way they aren't."

Hendricks stopped talking, and his chest heaved. He was beyond upset. Then he spoke again.

"How has Edison gotten away with this for so long?"

That was a question I could answer. "Because he has the goods. The couple of things I saw today through my mother's eyes was just a sample; that shoebox was packed full of stuff."

Hendricks' jaw muscles flexed as he considered this.

"You said it yourself, Jesse — blackmail is his way of getting people to do what he wants. And the stuff he has on key members of the River Junction and Greenhaven County law enforcement community is bad. Evidence of child pornography, gay sex and bondage…he has the ability to ruin these people's entire lives with a single phone call."

Hendricks' face didn't move at all, save for his lips. "This ends now. We're going to find the gold, we're going to nail Edison and Morgan Faust for Jack Hughes' murder, and we're going to hold anyone who has enabled the Fausts accountable. One way or another."

"Yes," I said.

"I'll take it all the way up to Chief Briggs if I have to," he said through gritted teeth. "He's a straight shooter."

I knew he wouldn't have to; Captain Sarah Bailey had made it clear she felt the same way he did.

"Might even have to bring in the BCA if the corruption runs deep enough at RJPD and GCSO. Which means the evidence will be even more important."

"Trust me — my mom is sitting on a goldmine," I said.

He nodded. "We'll verify and corroborate everything. Our case has to be absolutely watertight."

"We'll get him, Jesse."

Hendricks began to calm down, the muscles in his face finally relaxing. "We'll get him."

∞

Within the hour we were all seated around the table at my family's rental, noshing on a goulash casserole Mimi threw together with groceries she and Kieran had picked up at the supermarket. It was the definition of a simple yet hearty meal, and was a fan favorite in the O'Rourke family.

Hendricks had never tried goulash before. He looked suspiciously at the bubbling melted cheese that blanketed a hearty mixture of macaroni noodles, ground beef, tomatoes, and mixed vegetables before deciding it looked edible enough and scooping some onto his plate. A basket of store-bought bread rolls and softened butter in a dish completed the meal.

We ate in broody silence for several minutes, until Hendricks reloaded his plate for the second time. Then we had to give him crap. A little levity and laughter went a long way to improving everyone's mood.

"Did you kids learn anything new today?" Mimi asked.

Hendricks and I filled them in on Edison's Ponzi scheme, Laura Faust's sudden and unexpected death, and the Greenhaven Bank and Trust robbery. We also told them what Matt Starr had called to report about Ray Schuster, and the items Mom had found in Edison's shoebox.

"That letter to the Minneapolis police chief is troubling," my dad said.

"No kidding," Kieran said. "Is it typical for a police department to refuse to help another department with its investigation?"

"Not in my experience." Hendricks wiped his mouth with a napkin. "Law enforcement agencies pretty much always help each other out with investigations. I've never heard of an agency flat out refusing to assist. It's appalling. Chief Erickson, who wrote that letter, is on our list of people to talk to tomorrow."

Silence descended for a minute or two, until I realized we'd missed a couple things. "Mimi," I said around a mouthful of half-chewed macaroni noodles. "Matt Starr told us everything MPD knows about Pearl's death too."

"What, that there were no witnesses and they declared it a suicide?" she asked, with uncharacteristic sarcasm in her tone.

I nodded. "Yeah, pretty much. And there was one other thing. This actually came up from a River Junction case, the death of a fellow named Chester Lange in January nineteen eighty-one."

Blank stares from Mimi, my dad, and my brother.

"He was found shot to death in the parking lot of a bar here in town. Anyone want to guess who shot him?"

"Edison," they all said in unison.

I held up my fork. "Exactly. But here's the thing. These two drunken geniuses had an old-fashioned pistol duel, and Chester shot Edison too. He made it to the hospital here in River Junction, and they sent him to the trauma unit at Hennepin County Medical Center."

My dad blinked. "You said January of eighty-one?"

I nodded.

He gave Mimi a wide-eyed glance, then turned his attention back to me. "What was the date?"

"Edison was shot on the fifteenth."

My dad leaned back in his chair and rubbed his hands over his face and snowy hair.

"Wait," Kieran said. "I was born the next day."

"Yes. And at the same hospital," my dad said. "And the day after that a nurse tried to kidnap you."

Thunderstruck silence filled the room. "Holy shit," I murmured.

Kieran's eyes were huge. "Seriously?"

Liam nodded. "I noticed you weren't in your bassinet in the nursery and panicked. I ran all over the maternity ward looking for you, asking where you were, if anyone had seen you. The nurses checked all the rooms. Hospital security went all over the building. Finally I found an orderly who had just seen a young woman dressed as a nurse walking quickly toward the elevator with a redheaded baby in her arms." The lines on his face seemed deeper. "You'd better believe I went that way and chased the woman down before she could leave the building and disappear with my kid. I grabbed her, snatched you from her arms, and hospital security took her from there. The next – and last – I heard of it was the nurse refused to cooperate with Minneapolis police, and they discontinued the investigation due to a lack of evidence."

Roadblock after roadblock until the case dies, just like Captain Bailey had said.

"I did not know that Edison Faust was at HCMC at the same time we were," he said. "That…that changes everything."

"I'd bet dollars to doughnuts he was behind that nurse trying to take Kieran," Mimi said. "Maybe he bribed her."

I looked at Hendricks. "What would have happened to Edison after he was discharged from the hospital?"

He took a deep breath and blew it out through his lips. "Ah, well, he probably would have gone to jail. Likely Hennepin County first, then transferred to Greenhaven County to face charges in Chester Lange's death." He shoveled a big bite of goulash into his mouth. "This is excellent, Emily."

Mimi smiled.

I pondered this for a moment. "Who was the district attorney in Greenhaven County back in eighty-one?" They would have been responsible for charging decisions.

Hendricks frowned and wiped his lips again. "I don't know offhand, but I can find out."

My dad was stuck in the eighties. "Your arrival didn't go without a hitch either, Raegan."

"What happened?" I asked.

"Edison stalked us night and day for most of Dani's pregnancy. He'd sit in his big Chrysler and watch us – at home, at work, at the store, didn't matter. He was everywhere. We moved to different apartments twice during that time, and both times he found us within a couple of days."

"Oh, my god," I said.

"When the time came and we had to go to the hospital, I arranged for your bassinet to be in the room with your mom and Emily, and private security standing outside the room twenty-four seven. It cost a pretty penny, but I was determined not to have a repeat of what had happened to Kieran."

"It was when we left the hospital that things got really scary," Mimi said.

My dad nodded. "I had my entire family in the car, and as soon as we entered the highway, I glanced in the rearview mirror and there was Edison's big tank of a car right behind me and gaining fast. I knew right then that if we survived this, we wouldn't be going back to our apartment. We'd be starting over."

"Clearly we survived," I said. My head was spinning.

"He chased us for miles, and damn near ran us off the road twice. Finally I got off the highway and managed to shake him in a residential area. We spent the next two nights in a hotel."

"Tell them what happened while we were at the hotel, Liam," Mimi said.

My dad took a deep, watery breath. "I called our landlord to let him know we wouldn't be coming back, and he informed me that there had been a fire in the building the previous evening."

"WHAT?" Kieran and I both shrieked.

He nodded. "Of course it started in our unit and destroyed half the building."

"Starting over ended up being the only option," Mimi said.

"God, it's like the Fausts throw the ultimate tantrum when they don't get what they want and just burn the place down," Kieran said. "Uncle Carl's cabin, your apartment, the sunroom at Dad's house, probably that building on the U of M campus…I'm sure there are others."

I thought I knew what happened next. "Let me guess, the fire marshal either declared it an accidental fire or couldn't find a cause," I said.

My dad shrugged. "I never heard, but it wouldn't surprise me."

"What did you do?" Kieran asked.

"We had to move in with your Mimi while we looked for a new place. We ended up renting what is now my house in the Tangletown neighborhood of south Minneapolis from an elderly gentleman named Lloyd Farmer. His son Cooke became a close friend and took very good care of us. When Lloyd passed away in eighty-three, Cooke inherited the house and set me up with a contract for deed that allowed me to call the house my own without having my name on the deed. His act of kindness made it difficult for Edison Faust to find us for a long time."

I was impressed. "Nice work, Dad."

"That didn't stop him, of course. He just stepped up his stalking at my office. I had to go there if I wanted to feed my family, and he knew it. He managed to follow me home one day, and that was that."

Anger bubbled in my throat; I'd only been aware of a small fraction of the fear, pain and suffering my family had endured over the years. The more I heard, the madder I got. I swallowed hard, pushing that fiery ball down. Anger wouldn't help. I needed my mind to be clear.

"How did things go with the Gatlins today?" Hendricks asked. "Any better?"

"Much better today," Kieran said.

"I made some cookies and brought them as a peace offering," Mimi said. "I think they just needed to know we weren't there to harass them."

"Telling them we're also victims of Edison Faust helped too, just like it did with Paul and Jeannette Hughes," Kieran said. "Duke and Blanche calmed down and let us inside."

"They're very nice people," Mimi added. "And they're scared."

"Did you see anything inside the house that could help us find the gold?" I asked.

"I managed to take off a glove and touch the fireplace mantel," Mimi said. She described her vision of Edison and Morgan brutally beating Jack Hughes with their hands and the length of wood. It made my stomach turn.

"There was a brown and white dog that kept attacking their feet," she said. "Every time Morgan kicked it away, it came right back and kept on biting. It was trying to protect Jack."

"Yes, the dog was mentioned in the police reports," Hendricks said. "It was curled up next to Jack when his body was discovered. It was so aggressive the officers had to call Animal Control. Honestly, I can't believe the Fausts left it alive."

Inspiration struck. "Mimi, did you notice if the dog was wearing a collar?" I asked.

She thought for a moment, then nodded. "Yes, a red one with a silver tag."

I turned to Hendricks. "What would have happened to the dog?"

"It would have gone to the family, or to the River Junction Animal Shelter if the family didn't want it. Why, what are you thinking?"

I was thinking we'd possibly uncovered the key to finding Jack's gold. "I'm guessing either Jack's brother Paul or Arlene's sister Colleen would have taken the dog in. And if they did, I wonder if they might still have its collar."

"I bet that dog was with Jack everywhere he went," Mimi said, understanding dawning in her eyes. "Including wherever he hid his gold. That's brilliant, Rae."

"We're going to talk to Colleen and Teddy Campbell tomorrow," Hendricks said. "We'll ask about the dog."

Mimi looked at Kieran. "Looks like we'll be paying another visit to Paul and Jeannette tomorrow."

Kieran nodded.

"Oh. Two more things." Mimi turned her attention back to us. "After the awful visions of Jack being beaten to death, I caught a much older vision of a much younger Jack showing off a length of wood to Arlene. Oh, he was so very proud. I wonder if it's the same piece of wood the Fausts used to kill him. It looked like a beam of some sort, maybe from the original mill building."

Beaten to death with an item he'd procured from the workplace he was so proud of. Something about that made me so sad, I could barely stand it. I felt exactly the same way I had the day Hendricks and I found Mia Masterson.

"What's the other thing?" my dad asked.

"Duke and Blanche took us down to the basement of their home and showed us the big old cedar chest in the crawlspace under the stairs. They said it was there when they bought the house and they just never felt compelled to do anything with it."

"What did you see?" I asked.

"Several visions of Jack taking heavy-looking canvas bags out of the trunk and walking away with them."

We all stared at each other with wide eyes.

What was in those canvas bags?

Could the gold be real after all?

Saturday, July 24, 2021

CHAPTER 15

After a night of sweet lovemaking and blissful sleep, Hendricks and I woke with our alarms. Rather than jump out of bed and straight into the hustle of another day, we decided to steal a few more minutes from the morning. He wrapped his strong arms around me, pulled me close, and nuzzled the sensitive spot between my left ear and my neck. Shivers ran up and down my back and I sighed contentedly.

"I could lay here like this forever," I murmured. I couldn't think of a single time I'd ever felt this warm, safe, and happy with Nicholas.

"Me too," Hendricks' deep voice, rough from sleep, rumbled.

We spooned for a long time, breathing in sync, floating in the space between sleep and awake. It was quiet bliss until Hendricks' walkie crackled, startling us both. My heart jumped into my throat and my eyes popped open. His walkie and his alarm clock sat on the bedside table closest to me. According to the clock it was 7:55 in the morning. Later than I'd realized.

"Son of a bitch," Hendricks groaned as he rolled away from me, leaving cold emptiness along my nude backside. I propped myself up on my elbows and watched him search for his walkie as it crackled again.

"You there, Jesse? Over."

Hearing my dad's voice while I lay naked in Hendricks' bed was more than a little weird. Once again I felt like a teenager who'd been busted making out with a boy behind the shed.

"It's right there," I said and pointed Hendricks to the bedside table.

"Thanks." He walked around to my side of the bed. I admired the view; with his tight ass and solid muscles, he looked almost as good outside his uniform as he did in it. He caught me admiring, winked, and picked up the walkie. "Hey Liam, I'm here. What's up? Over."

"Just your morning check-in. The Fausts are back at Grotto Park for another day of searching. I have to be honest, though, I don't think there are many caves left to be searched. We're on borrowed time now. Over."

My heart pounded at the thought. Hendricks glanced at me, his eyes unreadable. "Ten-four, Liam. Let us know if they do anything unexpected. Over."

"Will do, over and out."

Hendricks sat on the bed next to me. I sat up and wrapped my arms around his neck from behind, resting my chin on his shoulder. "Think we can do this?" I hoped he felt more confident than I did.

He puffed his stubbled cheeks and forced air out between his lips. "We still have our work cut out for us."

Of course he was right. "Feels overwhelming," I said.

"I know it is. We have huge goals. But we have to keep pushing. We have to get there." He turned his head and kissed my cheek. "The alternative is – well, it's unacceptable."

That was almost all the motivation I needed to get up and get dressed.

"Can we grab Beananza on the way?" I asked as I slung my purse over my shoulder.

Hendricks smirked. "Coffee whore."

∞

Colleen and Teddy Campbell were in their mid-seventies and living out their retirement in a large 55+ apartment complex on the far west side of River Junction. Hendricks had called ahead, so they were expecting us.

We navigated a musty elevator and long hallways that smelled like chicken soup until we finally came upon apartment number 417. An oval-shaped braided rug made to resemble the American flag lay on the threshold, and a good-sized metal star painted red hung on the door. The woman who answered the door was surprisingly tall, with stooped shoulders and her fine white hair pinned to the top of her head. She inspected us with clear blue eyes, gave Hendricks' badge a cursory glance, and invited us inside.

"Come in, come in." Her voice was as deep as she was tall. She pointed us to a pillow-choked blue couch and said, "I put the coffee on, would either of you like a cup?"

"I'm good, but thank you," I said. I had fresh Beananza dark roast running through my veins.

Her gaze moved to Hendricks. "How about you, Officer?"

He shook his head and smiled. "No, thank you."

"Just one for me, then. I'll be right back."

While Colleen Campbell was in the kitchen, I looked around the living room. The decor on the front door was a hint of what to expect from the rest of the apartment. It was clear that Colleen and Teddy were going for a rustic Americana look for their home, but their sterile senior living apartment lacked any sort of rusticness at all. The result was just clutter: American flags, stars of various sizes and shades of red, white and blue, framed reproduced paintings of long-dead presidents, and other bric-a-brac covered every shelf and every surface of an otherwise perfectly ordinary apartment.

Hendricks stood next to the couch with a red pillow in each hand, debating where to put them so we could sit. I pointed to a spot on the cream-colored carpet next to the couch. He carefully placed the pillows there, and we sat just as Colleen Campbell emerged from the kitchen with a steaming American flag mug in her hands.

"Teddy will be back any minute." She sat primly in an antique-looking wooden armchair upholstered in maroon, cream, and navy vertical stripes. "He ran to the SuperAmerica to buy a newspaper. We have a subscription, but that Tom Parker across the hall keeps stealing our paper." She gave Hendricks a humorous look. "Any chance we can file a police report?"

He chuckled. "That would be a civil matter, Mrs. Campbell."

"Please, call me Colleen."

The door opened and a tall bald man with a wide nose and a perfectly shaped palate that suggested the presence of dentures loped in holding a neatly folded newspaper. "I'm going to send that asshole a bill for every goddamn paper I've had to –" He stopped short when he saw us. "Oh. Hello."

"Teddy, this is the River Junction police. Remember, I told you they were coming this morning."

Hendricks stood, flashed his badge, and extended his hand. "Jesse Hendricks."

Teddy shook it and cast a questioning glance in my direction.

"This is Raegan O'Rourke," Hendricks said, pointing at me. "She's consulting with us on the investigation into Jack Hughes' death."

"You mean his murder," Colleen said. Teddy made himself comfortable in an identical armchair next to his wife's.

Hendricks nodded. "That's right."

"There is absolutely no doubt in my mind that Edison Faust was involved." Colleen sipped from her cup. "In fact, I'm surprised it didn't happen a lot sooner."

"What makes you say that?" Hendricks took his notepad from his pants pocket.

"Because Edison was my sister's boyfriend for two years in high school." She set her cup on a round wooden table between her chair and Teddy's. "I was four years younger than Arlene, but even I could see he had a jealous streak and a wicked temper. He tried to control every aspect of Arlene's life." Colleen gave a dry chuckle. "As if she could be controlled."

"She was headstrong," Teddy chimed in.

Colleen nodded. "She was. And our daddy always said what a tenderheart she was. I'm sure you know Edison didn't have such a great family life, and she didn't want to give up on him. Even when he hit her."

"How did Jack figure into all of this?" Hendricks asked. His ballpoint pen scratched the paper as he furiously took notes.

"Jack and Edison were best buddies all through high school. When Edison and Arlene started dating, the three of them were thick as thieves."

I thought I could see where this was going. "A love triangle," I said.

Colleen nodded. "Valentine's Day nineteen-sixty. That's the day the you-know-what hit the fan." She sipped her coffee. "Edison took Arlene out for a romantic drive in his dad's black Chrysler Imperial. I watched them drive away from my bedroom window. I remember it started snowing outside while Arlene was off on her date." Colleen stared unfocusedly at a spot on the wall, then blinked and said, "Less than an hour later she came home, wet and cold and sobbing. Her mascara was all streaked down her cheeks."

"What happened?" Hendricks asked.

Colleen glanced at Teddy, who gave her a reassuring nod. She took a deep breath. "Edison parked the car on the land that used to be Faust Lumber and tried to force himself on her."

"He tried to rape her," Teddy clarified.

Colleen shook her head. "I don't know how she did it, but she got out from under that bastard and ran home in a snowstorm."

Teddy nodded. "See what I mean? Headstrong."

"Arlene immediately called Jack. He came over in his father's Buick and picked her up. She said they were going to Levendal's for a soda. Maybe they did that, maybe they didn't; it was snowing, after all. I just know the next day Arlene went to school wearing Jack's letter jacket."

Knowing what I knew about Edison Faust, I imagined this went over like a lead balloon. "Edison didn't take it well, did he?"

"That, my dear, would be the understatement to beat them all." Colleen picked up her coffee cup and sipped again. "He exploded when he saw her in Jack's letter jacket. Grabbed her by the hair and smashed her face into a locker. Broke her nose."

Hendricks and I winced in unison.

"Jack tried to intervene and Edison punched him in the throat. Jack couldn't speak for a week after that." Another sip of coffee. "The two phy ed teachers restrained Edison and dragged him to the office. He was suspended for two weeks. Life after that was difficult for Arlene and Jack."

"What do you mean?" Hendricks asked.

I remembered what Paul Hughes had told Mimi and Kieran. "He started stalking them, didn't he? He'd show up in unexpected places. Maybe a dead animal would appear in a desk or a locker. He was always watching."

Colleen stared at me, wide-eyed. "Yes. How did you know that?"

I smiled. "I have some experience with the Faust family myself, but we've also spoken with Jack's brother."

She gazed at me for a couple beats, then continued. "My sister got her very first job at Levendal's Five and Dime the spring of her senior year. She was a soda jerk there and she was so excited to start making some money of her own." Colleen paused, thinking. Then: "She had her dress for the spring dance all picked out at Lola's Dress Shop, and she was determined to buy it herself. But then, on her second day she was let go without explanation. I found out later that Jack was dismissed that same day from his job at Purmort's gas station. That was on Hughes Street back in those days."

"Edison," I said.

Colleen nodded. "Neither of them could keep a job. Until Jack went to work for Ainsley Mill that summer."

I remembered something Mimi said: *I don't know exactly how, but Jack caught Bernard Ainsley's attention, and he made sure Jack had a job after he graduated from high school.* Everything Colleen was saying tracked perfectly with what Mimi and Kieran learned from Paul Hughes.

"I worked there too," Teddy said. "Thirty-seven years. Jack and I became good buddies. That's how I met Colleen."

Colleen continued as if Teddy hadn't spoken at all. "Maybe Edison couldn't have Jack fired anymore, but that didn't stop him from following them, watching them, breaking into their house, and putting dead squirrels in their mailbox. Their backyard shed burned to the ground in eighty-four."

"But Jack and Arlene stayed together through all of that," Teddy said. "They never let Edison come between them."

Colleen nodded. "Thirty-two years they were together. Until Arlene passed in March of ninety-two. Leukemia. Took her in six months."

"I'm very sorry," Hendricks offered.

"Me too," I said.

Colleen stared off into space for a minute or two. Then she blinked and said, "I helped out as much as I could while she was sick. Jack was overwhelmed and grieving, and needed to work so they wouldn't lose their house. I was between jobs then, so I took care of her. Made sure she took her meds, made sure she was eating and drinking, got her to the bathroom, that sort of thing."

Teddy took his wife's hand. "You were a good nurse."

She gave him a grateful smile, then turned back to us. "There shouldn't be any doubt about who slaughtered my brother-in-law, Mr. Hendricks." Her eyes snapped. "None. That crazy bastard never let Arlene and Jack have a moment's peace."

Hendricks made a couple notes. "Thanks for that, Mrs. Campbell. Colleen. I do have two more questions for you, if that's all right."

"Shoot."

"Did Jack have a dog?"

Colleen nodded. "Scout. He got him from the animal shelter after Arlene died. Never went anywhere without him."

"What happened to Scout after Jack died?" I asked.

Colleen glanced at her husband. "I believe Paul took him home. Right, Teddy?"

Teddy nodded.

"Thank you," Hendricks said. "And finally, you two were interviewed on June twenty-third of ninety-seven, the day after Jack's body was found."

They both nodded.

"In that interview, Teddy, you asked Detective Shaw if they'd found Jack's gold yet. Can you elaborate on that for us?"

"I can," Colleen said. It was becoming increasingly obvious who wore the pants in this marriage. "I mentioned that I was my sister's caregiver, right?"

Hendricks and I nodded.

"At first she was in pretty good shape. She could take care of herself pretty well. But that damn cancer stole all of that from her, and fast. By the three-month mark the cancer and the chemotherapy had ravaged her body to the point she couldn't get out of bed. By about the last month of her life she was sleeping pretty much all the time." Colleen blinked several times in quick succession; I realized she was trying to hold back tears. "I kept her bedroom door open so I could hear her while I watched TV or tidied up around the house.

"One day I heard her voice and went to her, thinking she needed a sip of water or something. But she wasn't even awake. She was talking in her sleep. She said, clear as day, 'Jack, we're not safe with all that gold in the house. It's time to move it.'"

Holy crap, I thought. *Maybe this gold is for real after all.*

"Did you mention this to Jack?" Hendricks asked.

Colleen shook her head. "No. I chalked it up to delirium. The meds will do that to you, you know. So I didn't tell anybody. Except Teddy. I tell Teddy everything."

Hendricks turned his attention to Teddy. "Did you say anything to Jack?"

"Damn right I did," Teddy said. "Are you kidding? I wanted to know all about this mysterious stash of riches. By that time I was head miller, he was production manager. So he was my boss, but that didn't stop me from ribbing him about it all the time at work. He would just smile and shake his head, and tell me if I asked again he'd fire me." He grinned, showing dazzling white dentures. "Of course I always asked again."

Hendricks noted this. "So you two never actually saw any gold?"

"No," they said in unison.

"Okay, thank you. I don't have any further questions. Raegan, is there anything you wanted to ask?"

I shook my head.

Hendricks pocketed his notebook and stood, and the rest of us followed suit. "Thank you both for your time this morning," he said. "We can show ourselves to the door."

Teddy sat back down in his chair with his newspaper, but Colleen followed us. "Mr. Hendricks? If I could ask one favor?"

We stopped and faced her. "Of course," Hendricks said.

"Did you find a pin in your case files?" she asked.

"What kind of pin?"

"It's called a scarab pin, and it looks a little bit like a wreath. It has six stones that are carved to look like beetles set in a circle that's maybe an inch and a half across." She held her bony thumb and forefinger up to demonstrate how big an inch and a half might be. "It's an heirloom. My mother inherited it from her grandmother, and she gave it to Arlene as a sweet sixteen present." Her eyes misted over. "She let me wear it once. At her wedding. Edison Faust couldn't even let her have that day of happiness."

She sighed and her eyes cleared. "Anyway, her pin was lost after Jack died, and I would very much like to have it back."

Hendricks pulled his notebook out of his pocket and wrote this down. "I haven't seen it, but I will certainly keep an eye out."

We bid our goodbyes and stepped out into the hallway; the smell of chicken soup was even stronger. *Must be lunchtime*, I thought.

Colleen Campbell softly closed the door behind us.

CHAPTER 16

Our next destination was another senior living complex, this one just over River Junction's eastern border in the city of Soderton. This was the home of former River Junction Police Chief Patrick Erickson.

Hendricks and I navigated another set of elevators and long, dusty-smelling hallways until we arrived at unit number 357. Hendricks knocked on the door, this one devoid of any decorations.

"Coming." The muffled voice was deep but sounded very tired. When the door opened, I saw that the face looked every bit as exhausted as the voice sounded. The former police chief was of average height and build and bald like Teddy Campbell. He was about the same age as Campbell, but looked a decade older with deep lines at the corners of his downturned mouth and puffy dark circles carved into the skin under his heavy-lidded eyes.

This was a broken man carrying many heavy burdens. I thought we might be looking at the key to taking Edison Faust down.

"Yes?" He was confused and suspicious, and looked closely at Hendricks' badge. "What can I do for you?"

"Chief, my name is Jesse Hendricks, and I'm with River Junction PD. This is Raegan O'Rourke, she is consulting with us on a couple of cases. We're hoping for a few minutes of your time today."

"You have no jurisdiction here." He tried to close the door.

Hendricks blocked the door open with his foot. "I understand that, sir, but I just have a few questions for you. I –"

"Which cases?" Erickson barked.

Hendricks paid no mind to this blatant attempt to throw him off-kilter. He was going to keep control of this conversation. "There are several, actually. Do the names Chester and Pamela Lange mean anything to you? How about Robert Martin? Ray Schuster? Jack Hughes?" He paused for emphasis, then dropped his final bomb. "Edison Faust?"

Erickson's head and shoulders drooped, and he sighed. "Come in."

Where the Campbells' apartment was cluttered yet homey, Erickson's was bare and strictly utilitarian. Everything was brutally neat and nothing was out of place, making me wonder if he had a military background or maybe some kind of mental disorder with obsessive-compulsive tendencies.

He pointed us to a round dining table with four perfectly-spaced chairs situated just outside the kitchen. "Coffee?"

We both declined. Erickson retrieved his plain black mug from a spotless coffee table in the living room and joined us. "I was beginning to think nobody would come around asking about those cases."

Hendricks' face was stone. Even I couldn't read it. "You realize you have some explaining to do."

Erickson nodded. "I did my time so that bastard wouldn't have to." He sipped from his mug, and I wondered if there was booze in that cup instead of coffee. That's how unhappy he seemed. His eyes were resolute – and, I noticed, a lovely shade of cocoa brown. "I'm done keeping his secrets."

Hendricks and I exchanged heavy glances. *Here we go,* I thought.

Hendricks got straight to the point. "What did Edison Faust have on you, Chief?"

Erickson hunched over his coffee and took his time answering the question. Finally he spoke. "I had a gambling problem."

"Okay," Hendricks said.

"At first it was just a way to blow off steam from a stressful job. You know? I'd go to the casino and throw fifty bucks at a poker or blackjack table. Pretty soon fifty became a couple hundred, then before I knew it I was losing a couple grand a week. Or more." Another drink from his mug. "My excuse was always 'If I just try one more time, I'll win it all back.'"

Hendricks jotted this down in his notebook.

"A cop's salary isn't nearly enough to support that kind of habit, as you know. So I had to find…alternate sources of funds."

Hendricks looked up sharply.

"When I landed the chief gig at RJPD, I had access to the department's entire budget."

"Ohhh…no. Tell me you didn't," Hendricks said.

Erickson nodded miserably. "I did. I was chief of police for seventeen years, and in that time I managed to steal close to a million dollars without anybody, even the city manager, realizing it. And every penny of it went straight to the tribes."

Hendricks sat back in his chair and ran a hand over his head. "Let's go down the list of cases, what do you say?"

Erickson nodded and waved a white-haired arm in a "let's do this" gesture.

"Let's start with Chester Lange. Everyone knew Edison shot him. Why wasn't he investigated?"

"He was," Erickson said. "My team had a solid case. The district attorney declined to send him up on charges."

Hendricks frowned. "Who was the DA?"

"A fine, upstanding fellow named Scott Ridley."

Ridley. How did I know that name?

"My gambling problem was nothing compared to his…unnatural fascination with children."

Then it clicked: Scotty's Girls. The Instamatic and accompanying photographs of young girls in sexually compromising poses in Edison Faust's safe. It was Ridley's name scratched into the camera's black plastic case. *Holy shit.*

"Not too long after the Chester Lange case, Edison caught me in my office, closed the door, and told me, and I'm paraphrasing here, that if I ever tried to pin something on him again he would have my job and I'd be run out of Greenhaven County." He gave a dry, humorless chuckle. "To this day I don't know how, but he'd gotten his hands on evidence of my…wrongdoing. And he held it over my head for the next thirteen years."

Hendricks' face remained passive.

"That didn't stop me from continuing to 'borrow' money from the city," Erickson said dryly before sipping again from his mug. "You know about Chester, I'm sure you also know about his daughter Pamela. She and Edison dated for a while, did you know that?"

No reaction from Hendricks.

"I knew damn well he killed her and dumped her in the Bourbon River," Erickson said. "But I couldn't investigate him. Even if I did, Ridley couldn't bring him up on charges. It didn't matter anyway; the medical examiner ruled her death an accident so we technically didn't have anything to investigate."

"Tell me about this M.E.," Hendricks said.

"Winston Steele was nothing but an opportunistic crook. All Edison had to do was slip him a few bills and Steele would do whatever he wanted."

I thought of the old Majestic Saloon napkin my mom found in Edison's shoebox. "Pleasure doing business with you, Wint" had been written on it. I thought I now knew who "Wint" was.

Hendricks angrily shook his head and made notes in his notebook. I wondered if he was making the same connections I was.

"Where can I find Winston Steele?" Hendricks asked.

"In Greenhaven Cemetery. He passed about a year ago."

Hendricks took a deep breath and leveled an impatient look at Erickson. "Let's talk about Robert Martin for a minute."

Erickson's head and shoulders slumped again.

"Did you know about Edison's Ponzi scheme?" Hendricks asked.

Erickson nodded, mute.

"You were going to let that slide, weren't you?"

"You don't understand," Erickson mumbled.

"Then make me understand," Hendricks nearly shouted.

"He would have ruined me!" Erickson's voice matched Hendricks' in volume and tone.

"Instead you sat back and watched him ruin dozens of innocent people." Hendricks' voice dripped with contempt. "Some lost every goddamn penny they had, Chief. Including Robert Martin."

Erickson remained silent, but he at least had the decency to look ashamed of himself.

"Is it fair to say that Martin's suicide forced your hand on the Ponzi scheme?"

Erickson nodded and wiped his face with a trembling hand. "I didn't have a choice. I had to hand the Ponzi scheme over to the FBI. The U.S. Attorney's office prosecuted on federal charges." He took a deep breath. "I lived in fear that he would get out of prison and expose me. Do you have any idea what kind of hell that is?"

Hendricks had exactly zero sympathy for Erickson. "Let's move on. Tell me why you wouldn't help Minneapolis investigate the shooting of one of their officers. Ray Schuster."

Erickson winced. "Yeah, that's the decision that ended my career."

"What happened?"

"What you might think would happen. Edison warned me that if I cooperated he would out me faster than I could say 'embezzlement.' So I wrote a letter to Marty Alcorn declining to help him." He sighed. "I was so concerned with saving my own ass that I didn't think about the possibility that Alcorn would bring in the state cops. He looped the BCA in and they came around asking questions. By February of ninety-eight I was done. Exposed, fired, and eventually incarcerated. I spent eleven months in the county workhouse." He drank the last of his coffee and set the mug on the table. "No blackjack tables there. And the goddamn worst part of it all? Edison Faust *still* was never held accountable for Schuster."

"Morgan Faust was the one who killed Ray," I said, my voice tight.

Erickson lifted a hand and let it drop. "Yeah, well, he wasn't either."

The former chief had corroborated several pieces of evidence my mom found in Edison's shoebox: the letter to Martin Alcorn, the Instamatic camera and photos of Scotty's Girls, and the Majestic Saloon napkin. With his next words he casually dropped a bomb that validated that creepy hotel room photo.

"My predecessor was in Edison's pocket as well."

Hendricks' eyes widened. "You're kidding me."

Erickson shook his head and drank from his mug.

Hendricks looked at me. "Art Flanagan is a legend. He's widely regarded as the best police chief River Junction has ever had."

"He was also a card-carrying cross-dresser," Erickson said.

Hendricks' eyes widened even more in total disbelief. "Excuse me?"

Erickson calmly sipped from his mug again. "And he batted for the same team, if you know what I mean. He liked his boy toys young. The younger, the better."

Hendricks' jaw dropped.

Was it possible that "A.F." was Art Flanagan? I thought maybe it was.

"Of course Edison knew this and used it to keep Flanagan in line. Several cases gathered dust bunnies while Flanagan was chief," Erickson said.

An image of the Edison board in our war room at RJPD popped up in my mind's eye. "I'm guessing those cases include the deaths of Myrtle Conley, Lewis Porter, and Elaine Faust."

Erickson dipped his head in agreement.

"Oh, and the first bank robbery. The one where the bank manager died. What was his name?"

"Frank Barnale," Hendricks said, never taking his eyes off Erickson's face. "Do you mean to tell me that Flanagan hamstrung all of those cases?"

I finally realized why the bank manager seemed so familiar. My mother had mentioned it the day the Fausts came and took her. *The bank manager died, didn't he?* she'd asked.

"That's what I'm telling you. Edison also had the goods on the guy who succeeded me, Graham Kelleher."

Hendricks blinked. "That's the guy who hired me. Turned out he didn't need Edison to torpedo his career, he did that all by himself."

"What happened?" I asked.

"He got absolutely shitfaced and crashed his city-owned vehicle doing eighty on his way back from a convention up north. It was a miracle he survived. He went directly to treatment and the City Council fired him with a unanimous vote a couple months later."

"If he's still alive, he's probably drunk," Erickson said. "Another example of when blowing off steam grows into a grade-A problem."

I could relate. That was how my own alcohol problem had taken root and grown. It started with a drink here and there, socially, to help take my mind off my touch and the sometimes crazy things I saw because of it. After I met Nicholas it became a daily thing, the only way I knew to cope with the fears and insecurities that came with a highly forbidden and totally clandestine relationship. It finally got to the point where I didn't think I could make it through the day without a glass of wine. A glass a day grew to a bottle a day. And before I knew it, my habit threatened to interfere with my work.

Now, with Nicholas out of the picture and Hendricks in it, I thought I might have the capacity to heal. Hendricks modeled a much healthier approach to life; it was an approach I sort of wanted to emulate.

"Barton Briggs runs a clean ship," Erickson said. "He must not have any skeletons in his closet."

"Briggs is a great chief," Hendricks said. "He doesn't live in River Junction or in Greenhaven County, which probably helps."

It was an awkward end to an awkward conversation. Hendricks and I left Patrick Erickson just as we'd found him.

Broken, haunted, and alone.

CHAPTER 17

Hendricks and I were on our way back to RJPD when his radio crackled. "You there, Jesse? Over."

He handed the walkie to me.

I pressed the button and said, "Hi Dad, we're here. What's up?"

"The Fausts are packing up to leave Grotto Park." The worry in my dad's voice was unmistakable. I glanced at the clock in the dashboard of Hendricks' squad; it was just past two o'clock. Not good.

Shades of green suddenly started pulsing around the edges of my vision. I keyed in and said, "Hang on, Dad, Mom's calling. I'm giving you to Jesse." I handed the walkie back to Hendricks and opened the connection.

∞

I was surprised to discover that my mother wasn't back in Edison's office. Instead she was in what appeared to be the Fortress' master bedroom. It was much larger than her room, round, with big windows and vaulted ceilings. The furniture was heavy and ornate. The windows were covered with heavy drapes. It was clear that this room was not in regular use, and hadn't been for some time. A thin layer of dust coated all the hard surfaces, and the bed was a little too perfectly made.

Wasting no time, she beelined to one of the bedside tables and started rummaging through drawers. The first drawer opened to reveal a leatherbound book with a ribbon attached to its spine. A journal. My mother didn't take the time to look through it; instead she stuck it in the waistband of her jeans at the small of her back and covered it with her t-shirt. The second drawer contained the kinds of things someone would want to keep near them when spending an extended period of time in bed: a thermometer, a box of tissues, various bottles of over-the-counter meds, syringes, alcohol swabs, several battered paperback novels, empty prescription bottles, single-use ice packs still in their packages.

She closed the last drawer, and then knelt to check under the bed. A large object covered with a dusty white sheet lay there among the dust bunnies. It took some effort, but eventually she was able to slide it enough so that one end stuck out about eighteen inches. She pulled the sheet off to get a better look.

The object turned out to be made of wood and it looked quite old; this was no fresh four-by-four recently purchased at the local home center. It was pitted and cracked and darkened with age. My mother instinctively reached out to touch it, and stopped herself when she realized there was something on it. She leaned in for a closer look. Half of the wooden beam was covered with some kind of dried, flaky substance. It looked a whole lot like blood to me.

Suddenly my mother stood up and turned to the door. I caught a glimpse of all three Faust men standing in the doorway —

∞

I blinked. "What the —"

"Everything all right?" Hendricks asked. We were sitting in his squad, parked behind RJPD.

"No." My heart was doing strange things in my chest, causing my voice to tremble. "No, I don't think so. Edison just caught my mom in a room other than the one she's supposed to be locked in."

"Ah, shit."

"I'm going to see if I can get her back." I closed my eyes and pinged my mom. She did not respond. I tried again. And again. Nothing.

"Oh my god." My hands started to shake. Had he killed her already? "Come on, Mom. Come *on*." I tried again, still nothing. I looked helplessly at Hendricks, fighting tears of sheer panic. "What do we do?"

"If you think she's in real danger, we go in and get her," he said without hesitation. "Let's go inside. I can talk to Captain Bailey or Sergeant Rooney and get a warrant going." He took my gloved left hand, and his fingers found the lump of Grace's ring underneath. "But. You understand that if we get RJPD involved our plan goes to shit, right? We're authorized to investigate Jack Hughes' murder. All this other stuff, like letting them kidnap your mom and looking for Jack's gold, is strictly on the downlow. If RJPD takes over, we're going to lose our best chance to take Edison down for real and for good."

I chewed on my lip and let the tears fall. It was an impossible choice. Which did I want more: my mother's life, or the downfall of the man who had spent his entire life terrorizing my family?

Truth was, I wanted both.

If I saw past my panic and emotion and looked at this rationally, how likely was it, really, that my mom was dead? I had no doubt Edison was pissed that he didn't find Jack Hughes' gold in the caves at Grotto Park. But he wanted that gold so badly that he wouldn't be willing to kill the one person he believed could truly help him find it. Not yet.

I nodded and took a deep breath to steady my pounding heart and shaking hands. "Let's go in and I'll try one more time."

We went inside and walked straight to our war room. Well…Hendricks walked. My body was so jacked with adrenaline that I jerked along like some maniacal marionette. Hendricks closed the door behind us while I went to my chair. I sat and tried pinging my mom again.

∞

She was back in Edison's office, and this time she wasn't alone. She sat in a folding chair in front of Edison's massive desk. Nicholas and Morgan occupied each end of the couch. Edison paced around the room, shouting, arms waving, white hair messy and wild. I didn't like what I saw in his eyes: deep, dark, unrelenting madness.

Edison yanked a drawer open and withdrew a silver revolver. He held it in his hand for a solid minute while he spoke, then pointed it directly at my mother's face.

Nicholas jumped up from the couch and wrestled the gun away from his grandfather. Ignoring Edison's screams of protest, Nicholas opened the chamber, emptied the bullets onto the floor, and stuck the gun in the waistband of his shorts. Edison suddenly collapsed in his chair and closed his eyes; Nicholas ignored this and guided my mother out of the office.

He deposited her safely in her room and left without a word, gently closing the door behind him.

∞

I opened my eyes. Hendricks sat across the desk watching me closely, anxiety all over his face. "Well? Is Danielle all right?"

"She's fine," I said. My entire body tingled from the aftereffects of a cataclysmic adrenaline rush, which offset the fatigue that typically rolled in after a connection.

"Thank god."

"Edison's beyond pissed, though." And I told him everything I'd seen, my voice still trembling.

"Hooo, that was a close call," he breathed.

I nodded, glanced down at my hands, and realized I was wringing them in my lap. Hard. I forced myself to stop and splayed my fingers on my thighs.

The phone rang, making us both jump. Hendricks grabbed the receiver. "Jesse Hendricks." A pause, and then he said, "Detective Guilder, thank you for returning my call. As I mentioned in my voicemail, I was wondering what you could tell me about the nineteen seventy-one death of Catherine Parkay. I understand it happened in your jurisdiction."

So formal, I thought as I watched him grab a legal pad and a pen and begin furiously writing notes. "Wow, okay. What was the scene —" He didn't finish his question, just kept writing. "Cause of death?" he asked, then wrote that down too. I could just make out the words **BEATEN TO DEATH.** I winced.

This went on for at least fifteen minutes. Finally Hendricks sat up straight and said, "I really appreciate all this Dete—I mean, David. It sounds like McKenzie County did everything they could at the time. Good news is, I may have a lead for you. Mrs. Parkay's beloved niece Elaine had a husband." He paused, then nodded and said, "Right. Elaine's husband, Edison Faust, is the ne'er-do-well in my city. His whole family has been a thorn in the ass of this department for generations. And though I can't prove it yet, I strongly suspect he might have had something to do with this." Another pause, another nod. "Well, mostly because six months after Mrs. Parkay died, Elaine was found dead, floating in the Bourbon River behind her house. If Mrs. Parkay was as wealthy as you say she was, and Elaine was the sole beneficiary of her estate, well…it's not a stretch to believe Edison would drive nine hours each way to help the old lady along. As awful as that sounds."

I sat back in my chair, wide-eyed. *Holy crap, I was right.*

"We're investigating him for other crimes as well. I'd be happy to keep you posted. Mrs. Parkay's family deserves justice, you know? Even fifty years later." A pause and a nod. "Great. Thank you for your time, David. We will be in touch." He placed the phone back in its cradle and looked at me with blazing eyes. "That son of a bitch did this. I'd bet every penny I have. Which isn't much, but you get the point."

"The man really will stop at nothing to get what he wants," I said, mostly to myself. It was an absolute miracle that any of us Ainsleys were still alive. But what bothered me most was how many *other* people's lives were torn apart by Edison Faust's selfish greed.

"It's almost three o'clock," Hendricks said. "Let's call it a day here and go check in with your family," he said. The pensive look on his handsome face told me exactly what was on his mind: this would all be coming to an end.

And soon.

CHAPTER 18

By the time we got back to the house, my dad had filled Mimi and Kieran in on the current status of the Fausts' search for Jack Hughes' gold, and they were all panicked. They started peppering Hendricks and me with questions as soon as we walked in the side kitchen door.

"What happened?

"Is Dani all right?"

I raised my hands. "Relax, she's fine. Edison is not happy that there was no gold in the caves at Grotto Park, but it doesn't look like he's going to hurt her today." I went on to describe what I'd seen in my last two visions. They gasped when I mentioned the gun, then looked relieved but perplexed when I told them how Nicholas intervened.

"That's so weird," Kieran said. "It really is like he's protecting her. I mean, I'm glad, but….weird."

"Tell them what you told me about the beam," Hendricks prompted me.

"Oh, that's right. Mom called after Hendricks and I chatted with Patrick Erickson. She found that wood beam the Fausts used to kill Jack. It's hidden under a bed."

Mimi interrupted me. "Raegan? I'm seeing green. Does that mean Danielle's trying to ping me?"

"I see it too," I said. My mom's green colors seemed a little more faded than before, as if psychically connecting with two people at the same time required just a bit too much energy. "She's pinging both of us."

"That's new," Mimi said. She seemed pleased to be included. "Let's see what she's got."

I sat across from Mimi at the table, and, on a whim, took off my left glove and extended my hand across the table. She did the same and laid her hand in mine. Hand in hand, ring to ring, we closed our eyes and opened the connection.

∞

Danielle was back in her room, sitting in the rocker next to the window. She held the leather-bound journal she'd found in the big bedroom in her hands. It was roughly six inches by nine inches, and the word DIARY was stamped into the cover. She opened the book and examined the inscription on the paper liner inside the front cover: I, Simone Rich Faust, am of sound mind as I write in this journal. My body? Not so sound.

Then she turned to the first page.

January 4, 2002

The doctors say there's nothing more they can do for me now. They referred me to hospice care two weeks ago. I guess that means I don't have much time left.

My biggest regret? Well, I suppose it's that I won't be able to do what I should have done a long time ago. So I'm writing it all down here in hopes that someone will find it and help set the Universe right.

First, I want to make it clear that I love my husband. Edison has loved me without condition for nearly eleven years. I'm very sorry to leave him.

But Edison has done some terrible things, things that weigh heavy on my conscience. I've kept his secrets, possibly to my own detriment. Would I be lying here, dying of pancreatic cancer, if I'd simply acknowledged the truth and turned him in for what he's done?

It's impossible to know. But I'm going to use what little time I have left to help the Universe make things right.

So tired now. Must rest.

January 5, 2002

Someone asked me once what I'm most proud of. I've been thinking about that a lot as I lie here waiting patiently for the cancer to take me. If I had to choose one thing, it would be my store. Hippie Chick, River Junction's first "spiritual healing center" and headshop, has been a source of irritation for River Junction's conservative establishment since the day I opened the doors. That's a fact I'm terribly proud of.

A hippie like me had no business in River Junction when I landed here in mid-1990, after my divorce from Stuart was finalized. I took my half from that fat bastard, threw a dart at a map, and got the hell out of Chicago. River Junction seemed like a nice place, close to the Twin Cities but not too close, perfect for a newly-single woman to take another shot at life on her terms.

It turns out that divorcing a multimillionaire is a winning proposition. My settlement with Stuart was so substantial that I didn't need to work ever again if I didn't want to. But I needed something to keep me busy — and Hippie Chick opened in downtown River Junction in January 1990. Every town needs a good headshop. My store was the only one in thirty miles that sold marijuana paraphernalia. I also offered crystals, incense and essential oils, bohemian clothing, and jewelry.

The kids loved me. Their parents, not so much.

When I wasn't working, I was bored and lonely. So I started spending much of my free time at the Majestic Saloon. That shithole bar became my entire social life. I spent nearly all of my free time there, drinking, smoking, playing bingo, pulling tabs, and bullshitting with friends. We could smoke inside back then.

That's where I met Edison Faust in May 1990. He started pursuing me on day 1, but I was not interested. He – really, his whole family – had a terrible reputation in town. I was lonely, but I wasn't that lonely.

When Edison realized his slimy pickup lines and outlandish lies – a CIA agent? Really? Give me a break – weren't working on me, he finally dropped the act. And I grew to sort of like this brash, sarcastic, brutally honest, hard-drinking man. We had a lot in common. And being with him made me feel less lonely.

He had anger issues, still does, and he kept making the mistake of trying to isolate and control me. That might have worked on a weaker woman, but I did not – and still don't – have time for that kind of bullshit. If he hit me, I hit back twice as hard.

I got tired of the games and kicked his ass straight to the curb. He came crawling back within days. We had to do that dance several times before Edison finally learned his lesson: if you want to be with me, you will behave. Eventually we came to an understanding. Sometimes he still hits when he's pissed off, and I still hit back.

We were married on Valentine's Day 1991, and for the most part life with him has been pretty good. We've built a mutual respect and he loves me in his own way. That's good enough for me.

I'm certainly not lonely anymore.

January 6, 2002

Edison tells me all the time that I am nothing like his first wife Elaine. I don't take his shit and I will not be controlled. He says he likes the challenge. He also hasn't been shy about his love for my money.

But he lives in a constant state of resentment and anger, and I fear my strength may have pushed him to take that anger out on others.

Laura, for example. She raised her boy Nicholas away from the shadow of the Fausts, and she raised him well. Nicholas is a fine boy. But Edison wants him in his fold and under his thumb. So, nearly two years ago now, he had Morgan kill Laura to finally get her out of the way. They did it sneaky too. They used the sux. Laura had type 1 diabetes and Edison knew nobody would think twice about a needle mark. He also knew heart problems are common in people with diabetes so everyone would assume she had a heart attack. Even if he hadn't had Wint Steele in his pocket, this was damn near the perfect murder.

I still feel awful about it. Laura was just doing her job and protecting her boy — and she paid the price.

I worry about Nicholas now.

January 7, 2002

My belly feels like it's on fire all the time now. The only thing that helps is the morphine the hospice nurse gives me. I write while the pain is less, and then I sleep. I sleep a lot now. My body is so damn tired.

But I'm not done yet. There's one other awful thing Edison did that I cannot abide. He killed an old high school classmate. Why? Because Jack Hughes supposedly had a stash of gold and Edison wanted it. He was – still is – obsessed with it. Which I don't really understand. Thanks to my divorce settlement, we have more than enough money.

Well…maybe I do understand: Jack Hughes stole Edison's girl back in high school. And Edison doesn't forgive a transgression like that. Not ever.

I don't believe Edison showed up at Jack's house that day planning to kill him. I think he only meant to scare him into giving up where he was hiding that damn gold. But I'll tell you what: thirty-seven years is a long time to carry that kind of anger. At some point it's going to boil over. I think Edison lost control. Instead of making Jack bleed a little bit, he didn't stop hitting him until he was good and dead. Morgan told me Jack's head didn't even look like a head by the time Edison was done.

I found the piece of wood they used to kill Jack in the basement. It still has his blood all over it. One of the last things I did while I could still walk was drag that beam upstairs. I hid it under my bed. You'll find it there if you look. (Edison knows better than to mess with anything in my room, even after I'm gone.)

You know what I find most appalling about this whole thing, besides what happened to poor Jack? After Edison beat Jack to death, he stole Arlene's heirloom scarab pin. It's a beautiful piece, looks like multicolored beetles standing tip-to-toe in a perfect circle. Something like that would fetch a pretty penny in my store. But it belongs to Arlene's family. Instead it's locked inside Edison's safe – the one thing in this entire house I cannot access.

January 9, 2002

Dear Universe, I hope you will do what I couldn't muster up the courage or the strength to do myself. I hope you will hold Edison accountable for these terrible things he's done.

Danielle closed the book and laid it in her lap.

∞

By the time Mimi and I disconnected from Danielle, the quality of the vision had deteriorated considerably. It was so dim by the end that I could barely read the last entry in Simone Faust's diary.

I let go of Mimi's hand and laid my head – which suddenly felt like it weighed a metric ton – on my arms. "My god, I just want to go to bed," I said.

Mimi stared in my general direction, her eyes glassy. "I see what you mean now," she said. "I can only imagine how Danielle feels."

"Let's go sit in the living room," I yawned. "More comfortable in there."

My dad, Kieran, and Hendricks were already in the living room, each holding a sandwich. They must have made them while Mimi and I were connected to my mom.

"How did it go?" Hendricks asked as I claimed the spot next to him on the couch.

"It was…interesting," I said. I inspected the sandwich in his hand with great interest. "Whatcha got there?"

Hendricks held it away from me. "Back off. Go get your own."

"What did you see?" Kieran asked before taking a huge bite of his sandwich.

Mimi and I described what we'd read in Simone's journal.

"Holy shit," Hendricks said.

Kieran was stuck on something else. "Edison Faust was *married?*" he asked, aghast.

I chuckled. "Twice, it sounds like."

"What woman in her right mind would marry that psychopath?" he muttered.

"Maybe they weren't in their right mind," I said. "But it seems this Simone had her shit together enough to realize what Edison was capable of."

Speaking Simone's name out loud pulled at something in my brain. Where had I seen that name before? Then I remembered: my mother had found Simone's will in Edison's safe on her second day as a guest of the Fausts.

"Killing Jack wasn't enough," Mimi said. "He had to take Arlene's pin, too. That–that's really low."

Hendricks jerked a little. "Did you say Arlene's *pin?*"

"I did."

"What did it look like?"

Mimi described it.

"Holy shit." Hendricks glanced at me. "That's the pin Colleen asked about this morning."

I nodded. "Sure sounds like it." Then I made a connection — one I should have made way before now. "That's also the pin my mom found in Edison's safe. Simone was right, it is beautiful."

"Emily and Kieran, did you visit Jack's brother today?" my dad asked.

"We did," Kieran confirmed around his last bite of sandwich. "Jack did have a dog. A terrier mutt named Scout."

"That's what Colleen and Teddy Campbell said too," I offered.

"He was incredibly protective of Jack," Mimi said. "He went to live with Paul and Jeannette after Jack died. He lived another five years, but Paul said he was never the same."

"I'm sure," I said. "He must have been traumatized." I thought briefly of another dog I'd once known: Baxter, my neighbors' elderly cocker spaniel. His untimely death was what sent me up north to Catclaw Lake a few weeks ago to investigate — and ultimately solve my first two cases as a private eye. So much had happened since then; felt like a hundred years ago and just yesterday.

"Your gut was right about Scout's collar, Rae," Kieran said. "Paul still had it. Said he didn't keep it with Jack's things and it never occurred to him to give it to the Fausts."

"Scout was Paul's dog those last few years, after all," Mimi chimed in.

"Did you touch it, Mimi?" I asked.

"Of course I touched it," Mimi said. "Took off my glove and held the buckle and tag right in my hand." She grinned, letting us stew in anticipation for a moment.

I caved. "Well, what did you see?"

"I saw Jack carrying those canvas bank bags across a very dimly-lit room."

She was talking about the bags she'd seen him, in a separate vision, remove from a cedar chest in his basement. My heart jumped. "Could you see anything else in the room?"

"It was pretty dark in there, but Scout did a great job of exploring the whole place. Gave me a touch of motion sickness." She smiled. "There were wooden and steel beams on the ceiling and walls, and what looked like a canal or a ditch dug into the dirt floor. The ditch led to an enormous wooden wheel, probably twenty feet tall."

"Like in Paul's photo of Jack," I murmured.

"I had four, maybe five visions, and Jack wore a different shirt in every one. He would carry a couple of bags over to that wheel, disappear behind it, then emerge without them. I think those bags were so heavy that he had to make several trips. Scout never got too close to the wheel, though. He would have had to walk across a board that was being used as a little bridge over the ditch and I think he was scared of that."

"I read somewhere once that gold weighs almost twenty times more than water," Kieran said. "It would have been hard to move." He stood. "I'll be right back, I'm going to grab a sweater."

It was a bit chilly in the house, I realized. Despite the scorching July temperature outside. *Dad and his thermostat,* I thought.

Kieran returned wearing his Oregon hoodie. "Dad, we need to talk. The thermostat is set absurdly low. How are you not freezing to death in just a t-shirt and shorts?"

Liam smiled and sipped his coffee. "You can always put more clothes on. You can only take so much off."

Kieran and I rolled our eyes in unison. It was a line we'd heard thousands of times. Kieran stuffed his hands in his hoodie's front pocket and frowned. "What's this?" he muttered and pulled out what appeared to be a yellowed scrap of newspaper. He laid it on the table to flatten it out, and I could see the headline: **General**

Mills completes purchase of Ainsley Mill, plans to build modern facility.

"Let me see that." I slid the clipping toward me and scanned it. It was from the River Junction Gazette, dated May 12, 1967. The photo showed smiling men in suits and browline eyeglasses shaking hands in front of the entrance to the old Ainsley Mill. I scanned the article. "It says here that General Mills planned to demolish most of the Ainsley Mill and build a new, modern flour mill in its place." I paused, reading. "But the cost to dismantle and remove the nineteenth-century waterwheels and race system was prohibitive and the city wouldn't issue a demo permit for that part, citing concerns about the potential impact to the Bourbon River. So General Mills decided to just mothball the turbine room and build around it." I looked at Kieran. "Where did you find this?"

"It was in Jack's cedar chest," he said, wide-eyed. "I picked it up to read it and must have stuck it in my pocket without realizing it."

That's when everything started falling into place.

The photo on Paul Hughes' mantel had shown a young Jack in the very turbine room I'd just read about. "Jack almost certainly took that wooden beam home as a souvenir when they demolished the old mill," I said. "He was a loyal employee and would have wanted a keepsake of the original mill where he'd started his career."

"And that decommissioned turbine room is where he hid his gold. I'd bet my life on it," Hendricks said.

We sat in absolute, disbelieving silence. We'd found Jack Hughes' legendary gold.

Now we had to figure out how to get our hands on it.

"How do we get in there?" Liam asked.

A perfect vertical line formed between Hendricks' eyebrows as he considered this, then his face brightened and he snapped his fingers. "I got it!" He turned to me. "Teddy Campbell."

"That's right!" I backhanded Hendricks' chest, and he grunted. "He worked with Jack at the mill!"

"I think he's retired now, but I bet he still has contacts there." He rubbed his chest. "Would you quit hitting me?"

"I'm sorry," I said, grinning and not all that sorry. "I just get so excited."

"I'll call Teddy," Hendricks said, starting to get up.

I pulled him back down. "Hang on a sec. I know our goal was to get the gold before the Fausts do, but what if we use it to capture them?" I asked. "Lure them to Ainsley Mill and be there ready to take them down?" I glanced at Hendricks. "Would it be possible to arrest them?"

He pondered. "Not for any of the murders, no. All of that evidence is locked inside his house and the only reason we know it's there is because of your mother."

Everyone's shoulders dropped.

"But we can certainly arrest all three Fausts for kidnapping Danielle. Our eyewitness accounts plus that text Nicholas sent Raegan will be plenty enough for an arrest warrant."

Mimi clasped her gloved hands in front of her chest. "Oh, thank god!"

I was happy too, but hearing that Nicholas would be arrested twinged my heart a little. I knew he was a reluctant participant in all this, but, as was Edison's way, Nicholas would pay the price for it.

"I'll call Teddy and see if and when he can get us into that turbine room," Hendricks said, standing up. "Then I'll call Sergeant Rooney and get that arrest warrant rolling. We'll all need to stop by RJPD and submit sworn statements, so I probably won't have it in hand until about ten o'clock tomorrow morning."

I took a screenshot of the text Nicholas sent me on Tuesday (**We're coming for her. Give her up and nobody gets hurt.**) and texted it to Hendricks. Then I realized something. "We have to loop Mom in," I said. "She can help us get the Fausts to Ainsley Mill."

"Good call, Rae," Kieran said.

I got up off the couch and went to the kitchen, where I found the notepad and pen I'd used to scrawl a note to my mother on Thursday.

I wrote a new note: GOLD IS IN OLD WATERWHEEL ROOM UNDER AINSLEY MILL. WE WILL BE THERE 10:30AM TOMORROW READY TO ARREST ALL 3 FAUSTS. CAN YOU HELP GET THEM THERE? Then I closed my eyes and pinged my mother. When she connected I opened my eyes and stared at my note, giving her ample time to read it. When she disconnected I tore the note and the sheet underneath it into tiny shreds and sent them down the garbage disposal piece by piece.

My mother pinged me back right away. I opened the connection and saw a note written in her spidery handwriting: SAFE COMBINATION IS 98-47-13-62 TURN WHEEL 4 TIMES BEFORE COMBO. I blindly grabbed for my pen and scribbled the numbers and "4 turns" on the notepad. Then I disconnected.

Danielle had just given me the key piece of information we would need to nail Edison for the trail of destruction he'd left behind him over the last sixty-plus years. She knew the gig was up.

I just hoped she could stay alive until then.

172

PART 2:
DANIELLE & NICHOLAS

Tuesday, July 20, 2021

CHAPTER 19

Danielle O'Rourke stared out the window, not seeing the urban scenery whiz by as Morgan Faust piloted the Suburban at breakneck speeds through Minneapolis. After a lifetime of cat-and-mouse and thirty-two years of hiding, her nightmare scenario had come to pass: Edison Faust had her in his clutches. He'd triumphed.

Or so he thinks, Danielle thought. *Little does he know we orchestrated this whole thing. We're the cats now — the ones who will triumph in the end.*

Still. Without her family she felt desolate. Empty. It was a feeling she'd learned to live with during her time in hiding, but it was bigger now. Twenty-four hours with Emily, Liam, Kieran, and Raegan had finally filled that hole within her like nothing else could — and Edison Faust had cruelly ripped her away from them again. The wound inside her was gaping and raw.

The inside of the Suburban was hot; the air conditioning blew half-cold air that couldn't blunt the late July heat outside. It also stank like unwashed skin and stale cigar smoke. She sighed and glanced to her right, where Nicholas, Edison's grandson, sat stone-faced. Despite his pallor and the dark circles around his slightly sunken eyes, Danielle could see how he would have appealed to Raegan. *He must have some kernel of good inside him, or*

Raegan wouldn't have stayed with him as long as she did, she thought. *This could work to my advantage.*

Edison, seated in the front passenger seat, turned to look at her over his bony left shoulder. "So. Danielle."

Pulled from her reverie, she glared defiantly at him. The boastful gleam in his black eyes made her sick.

"I believe you'll find your accommodations to be acceptable during your stay with us. Much more comfortable than that shack you'd been living in up north," Edison said.

Danielle said nothing.

A sly smile spread across his hawkish, liver-spotted face. "It's a shame what happened, though."

Danielle remained mute, but her heart quickened. *Oh, god. Carl.*

"I'm sorry to say that old shack had an unfortunate fire."

"You son of a bitch," Danielle said through clenched teeth.

All pretense of friendliness disappeared from Edison's face. "Let me give you a piece of friendly advice, Danielle. Don't fuck with me. You're here to serve a specific purpose. I would strongly advise against any shenanigans if you want to see your family again."

He is a truly ugly man, inside and out, Danielle thought. "What's this specific purpose?" She already knew, but wanted to see what Edison would say. Would he tell her the truth?

"Gold," Nicholas said, thwarting any attempt by Edison to lie or put a spin on the truth.

"Shut your goddamn mouth, boy," Edison snarled.

Nicholas glared at his grandfather, then looked at Danielle. "He wants you to help him find a stash of gold that may or may not exist."

Edison started yelling then, launching into a tirade. Various shades of blue began to pulse across Danielle's vision. She wasn't sure if it was Emily or Raegan trying to connect; she concentrated on Raegan first and the connection was established. *Blue means Raegan,* she thought.

"Oh, it exists. Don't you doubt that," Edison shouted, bony arms waving. "It's out there, waiting for *me* to find it." He jabbed a finger in Morgan's direction. "That fucker Jack Hughes stole Arlene from me. I *deserve* that gold." He pointed at Nicholas. "He *owes* it to me. It's *mine*." His blazing eyes and gnarled finger settled on Danielle. "And *you're* going to help me find it."

Nicholas shook his head and tossed a sour glance at Danielle. "Edison here believes in fairy tales, I guess. Nobody's ever seen this gold. There is *zero* evidence it exists. But he's willing to brazenly kidnap somebody, hold her against her will, and force her to do his bidding to find it. As if that isn't a pile of felonies just waiting to put him in prison for the rest of his worthless life."

Edison waved this away. "I am untouchable. Nobody in River Junction or Greenhaven County has the cajones to pin anything on me."

Except you kidnapped me from Minneapolis, Danielle thought but did not say. A quick glance at Nicholas confirmed he had the same thought. Edison didn't seem concerned at all that her family might call the police and report her kidnapping. He was supremely confident indeed.

She turned back to the window and saw a wooden sign that said GREENHAVEN GROTTO PARK standing next to a short driveway and a long, skinny parking lot along the Bourbon River. *Caves,* she thought randomly.

The sign disappeared behind them and Morgan, ever silent, turned into a long driveway lined with gnarled old oak trees that led to a sinister-looking three-story mansion with a gray granite exterior and a tall turret. This creepy house, built in the late nineteenth century, was known as The Fortress and was where generations of Fausts had called home. He parked and Edison told Nicholas to take Danielle inside.

Danielle got out of the truck and allowed Nicholas to lead the way. She was mildly surprised to discover that the inside of the Fortress did not, in fact, look like a medieval castle. It looked like a regular house with a decidedly apathetic male ambience. Nicholas led her up a staircase and down a long second floor hallway. She counted six closed doors, three on each side of the hall. He stopped at the last door on the right and opened it. "Here's your room," he mumbled, refusing to make eye contact.

"Thank you, Nicholas," Danielle said with as much warmth as she could muster given the circumstances. Suddenly she felt very tired.

Nicholas dipped his head and gestured for her to go inside. She did, and turned around just in time to see the door shut firmly behind her.

She went to the door and tested the doorknob. She didn't really expect it to move, and it didn't. She sighed and turned to survey her room. It was a decent size, with a queen-sized bed, a rocker next to the window, a TV, and its own bathroom. The white walls were devoid of any decoration and the window was covered with cheap aluminum miniblinds. The room was comfortably cool.

It's better than a dungeon, I suppose, Danielle thought, then sat on the end of the bed. The tears came and she covered her face with her gloved hands. *Oh god, what have I done?*

She disconnected from Raegan, had a good cry, then climbed into the bed and pulled the covers over her head. *I'm so tired, but I don't know how I'll ever sleep,* she thought.

Despite the late afternoon sun blasting through the chinks in the miniblinds, Danielle was asleep in seconds.

Wednesday, July 21, 2021

CHAPTER 20

Danielle woke with the sun the following morning, feeling stale in yesterday's clothes and desperate to brush her teeth. She got out of bed and wandered around the room, looking through drawers and peeking into closets. She was surprised to find clean clothes in the dresser; she pulled out a pair of basic gray sweatpants and a tie-dyed cropped t-shirt with a big white peace sign on it. *The shirt is a little shorter than I'd like, but it will do.* She laid the clothes on the bed and headed for the bathroom.

She found it stocked. *They were certainly prepared for me,* she thought as she finally brushed her teeth. *I wonder for how long.* The clothes in the dresser were out of style and the toothpaste was a brand that had been discontinued years ago. *Even I know that, and I was a hermit for thirty years,* she thought. She spit and rinsed, then turned on the shower.

Cleaned up and dressed, her long, curly white hair held back by an old-fashioned cloth headband, Danielle felt a bit more put together. She went to the window and opened the blinds. The view was breathtaking. This side of the house overlooked the Bourbon River, which sparkled like sequins in the distance. Enormous old oak and maple trees provided shade while still allowing a view of the huge, if a bit overgrown, backyard. She watched a couple of squirrels chase each other and then disappear up a tree.

Danielle sat in the rocker and stared out the window, occasionally watching the birds but mostly lost in her own thoughts: of Liam, of her kids, of her twenty-four-hour taste of normalcy. Of Edison and a lifetime of playing cat-and-mouse in an effort to keep him from exploiting her touch for his own gain.

Danielle couldn't remember the last time she had used her touch. She lived alone in Carl's cabin up in Isabella, and she made a concerted effort to never use it. Her own memories of nearly being snatched by Edison and subsequently leaving her children were hard enough to live with; she didn't need the added stress of touch visions, future or past. So almost as soon as she'd arrived at the secluded cabin that would be her home for thirty-two years, she put on her sheepskin gloves and only took them off to bathe, clean, and wash the dishes. They became a part of her, as much as her nose or her hair. Liam and Carl made sure she always had a supply.

She lifted her hands and inspected the gloves she was wearing now. They were still in pretty good shape. *These should get me through,* she thought. She noticed the extra bulge around her left ring finger and felt comforted knowing she could still connect with Emily and Raegan. The psychic connection could never replace actual human contact, but would do for now.

Shades of blue pulsed around the edges of Danielle's vision, and she smiled. She closed her eyes and connected with Raegan, then opened them and treated her daughter to a glimpse of the view outside her window.

Commotion at the bedroom door caught her attention and she turned. The door was open and Edison shuffled in, holding something in his right hand. He was scowling.

Danielle wasn't sure if she should stand or stay sitting. She chose the latter and warily watched him approach.

Edison stopped in front of her and held his fist out. "Touch this and tell me what you see." A foul odor like decades of rotten coffee emanated from his mouth. Danielle had to swallow hard to stop herself from gagging.

"What is it?" She couldn't quite tell; all she could see were glimpses of gray between liver-spotted fingers.

Edison held the object so close to Danielle's face that it nearly touched her nose. Then he shook it. "Are you fucking blind? It's a belt buckle."

Danielle leaned back a bit and held her hands up defensively.

Another voice came from the door. "Calm down there, Grandpa."

Danielle and Edison turned. Nicholas stood in the open door, his hair wet and his face freshly shaved. He held his own hands up in a calming gesture.

"Fuck you," Edison said, then turned back and resumed shaking the belt buckle in Danielle's face. The hanging skin on his neck was turning red. "Touch this, I said."

"I have an idea. How about you ask the lady nicely?" Nicholas asked, advancing a few more steps into the room. "You ever heard the term 'You get more bees with honey than vinegar?' Nobody wants to help you when you're an asshole."

Edison glanced at Danielle and pondered this. Then he took a deep breath to steady himself and tried again. "Touch this and tell me what you see." He cleared his throat. "Uh, please."

Danielle decided to humor him, mostly to show Edison that his grandson gave sage advice. "Yes, Edison. I can do that." She held out her gloved left hand.

"You gotta take that off," Edison grumbled, but he placed the buckle in Danielle's gloved hand. It was a custom-made silver Western-style belt buckle with the name JACK and an old-fashioned gristmill waterwheel embossed on it in a gold metal. An engraved inscription on the back read **Congrats on 25 years! From your Ainsley Mill family.**

Danielle made a show of using her teeth to remove her right glove while she wracked her brain for some idea of what she would tell Edison. She had to buy enough time for Raegan, Kieran, Officer Jesse and Liam to find the gold before Edison could.

Her mind was blank for a couple of panicky seconds, and then, blessedly, an idea came to her. She remembered the sign she'd seen from the car the day before. *Caves.* She didn't know anything about Greenhaven Grotto Park, but she hoped there were multiple grottos there for the Fausts to search while her family worked to put them behind bars.

She finally got the glove off and wrapped her bare fingers around the metal belt buckle. She spontaneously disconnected from Raegan when a faded vision appeared behind her eyes.

∞

At first there was nothing but black. Just as Danielle began to wonder if her touch was broken, the black gave way to a large, dim, dirt-floored room.

A smallish brown and white dog trotted around, sniffing everything and occasionally stopping to check on the buckle's wearer. A canal had been dug into the floor, and straight ahead was a huge, hulking wood structure that she didn't recognize at first. Then she started moving toward it, purposefully but slowly. The buckle's wearer stopped once, and her vision went black for a second. It went black again a minute or so later, and she slowly made her way toward the big structure again.

She realized that the buckle was on Jack Hughes' belt and he was trying to carry something heavy across the room. He'd stopped to rest, and when he bent over to set his load down, the belt buckle was covered and everything went black. It happened again when he bent to pick his load back up.

As Jack drew nearer she could see that the enormous wooden structure was a huge waterwheel, the kind used in old gristmills. He made his way across a rickety old board that served as a bridge across the trench — which she could now see was a fairly deep canal — then stopped and looked back. The dog stood on the far side of the board bridge and stared intently, then sat.

Jack resumed his journey, finally stopping in front of an old wooden door set into the stone wall at the base of the wheel. He set one of his loads down and grasped the knob with a thick, callused hand. It turned and he pulled the door open, then stepped inside the pitch black room. A light suddenly popped on — from a headlamp, perhaps — and she could see that the room was more of a closet: small, cramped, and full of various tools and materials that a worker might need to fix and maintain a nineteenth-century waterwheel. On the floor in one corner sat six heavy-duty canvas bank bags with reinforced vinyl bottoms and handles, each about two feet tall and eighteen inches wide. Those bags looked secure and able to withstand punishing environments. Jack moved toward the pile and bent to add his current load to it. Then he stood and stepped back; now there were eight bags.

Jack backed out of the room, closed the door behind him, and walked back to where his faithful dog still sat, waiting patiently.

∞

Danielle opened her eyes. Edison still stood directly in front of her, his wrinkled face now eager. "Well? What did you see?"

She blinked and frowned, pretending to think really hard. "Ah, well, I saw Jack Hughes carrying something heavy into a…well, I guess it must have been a cave."

It was Edison's turn to frown. "A cave?"

Danielle nodded. "Yes. There was a sign nearby." She pretended to concentrate. "I believe it said 'Greenhaven Grotto Park.' Do you know what that is?"

"What else did you see?"

"It was pretty dark once he entered the cave, so I didn't see much else. He left his item deep inside and then walked back out."

Suspicion bloomed in Edison's eyes. "What happened after that? Which cave is it in? Is it still there?" His poorly-hidden accusation: *Are you lying to me, bitch?*

At first Danielle didn't know what he was talking about. Then it hit her: he was expecting that her future touch would tell him exactly where to go. The only problem: she didn't have a future vision. Only a past one. Her stomach dropped. She would really have to make something up — but she could use Jack's untimely death to her advantage.

"I don't know if it's still there," she said. "And I can't tell you exactly which cave it's in. There are so many." She hoped. "But I can tell you Jack never went back there before he died. The psychic trail ends for me with his death. There's nothing to see after that." She gave the old man the buckle.

Edison's neck started to flush red again, and his thin lips worked over his crooked yellow teeth. "You —"

Nicholas crossed the room, grabbed his grandfather's bony upper arm, and led him to the door. "Come on, Grandpa, you got what you wanted. Let's go."

Danielle appreciated Nicholas' sarcastic use of the term "Grandpa." She wondered if Edison even noticed.

CHAPTER 21

Nicholas returned a few minutes later with a big blueberry muffin and a hot cup of coffee. Danielle accepted both gratefully. "Thank you," she said. "I'm starving."

He nodded, eyes on the floor, and left. The doorknob locked with a quiet *click*.

Danielle sat in the rocker and devoured her breakfast. *Nicholas won't make eye contact with me*, she thought as she ate. *Is he ashamed of himself after what he did to Raegan?* She thought about the bruises on her daughter's neck and her heart skipped a beat. *Maybe. Although I suspect it's more than that. Maybe he still loves her. And I remind him of her.* She thought that was much more likely.

Suddenly a door elsewhere in the house slammed and a car outside started up. She couldn't see the front of the house from her window, but she guessed that Edison, Morgan, and Nicholas were on their way to begin searching caves at Greenhaven Grotto Park.

Danielle stood and set her dishes on the bedside table. *Ah, perfect*, she thought. *Let's take a look at this lock.* She had to get out of this room if she hoped to find any evidence to help bring the Fausts down. That was the key to this whole plan.

Danielle went to the door and bent to inspect the doorknob. To her surprise – and delight – it was a basic home center variety doorknob that had been installed backwards and upside down so the locking mechanism was on the hallway side of the door. There was a small hole on the room side that could be jimmied. When installed properly, this hole would allow for emergency access to a room. For Danielle, it would provide her way out.

What a bunch of noobs, she thought as she walked into the bathroom. *All I need is a couple of bobby pins or paper clips and I'm a free woman.* The ancient doorknobs at Carl's cabin were finicky, and the key had long ago been lost. She was locked out of the bathroom one time and had to teach herself how to pick the lock. That was a challenge. This would be a breeze.

She rummaged through bathroom drawers, pushing aside brightly-colored scrunchies, smaller hair ties, a pair of tweezers, and a hairbrush until she finally found what she was looking for: three or four old bobby pins hiding at the far back of the drawer. *Wow…what are the odds?* She used the tweezers to pick up two of the pins and lifted them out. She bent one into an L-shape and straightened the other before putting a small bend in the tip. Then she went back to the door and got to work. Within two minutes the knob was unlocked and the door opened.

Danielle hid her new lock-picking tools in the bathroom, then tiptoed to the door and poked her head out. She stood very still and listened for a long time, just to make sure the Fausts had really left the house. She heard nothing, so, heart pounding, she finally stepped out into the hallway. She was careful to leave her door cracked open. She didn't completely trust the doorknob, and she didn't want to find herself on the wrong side of her locked door.

All of the other bedroom doors were closed, but that didn't stop Danielle from opening them and exploring each room. The first room she entered appeared to be Edison's. It smelled like him, anyway: unwashed skin, stale cigar smoke, spilled alcohol, rotten breath. Danielle covered her mouth and nose with a gloved hand as she looked around. The room was laid out much like hers, but was darker; a light-blocking curtain covered the window. The bed was unmade and dirty clothes were strewn all over the floor.

Let's test my touch again, she thought. Although she wasn't sure if she really wanted to see any visions from inside this room, she forced herself to remove a glove, closed her eyes, and laid her bare fingertips on the lightswitch next to the door.

She caught a vision and it popped up behind her eyelids. In it, Edison was lying on his bed wearing nothing but pee-stained boxer shorts, holding a drink and trying to figure out how to work the TV remote. His wrinkled and wasted body was covered in white hair. He pointed the remote at the TV, then shouted something and shook the remote hard, causing his drink to slosh out of the glass and onto his dirty sheets. When the channel still didn't change, he angrily chucked the remote against the wall. It fell to the floor in pieces.

With her fingers still on the lightswitch, Danielle disregarded the other visions floating around her and concentrated on connecting with Edison's spiritual energy. If she could find that, she could follow it, much like a dog follows a scent, to see his future.

She couldn't find any trace of his energy. It was like her antenna was broken.

She lifted her fingers from the lightswitch, backed out of the room, and quietly closed the door. *Let's try another room,* she thought.

The next door opened on a room that was so cluttered she couldn't push the door all the way open. It was even darker than Edison's, but she could make out an enormous TV hanging on the wall. Boxes and bags were piled on every surface, including the floor and half of the bed. She could just make out the spines of VHS tape cases that filled a box on top of a cattywampus pile next to the bed. The movies had titles like The Slutty Professor, Schlong Blade, and Star Whores. Danielle's stomach turned and she was tempted to just close the door and move along, but she forced herself to take her glove off and touch the lightswitch.

It was a decision she instantly regretted. The first vision she caught was of Morgan Faust sitting on the uncluttered side of his bed in the bright glow of his massive TV, propped up against the wall and watching intently. He was shirtless and his pants were pushed partway down. He was vigorously masturbating, the scarred side of his grizzled face contorted with effort and ecstasy.

Oh my god. Danielle yanked her fingers from the lightswitch and immediately left the room. She had no desire to look for Morgan's spiritual energy; she'd seen enough. *I wish there was a way I could unsee that.*

She crossed the hall to the room next to hers and peeked inside. It was empty. She opened the next door down, closest to the stairs, and discovered the room Nicholas was apparently occupying. It was bare, like hers, and furnished almost identically. An open bag with clothes folded neatly inside sat on the floor next to the dresser. She noticed a couple of fist-sized holes in the wall next to the television. *Ooo, I wonder what happened there,* she thought as she touched the lightswitch.

She caught a vision of Nicholas, wearing a black t-shirt and black athletic shorts, his black hair slicked back, pacing the room with his cellphone against his ear. He was talking animatedly, clearly upset. Suddenly he stopped, looked at the phone's screen with wide angry eyes, and threw it against the wall next to the TV like a pitcher throwing a baseball. He looked remarkably like his grandfather at that moment. Then, one right after the other, he punched two good-sized holes in the drywall. *A temper passed down through generations of Fausts,* Danielle thought. *I bet he was talking to Raegan.* Nicholas turned to face the window and stood there for a couple of minutes, clearly working to get his emotions under control. Then the vision flitted away.

Danielle focused in and tried to find Nicholas' spiritual energy; but, like with his grandfather, she saw and felt nothing. *My god, I think my future touch really is broken,* she thought. *Atrophied from so many years of not using it.*

This explained why she hadn't known they were on their way to get her. If Nicholas hadn't sent Raegan that text, they wouldn't have had time to prepare. She shuddered and closed the door to Nicholas' room, then made her way down the stairs.

The stairs ended in the large foyer, and directly opposite was another staircase. Curious, Danielle crossed the foyer and ascended. She found herself in another, shorter hallway. This one had only one door: heavy, wooden, and locked tight. A brief inspection confirmed the presence of a deadbolt. She wouldn't be able to pick this lock with her bobby pins.

She took off her glove and touched the knob. There weren't many visions to choose from, so she grabbed the most recent. It showed a much younger Edison, his black hair only just starting to turn white at the temples, locking the door tight and slipping the key in a pants pocket as he turned away.

Danielle needed that key and made a mental note to keep an eye out for it. She sighed, frustrated, and turned back.

The main level boasted a messy, neglected living room and a filthy kitchen. Danielle touched various surfaces in both rooms, curious about what she might see. Most visions in the living room were of Edison or Morgan lounging on the decrepit couches, watching TV. She managed to catch one interesting vision: a faded old clip of a woman with a friendly face that showed all the signs of a hard-living lifestyle. She was dark-eyed, olive-skinned and raven-haired, dressed in a long blue maxi skirt and the exact tie-dyed t-shirt Danielle herself was currently wearing. Her long hair was pulled up into a half ponytail held with a bright yellow scrunchie. She puffed on a cigarette and paced the room. Edison, roughly the same age as he was when he locked that heavy wooden door, sat on the couch. They were deep in an animated conversation. *Who is this gypsy woman, and why am I wearing her clothes?*

She tore herself away and resumed her trek through the Fortress, suddenly aware that time may be running short. She focused on looking for a room where Edison might keep important documents, like a den or an office — and she found it at the front of the house, next to the main entrance.

Danielle stepped into the office and decided to see if she could get a hold of Raegan. *She'll want to see all this*, she thought as she closed her eyes and concentrated on her daughter's beautiful face. Raegan opened the connection within seconds.

Edison's office was a good-sized room with wall-to-wall bookshelves and a huge picture window. An antique mahogany desk, upon which sat a very modern computer, faced the wall opposite the window. A basic rolling desk chair sat in front of the desk. An old electric typewriter had been relegated to a far corner of the room, and a shabby red couch sat perpendicular to the right of the desk. Newspapers and documents and yellow legal pads and pens littered every horizontal surface in the room, including the worn rug that covered most of the scuffed wood floor. Like the rest of the house, the office was a mess.

But what truly caught Danielle's eye was a massive portrait in a gaudy frame hanging on the wall to the left of the desk. It was of a clean-shaven young man in a black suit with a high white collar, black buttoned waistcoat, and a black tie. *A Faust, no doubt about it,* Danielle thought. *Stefan.* The young man held a straw boater hat in both hands below his waist, and his black hair was slicked back. She could see traces of his great-great grandson Nicholas in his carefully neutral face. The artist had captured an intensity in his deep black eyes that sent shivers up and down Danielle's spine.

The one who started it all. Bitter anger bubbled up into her throat. *This man caused generations of suffering. It's too bad his wife dispatched him all those years ago. I'd love a crack at him myself.* Danielle breathed deeply and swallowed the anger back down. It wouldn't help her now.

She noticed an unusual space between the portrait's frame and the wall and went to investigate. She felt around the edges of the frame until her fingers hooked into a slight depression in the wood. She gently pulled and the portrait swung on hinges, revealing a safe with an intimidating combination dial set deep in the wall.

Ah, jackpot, Danielle thought. The enormous combination dial didn't faze her; she simply removed a glove, touched it with her bare fingers, and watched as many Edisons throughout the years spun it back and forth. She memorized the combination, then put her glove back on and easily opened the safe herself.

Just as she reached in to pick up an item inside, bright lights washed across the darkening room. Danielle's heart thumped. *Oh god, they're home.* She quickly shut the safe and closed the portrait over it, then ran back to her room.

She heard their voices just as she closed her bedroom door. She realized almost too late that she'd forgotten to set the lock. She cracked the door, reached out, and turned the button on the knob. Then she quietly closed it again and beelined for the rocker next to the window. She sat, pulled a blanket over her lap, and tried to look like she'd been sitting there all day bored out of her mind.

Within a minute her door swung open. Danielle turned and there stood Edison, red-faced and scowling. When he noticed the tie-dyed t-shirt she was wearing, his eyes widened and some of the color fell out of his face.

"Hello, Edison," Danielle said calmly.

Edison recovered himself and the flush crept over his entire head. "You'd better not be lying to me, woman."

"I don't know what you're talking about."

Edison stormed into the room, holding Jack Hughes' belt buckle out with a skeletal arm. "You said the gold would be in the caves!" His raspy voice strained with the effort of shouting.

"I did say that," Danielle confirmed.

"Well, we didn't find it there. Which makes me wonder if you're lying to me. Or perhaps trying to divert our attention elsewhere." He glanced around the room with suspicious eyes.

"I don't care about your gold, Edison. I just want to go home. I have no interest in prolonging my stay here." Danielle resumed staring out the window.

"A mighty big assumption for such a little lady," Edison snapped, put out by Danielle's snub. "Let me be clear: you go home when I have the gold. But that's not a guarantee. If this takes longer than I think it should, I may feel less compelled to send you back to your family."

Danielle's heart pounded, but she kept her face perfectly still. Except her eyebrows. She couldn't stop them from knitting together.

"I'm going to ask you one last time, Danielle. Where's the fucking gold?"

Anger bubbled up into her throat, but she held steady. "It's in one of those caves. If you didn't find it, you weren't looking hard enough."

Edison clenched his bony hands into fists and for a brief second she thought he was going to hit her. Instead he turned and stalked out of the room, slamming the door behind him.

Danielle briefly covered her face with her hands to steady her nerves, then took a deep breath and blew the air out. *I bought us another day,* she thought, then turned back to the window to watch dusk descend through the oaks and maples outside.

She felt Raegan disconnect, leaving her feeling desolate again. Exhaustion crept over her, and she sighed. *One would think I'd be used to being away from them by now.* But the truth was, she never got used to it. The emptiness never faded, not once in thirty-two years.

A knock at the door pulled her from her thoughts. Nicholas entered carrying a black metal serving tray with flowers painted on it. *An interesting choice for a house full of men,* Danielle thought as he set the tray on her bedside table. He'd brought her a turkey sandwich, a handful of potato chips, and a glass of milk. Her stomach growled.

"Thank you, Nicholas," she said.

He nodded, still reluctant to meet her gaze. "You're welcome."

"Can I ask you a question?"

Fear — or dread, she couldn't tell which — flashed across his face and he glanced at the door as if he were calculating his chances of escaping. Then he sighed. "I guess."

"Do you think this gold your grandfather wants so badly is real?"

Nicholas thought about this, eyes still on the floor. Then he shrugged. "I don't know. Nobody knows."

"Then why all the fuss?" Danielle asked. "Doesn't this seem like a lot of effort for something that *might* exist?"

"Because it's Jack Hughes' gold." Nicholas leveled his gaze on Danielle. "I mean, nobody has ever accused Edison Faust of being a reasonable man."

A surprised chuckle escaped Danielle. "You have a point there."

Nicholas turned and headed toward the door. "I'll be back later for those dishes," he said, and was gone.

I'm going to make that boy my friend if it kills me, Danielle thought as she bit into her sandwich.

It wasn't half bad.

Thursday, July 22, 2021

CHAPTER 22

Danielle had been up for hours, gazing out her window and missing her family, when Nicholas arrived with her breakfast: an english muffin with strawberry jelly and a steaming cup of coffee. He set the tray on her bedside table and turned to leave.

"Nicholas," Danielle said.

He stopped, back to her.

"I wanted to thank you."

He turned, curious in spite of himself. "For what?"

"For your kindness."

He frowned. "I don't understand."

"You're the only one who tries to make my stay here at least tolerable. You bring me decent meals. It means a lot. Thank you."

Uncertainty clouded his dark eyes, and Danielle thought her seed might have finally found fertile ground. He cleared his throat. "I mean, we can't have you starving to death before we get that gold," he said. "That's all."

"Well, I appreciate it." She smiled.

Nicholas dipped his head and left, closing the door tight behind him.

∞

She heard the Suburban start up about an hour later, and she was ready. She picked the doorknob lock and was free from her room in minutes. She beelined for the office, and reached the front of the house just in time to see the Suburban's taillights disappear down the long, tree-lined driveway. She breathed deeply and the knots in her stomach eased a bit; she had time to explore, but she had to be careful.

She saw the briefest flash of light from within the thick foliage surrounding the house and her heart soared. *Liam.* Of course her beloved would be out there, watching, making sure she was all right. At their simple courthouse wedding in 1980, he'd gone off script during their vows and added one of his own: "I will never leave you alone. No matter what." The judge had nodded his approval. And it was a promise Liam had faithfully kept for forty years – even when she was in hiding.

She blew him a kiss through the window and hoped he saw it. Then she went into Edison's office. Wasting no time, she swung the Stefan portrait away from the wall, spun the combination dial back and forth, turned the handle, and pulled the safe open. *All right, let's get a look at what's in here,* she thought, reaching into the black recess with both hands.

She pulled out a pile of items and took them to the couch, where she could sit while looking through them. Just as she was about to start inspecting her haul, shades of blue pulsed around the edges of her vision. *Raegan.* She opened the connection, then began looking through the safe's contents in earnest.

There was a stack of file folders labeled with the names of the important documents they contained: Faust Lumber Property

Deed. 102 River Street Deed. 2015 Chev Suburban Title. Nicholas. Simone Will & Testament.

Simone. Danielle turned this name over and over in her head and decided it might be just right for a beautiful, olive-skinned gypsy woman who favored bohemian clothes, including the loose floral top Danielle had scrounged from the dresser after her morning shower.

The Nicholas folder was empty. *I wonder what was in there.*

She set the stack of folders aside and picked up a large wad of cash bound by a thick rubber band. She flipped through one end of the stack and guessed she was holding twenty or twenty-five grand in her hands. *That's-a lotta dough,* she thought in a random Italian accent and smiled at her own silliness.

Danielle set the cash on top of the file folders and pulled a battered red shoebox toward her. It had once contained a pair of thick-soled white sneakers, but now was stuffed full of notes, newspaper clippings, photos, printed emails, and memorabilia. It looked to be a treasure trove, but she decided not to spend precious time inspecting the contents of the box just yet. She went back to the safe, eager to see what else was inside.

She picked up an old pocket watch by its chain and held it up, watching it dangle and spin. It was silver, slightly tarnished, and intricately engraved with a leaf-and-vine pattern on the back and front. She set it carefully in the palm of her left hand, examined it closely, then flipped the watch cover open. There was nothing remarkable about the clock face, but something was written on the inside of the cover. She brought the watch close to her face and squinted. Engraved in delicate, worn, nearly unreadable cursive writing was the name Stefan Alexander Faust and the year 1910.

Stefan would have been…fifteen or so when he came into possession of this watch, Danielle thought. Curious, she peeked at Stefan's portrait on the wall and there it was: a silver chain hung between a buttonhole and a lower pocket of his suit vest. It occurred to her that if Stefan passed his watch to his son Benedict, who then passed it to Edison, that watch could be a goldmine of information. *I'll spend some time with that tomorrow*, she thought, glancing anxiously at the clock sitting on Edison's desk.

She carefully set the pocket watch back inside the safe and picked up the last artifact: a gold circle pin with multicolored carved gemstones set in it. It too was fairly tarnished, but it was still lovely. Danielle removed a glove and laid her bare fingertips on the pin, curious what she might see.

The pin must have been sitting in Edison's safe for a long time; all of the visions floating around her were very old and worn, like a well-loved, threadbare blanket. She disconnected from Raegan, then grabbed a few visions and watched just enough of each to get the gist.

∞

Vision: A teenaged Edison Faust leaned against a wall of red steel lockers with another young man in the hallway of a high school. His black hair was slicked back from his face and he wore a white short-sleeved button shirt, sleeves rolled and tucked into a pair of belted bluejeans. The skin on his face was much smoother, but that hawkish look was still there. He chatted with another young man who was similarly dressed, but in sharply pressed trousers instead of jeans. He was fit and muscular and towered over Edison. Both young men occasionally faced the pin and spoke jovially with its wearer;

this was a trio of good friends. Edison held his hand out to the pin's wearer and they headed to their next class. He slung an arm around the pin wearer's neck as they walked.

Vision: The pin's wearer stood against the same wall of lockers next to the other young man, facing the hallway. Throngs of kids jostled by, trying to get to class before the bell rang. Edison Faust pushed through the crowds toward them, his black eyes ablaze. He went directly to the pin's wearer and got in her face, screaming. Bits of spittle flew from his lips. He was still yelling as he yanked a black and red River Junction High School letter jacket off her shoulders. The name Jack was embroidered on the chest. Edison threw the jacket on the floor, then grabbed the pin's wearer by the hair, spun her violently, and everything went dark for a split second. When the light returned, she was holding her bloody hands in front of her face. The tall young man — this must have been Jack Hughes — intervened, taking Edison by the upper arm and pulling him away from the pin's wearer. Edison blindly wound up and threw a mighty roundhouse; he may have been aiming for Jack's face, but the height difference was too great. Instead his fist connected with Jack's throat. Jack staggered backward, gagging, eyes bulging. Two beefy male teachers pushed through the silent crowd and subdued Edison before dragging him away, still screaming.

Vision: The pin's wearer was inside a 1955 Buick Roadmaster. She and Jack sat on the front bench seat, holding each other tightly. Even in the dim glow of the dashboard lights it was obvious that Jack's throat was terribly bruised, his adam's apple swollen.

Vision: The pin's wearer opened her locker to find a dead rat hanging by its tail from the coat hook inside. The locker door quickly slammed shut.

Vision: The wearer of the pin was sitting in the front row of a church, watching Jack Hughes exchange vows with a pretty blonde woman wearing a simple white gown. A veil cascaded down her back from the tiara on her head.

Suddenly the view changed as the wearer turned to look toward the back of the church. There was Edison Faust, piss drunk, stumbling up the aisle and yelling, I object! Two of Jack's tuxedoed groomsmen, as tall and muscular as he was, left their spots and rushed down the aisle like a couple of running backs. They lifted Edison off his feet and carried him, still yelling, out of the sanctuary.

Vision: Jack Hughes, a few years older, hair longer, muttonchop sideburns along his jawline, stood in the dark-paneled living room of his home. The pin's wearer – presumably his wife – was seated on a brown and tan floral couch and looking slightly up at him. A box sat on the brown shag carpet at his feet, and one by one he lifted objects from it and proudly showed them off: various tools including an antique-looking handheld scoop carved from wood, an iron scraper, a flour sifter made of tin, and a neatly folded cotton flour sack. The last item, clearly his prized artifact, was a three-foot-long length of pitted six-by-six wood. A beam. How Jack smiled as he showed off his finds.

Vision: Darkness turned to light as the lid of a jewelry box opened, revealing Morgan Faust's scarred and blood-covered face. Blood was in his hair and all over his shirt, and it completely drenched the hand he used to reach in and pick up the pin. He examined it for a moment, then brought it out to the destroyed living room, where Edison waited with Jack's badly beaten body and unconscious dog. The wood beam Jack had so proudly shown off years before lay on the floor, almost its entire length covered in blood. There was blood on every surface of the room, including the ceiling and the glass fireplace doors. Morgan placed the pin in Edison's hand, and he too examined it. The deepening lines next to his mouth and across his forehead were visible, even through the blood that coated his face. He grinned, exposing crooked yellow teeth, then pocketed the pin.

Vision: Edison Faust, older now, his eyes bloodshot and bleary, removed the pin from the safe and took it to his desk. He looked at it for a long time with tears in his eyes, turning it over and over in his shaking hands.

∞

Danielle glanced at the clock on Edison's desk as she placed the scarab pin back in the safe. She went to the couch and gathered up the rest of the safe's contents. They could be back anytime now, and she did not want to get caught outside her room.

Before she loaded everything else back into the safe, Danielle took a moment to scan the safe's interior one last time. She was looking for the key to the locked room. No dice; Edison had no keys stashed in his safe. She quickly but carefully returned the safe's contents exactly as she'd found them, shut the door, spun the dial, and closed the Stefan portrait over it.

CHAPTER 23

Danielle had every intention of going back to her room to await the Fausts' return from Grotto Park. Instead she left Edison's office and wandered through the main level again. She couldn't stop herself, as if her subconscious knew she was missing something. And as soon as she set foot in the messy kitchen she saw it: a heavy wooden door just like the one keeping her out of the locked room upstairs. Unlike that door, however, this one was unlocked. She pushed it open and found herself in a ramshackle old sunroom. Its half-walls were constructed of the same granite as the house and topped with granite columns, latticed windows, and large skylights. A door led to the backyard. The floor was covered with large, cracked clay tiles. Dead plants lined the ledges, broken clay pots with dirt spilling out of them lay all over the floor, and an enormous urn planter in the center of the room held the skeletons of long-dead roses.

It was clear to Danielle that this place was once dearly loved, but had been long neglected. She removed a glove and laid her fingertips on the granite, which was surprisingly cold even in a solarium on a bright and hot July day.

There were even fewer visions to choose from in here – that's how neglected this room was – and they were old and faded.

Danielle grabbed three, and they all showed women in different times tending a riotous collection of thriving green plants.

∞

Vision: A slender woman with darkish hair curled and pinned back from her face, exposing a dark bruise on her left cheekbone and around her eye. She wore a simple skirt and blouse and used a dainty aluminum watering can. Based on the faded condition of the vision and the clothing she wore, Danielle thought this was Katherine Faust — wife (and killer) of Stefan, mother of Benedict, and grandmother of Edison.

Vision: A different woman in a different time. This one wore a white short-sleeved knit top tucked into a pair of maroon bellbottom pants. Her long brown hair was straightened, parted down the middle, and tucked behind her ears. Her watering can was much bigger than the first woman's, also made of metal, and painted a bright green. The woman's eyes were downcast and she seemed listless as she tended to her plants. Scratch that — she looked sad. Very, very sad. Danielle's heart went out to this nameless woman from the past.

Vision: The whimsical gypsy woman — Simone? — tending to an even bigger collection of plants. She wore her typical bohemian garb and her long black hair was pulled back with a banana clip. She held a pair of garden shears and appeared to be humming as she snipped dead flowers off the huge rosebush in the urn.

∞

Danielle lifted her hand from the granite, and as she put her glove back on she noticed the sun's low angle in the sky. *Now I really do have to get back.* She closed the door behind her and made her way upstairs.

Once she was locked safely back in her room, Danielle sat in the rocker next to the window and contemplated everything she'd seen. It was a lot, but two questions loomed large in her mind:

Where is that wooden beam?

And who is Simone?

∞

It wasn't long before the Fausts arrived home. The shouting and slamming of doors told Danielle that once again they had not succeeded in finding any gold. Her heart skipped a beat; she probably wouldn't be able to hold them off for much longer, especially with her future touch out of order. She would have to make the most of whatever time she had left to find what she and her family needed to take these bastards down for good.

Things eventually quieted down. While Danielle waited for Nicholas to bring her some dinner, shades of blue pulsed across her vision. *Will I get to see my family?* she wondered, suddenly desperate to lay eyes on them. *I'm sure they're all together right now.* Excitement building in her gut, she opened the connection with Raegan. She didn't see any faces, however; Raegan was holding a handwritten note right in front of her nose, obliterating everything behind it. Danielle read it as she swallowed back bitter disappointment. LOOK AROUND FOR A HEAVY LENGTH OF WOOD. MIGHT HAVE BLOOD ON IT.

Jack's beam. She'd had two visions of it: the day Jack brought it home from Ainsley Mill and proudly showed it off to whoever was wearing the scarab pin, and in Jack's blood-soaked living room the day Edison and Morgan beat him to death and then stole the scarab pin. *They think it's here in this house.* She would keep an eye out for it on her expeditions.

A knock on the door interrupted Danielle's sadness over not getting to see her family. "Come in," she called.

Nicholas entered carrying the black metal tray, and it was laden with a hot fried chicken TV dinner, complete with brownie, and a glass of milk. He set it on the bedside table. Instead of turning to leave, he stood and looked contemplatively at Danielle. His black eyes were dark-ringed, almost hollow.

Stomach growling, she left the rocking chair and went to the food. It smelled delicious. She caught his gaze and smiled. "Penny for your thoughts," she said. Now that she was closer to him, she noticed a ballpoint pen stuck behind his ear.

Nicholas tilted his head side to side as he debated his next words. "Edison thinks you're lying to us."

Danielle frowned. "Still?"

He nodded. "Because we haven't turned up any gold yet. He's becoming more and more convinced that you're deliberately distracting us."

"Well, he should know better. I don't want to be here any longer than I have to be. Trust me, I'm as surprised as you guys are that you haven't found it yet." She gave him a sly smile. "Maybe *he's* the reason he can't find it, not me."

Nicholas' nostrils flared in a failed attempt to hide a grin. He pulled the pen off his ear and began fiddling with it. "In the IT world, we call that 'user error.'"

"You're a computer guy, huh?" *Oh my heavens, that click-clicking noise is enough to drive anyone crazy.*

Nicholas nodded slowly. "I was, until about two weeks ago. I left a solid corporate job and moved in here to spend all my time helping Edison find Jack Hughes' mythical gold."

Danielle's eyebrows drew together. "Why would you do that?"

"Because he promised me a cut. One-third of the take is mine if I help him find it." He paused and looked at the pen in his hand, as if he were surprised to see it there. "I was going to use the money to get the fuck out of the Twin Cities and take Raegan with me. Start fresh somewhere else."

Raegan would never leave her dad and her Mimi, Danielle thought but did not say. She suspected Nicholas understood this as well – albeit too late. "So he says," she said.

Nicholas looked up sharply. "I don't think my grandfather would lie to me, especially–"

"Nicholas," Danielle interrupted as gently as she could. "Your grandfather lies to everyone about everything. It's one of his many tools for getting what he wants."

Nicholas sighed and his shoulders slumped. He set the pen on the bed. "I know you're right, Mrs. O'Rourke –"

"Please call me Dani."

This made him smile like a bashful teenager. "All right. Dani." He sighed. "I guess I would rather believe that Edison means what he says than think about all the ways I've fucked my life up over this gold."

"Including your relationship with Raegan?" She was taking a chance here, hoping he would open up a bit.

Instead his face closed like a steel trap. A dark curtain fell behind his eyes, concealing everything. "I gotta go." The doorknob clicked as he locked the door behind him.

After he'd gone, Danielle realized he'd left his pen sitting on her bed. She tossed it in the bedside table drawer, then she sat on the bed and ate her fried chicken dinner while she pondered the roughly two dozen new things she'd learned today. She was getting closer; she could feel it. Soon, hopefully tomorrow, she would find the one magic thing that would tie everything together and make it all make sense.

She just hoped she'd find it before the Fausts ran out of caves to search.

Friday, July 23, 2021

CHAPTER 24

Danielle was up with the sun after a sleepless night, rocking in the chair next to the window. She missed her family terribly. Oh, sure, this harebrained idea to let the Fausts finally take her had been her own, and it was starting to bear fruit – but she hadn't realized how hard it would be to be away from them again. *How did I do this for thirty years?* she wondered.

Truth be told, she didn't really know. Looking back, she remembered spending copious amounts of time outside, hiking or snowshoeing in the woods, just existing with nature. She painted. She took photos and even sold a few. She gathered mushrooms and berries. Pinecones were plentiful in the forest, and she made beautiful wreaths and other decorations with them that nobody would ever see. She fixed and maintained things around the cabin. She took the snowmobile or ATV six miles into tiny Isabella for groceries and basic supplies and gabbed with Paula Barnes, the owner of the general store and her only friend. *Well, besides Carl,* she thought.

Carl Engelman was her former brother-in-law, long divorced from Liam's sister Deirdre. He was a gentle giant, the sweetest man, and she'd always regretted how Deirdre had treated him, ultimately leaving him for someone else. *I think she's on husband number four now,* she thought.

Nevertheless, Carl had remained friendly with the O'Rourke family, and when Liam and Danielle called him up in the wee hours of a late August morning in 1989, he hadn't hesitated for even a second. He had a safe place for Danielle, and she could stay there as long as she needed.

His family's longtime hunting cabin was nestled smack in the middle of eighty private acres in the heart of the Superior National Forest. It was so secluded that getting in and out – especially in the winter – was often very difficult. The cabin itself was quite old and pretty basic; one bedroom, one bathroom, a kitchen, and a living area. It had electricity, a well and septic system, a small electric water heater, and a woodburning stove to keep her warm during the cold northern Minnesota winters. The furnishings looked like they'd been scrounged from someone's grandparents' basement. A second structure on the property had once been used as a bunkhouse. There was even a little ramshackle garage with a perfectly serviceable snowmobile and four-wheeled ATV inside.

As much as she didn't want to, Danielle knew she could make this little place her home. And after Carl dropped her off and she watched his car drive away, she got to work unpacking, cleaning, painting, reupholstering, and rearranging. The old bunkhouse became a studio for her creative ventures. Carl even installed a compact stacked washer and dryer in the kitchen for her, and that was a game-changer. Ten years into her stay, after making do with three snowy local channels on her rabbit-ears antenna, Carl set her up with satellite TV. A couple years after that he gave her a cell phone to be used only in an emergency. The service this far north was crap back then, and she had to climb to the top of the nearest ridge just to get a bar or two. Luckily she never had to use it. Ten years after that she got a new phone and satellite internet access, and the world opened up to her even more.

I'll never leave you alone. No matter what, Liam had promised. And he didn't, even when Danielle was in seclusion up north and he was in Minneapolis with Emily and the kids. Carl lived in Duluth and visited every week, bringing supplies and generally making sure she had everything she needed. He took her to doctors and dentists when needed, where she used the name Darcy Engelman. Weekly coffee with Carl and monthly visits with Paula kept her sane until technology advanced enough to finally allow daily calls and emails with Liam. She asked Carl once if he was afraid the Fausts would pick up on the trail left by all this technology. He just gave a deep, throaty chuckle. "Nobody's gonna find you up here, darlin. I've made sure of it."

The nights were the hardest. Sleep did not come easy for Danielle; the woods were too dark and too quiet, and that gave her darkest thoughts all the space they needed to move in. She spent a lot of time just being angry: angry at Edison Faust, angry at her touch, sometimes even angry at Liam or Emily. But even more than the anger, she carried bone-crushing guilt for abandoning her children. It didn't matter that she'd been forced into making such a drastic choice in an effort to keep herself and her family safe. *No mother worth her salt ever leaves her children behind,* she would think as she watched her hair gradually turn from blonde to platinum and the lines on her face deepen with every passing year. She was missing watching her kids grow up, every single one of their milestones, and some days the emptiness was so great she didn't know how she would cope.

That was how she felt right now, sitting in this rocking chair, locked in a room inside Edison Faust's creepy house. She felt empty and desolate to her core. *I don't know how much longer I can do this,* she thought, blinking back tears.

A knock on the door startled her out of her self-pity. "Yes?" she called, her voice a bit shaky with the shot of adrenaline.

Nicholas walked in with this morning's breakfast: scrambled eggs, buttered toast, a glass of milk, and coffee.

"Good morning," Danielle offered. She wasn't sure how he would react given his abrupt departure last night, but she had to keep trying.

"Good morning," he said, unable to meet her gaze.

"How are you?" she asked cautiously.

"I'm – Dani, I'm sorry." He looked at her, and Danielle's breath caught in her throat. There was so much sadness in his eyes.

"You have nothing to be sorry for, Nicholas," she said gently.

"It was rude of me to just shut you down like that last night. You were just trying to make conversation. It's–" He took a deep breath and sat on the end of the bed. "It's just that my relationship with Raegan is hard for me to talk about."

"I understand."

"And you – you look so much like her. My heart breaks every time I walk through that door."

"Then why not send Edison or Morgan in?" she asked.

"I doubt they would bother to make you scrambled eggs," he said with a dry little smile. "I volunteer to bring your meals because seeing you makes me feel closer to Raegan. Even though it's so hard." Nicholas looked at his toes. "I wish I could tell her…just…just how fucking *sorry* I am."

"Maybe you'll get a chance," Danielle said.

Nicholas' eyes were so full of shame that tears spontaneously started to effervesce behind her own eyes. "I spent eleven years promising Raegan that I would never hurt her," he said. "And then I did. I still can't believe I did."

Danielle felt for him. She knew Raegan was suffering too, even though she and Officer Jesse seemed to have a strong connection. "Edison got into your head, didn't he?"

Nicholas nodded. "Everything my mother told me about my dad and his family was the absolute truth. 'They're bad people,' she would say. Told me they would ruin my life if I gave them half a chance. She shielded me from them pretty well growing up, but then she died and Morgan was the only family I had left. He and Edison gave me a place to live, showered me with gifts, and paid for my education. I couldn't figure out what was so bad about them." A dry laugh. "I was a stupid eighteen-year-old kid who didn't see the forest for the trees until it was too late."

Danielle thought this was only partially true. "Clearly you weren't always riding the Faust train," she said. "Raegan wouldn't have stayed with you for as long as she did if you were."

Nicholas' eyebrows went up and he nodded, considering this. "I suppose that's true. All the time we were together, there was nobody else. She was my *life*. I had to fake it with Morgan and Edison, though, because by the time Raegan and I got together I knew what could happen to me if Edison got even a whiff of disloyalty." A smile came back to his face. "Fortunately I was able to use my computer skills during that time to low-key sabotage his plans to find you or hurt your family."

Danielle grinned widely. "See? You're not a bad Faust. Not by a long shot."

"I don't think there's such a thing as a "good" Faust," Nicholas corrected her, using his fingers to make air quotes. "A couple decades of Edison yammering in my ear and the lure of Jack Hughes' gold sort of overwhelmed any good sense my mom instilled in me."

"It's still in there." Danielle knew this was the truth as soon as the words were out. "You wouldn't feel so bad about hurting Raegan if it weren't."

He stood and turned toward the door.

"Nicholas?"

He stopped and looked over his shoulder. "Yeah?"

"Who is Simone?"

He turned to fully face her. "How do you know that name?"

Her mind scrambled to think of a believable excuse. Then she remembered the tie-dyed peace sign shirt and decided to take the gamble that the gypsy woman was, in fact, Simone. "From the clothes I've been wearing since I arrived," she said. "Every time I touch them with bare hands I see her face. I saw her name once. But I don't know who she is."

"Simone was my grandfather's wife."

Danielle couldn't stop her eyes from widening. "Edison was *married?*"

Nicholas smiled. "Yeah. Twice, actually. The first time was to a woman named Elaine. She passed away in the early seventies."

Brown hair and bellbottoms, Danielle thought, remembering her sunroom visions.

"He met Simone at the Majestic Saloon in the early nineties. She ran the local headshop back then. I knew her a bit. She was always nice to me. She died in two thousand two. Cancer."

"Oh, I'm sorry," Danielle said.

"Me too," Nicholas said. "I really think Simone and Edison loved each other, in their own strange way. Edison hasn't been the same since she died. He's even more of an asshole, if that's possible." And with that he was gone.

Less than half an hour later she was piling the last bite of eggs onto the last bite of toast when she heard the front door slam and the Suburban start up. The Fausts were off on another gold-digging expedition at Grotto Park. Danielle let herself out of the room and went to the window at the front of the house. The Suburban was already well out of sight by the time she got there. She blew a kiss in the general direction of the thick brush along the driveway and hoped Liam was there to see it. Then she went into Edison's office and opened his safe.

She immediately noticed that the scarab pin was not where she had left it the day before. Curious to know why, she picked the pin up, removed a glove, and touched it. A bright and shiny vision immediately appeared, and it showed Edison Faust's tear-streaked face as he sat at his desk and turned the pin over and over in his bony fingers. Once Danielle got over her shock that the old man actually had emotions, all she had to do was make a couple simple connections to understand that the scarab pin had belonged to Jack Hughes' wife. Arlene was the pin-wearer who was wearing Jack's letter jacket and had her face smashed into the lockers by

Edison. She was the bride in the wedding that Edison had interrupted while inebriated; someone else must have been wearing the pin that day. She was the Arlene Edison had accused Jack of stealing from him, thus entitling him to Jack's gold.

Holy moly, Danielle thought as she set the pin on Edison's desk and put her glove back on. *Could it be that Edison really did love Arlene?* She just couldn't make herself believe he loved anyone but himself, and that his behavior was about anything other than possession and control. But the tears…the tears did make her wonder a little bit.

Danielle set the scarab pin and the pocket watch on a corner of Edison's desk, then reached into the safe and brought out the old red shoebox. It was time to see what these bits of paper and memorabilia were all about. She closed her eyes and pinged Raegan, thinking she'd like to see this stuff as well. Relief washed over her when Raegan opened the connection, and she wished she could see her daughter live and in person. *Soon,* she thought. *Very soon.*

She rummaged through the box's contents, catching glimpses of photographs, napkins, torn scraps of paper, envelopes, matchbooks. Finally her fingers settled on an item and lifted it from the clutter. It was a square black and white photo with a white border and scalloped edges. APR 62 was stamped on the bottom. The photo showed two men in what looked like a seedy motel room. One of the men was big and burly and covered in curly black hair, including a thick walrus mustache. He wore mirrored aviator sunglasses, a lacy bra and panties, fishnet stockings, and spiky heels. He stood with his hand on the shoulder of a much younger and hairless man, who was seated on the bed. Danielle thought she could guess what was about to happen when the photo was taken, and her stomach turned. The words "A.F. & boy toy @ Rainbow" were written in blue printed letters along the bottom, to the left of the date the photo was developed.

Danielle set this photo aside and resumed digging. She pulled out another, larger item: an old Instamatic pocket camera with a paper envelope wrapped around it and held in place with a rubber band. She carefully removed the envelope and looked closely at the camera; S RIDLEY was crudely scratched into its black plastic case. She set the camera on the couch next to her and opened the envelope; inside were about half a dozen photos, some black and white and some color. They showed young girls, ranging in age from maybe five to about twelve years old, all in various states of undress and sexually explicit poses. Danielle's stomach turned again, and for a panicky second she thought she might throw up. Another peek inside the envelope revealed a scrap of paper with "Scotty's Girls" and a series of names and ages of the subjects scrawled on it in fading blue ink. *Scotty. I wonder who that is.*

She lashed the envelope to the camera again and set it aside. Her fingers found another envelope, and inside was a typewritten memo on official-looking letterhead:

RIVER JUNCTION POLICE DEPARTMENT
FROM THE DESK OF
CHIEF PATRICK J. ERICKSON

```
To: Chief Martin Alcorn
Minneapolis Police Department
```

October 15, 1997

Chief Alcorn –
Due to conflicts that are beyond the control of
the RJPD, I regretfully inform you that we are
unable to assist the MPD with its investigation
of Edison or Morgan Faust in relation to the
shooting death of Washburn High School Resource
Officer Raymond Schuster. On behalf of the
entire RJPD, please accept my condolences for
the loss of your officer. I have no doubt he was
a fine man and a dedicated law enforcement
officer.

Regards,
Patrick Erickson

Danielle frowned, troubled by the abrupt and dismissive nature of the note. She didn't know who Raymond Schuster was or whether Edison and/or Morgan shot him, but at the very least the two law enforcement agencies should have worked together. Patrick Erickson's refusal to do so raised all sorts of red flags in Danielle's mind. It implied that RJPD was protecting Edison. *He has a network of insiders,* she thought. *Just as I suspected.*

She folded the memo and stuck it back inside its envelope, set it aside, and went back to rifling through the contents of the shoebox. She pulled out a wrinkled old white napkin from the Majestic Saloon. "Pleasure doing business with you, Wint" was scrawled across the napkin in black ink. *What's a 'Wint'?* Danielle wondered.

She glanced at the clock and began gathering up the items to put back in the shoebox. Raegan disconnected, and she hoped her daughter found this stuff useful; Danielle herself didn't see the value in most of it. Yet, anyway.

As she placed everything in the safe exactly the way she'd found it, the old pocket watch caught her attention. She really wanted to take off her glove and spend some time with it, but she worried that, given its age, she would need more time than she had.

First thing tomorrow, she promised herself.

CHAPTER 25

Instead of going straight back to her room, Danielle decided to see if she could find the key to the locked room upstairs. *I'll be able to hear them coming if I'm not stuck in a vision,* she reasoned. She looked in every drawer and cupboard she could find, except in the bedrooms. *If it's in Edison's or Morgan's room I'll never find it.* She found numerous keys in her search, but not a single one would fit the lock on the mysterious door.

Frustrated, Danielle slid the last kitchen drawer closed and ran her hands over her coarse white curls. Her gaze landed on the solarium door, and she remembered the few visions that remained in there. Now that she knew who Simone and Elaine were, she was curious to see if she might be able to glean more information about them from the room they had both clearly loved. *I have time. There aren't that many left to see.*

She opened the door, stepped inside, removed a glove, and touched the same granite wall she had before. One by one she grabbed each vision and watched them in order from most to least faded.

∞

Vision: A young girl ran into the solarium, laughing, and hid behind the giant urn planter. Judging by her knee-length shift dress and dark blonde hair that brushed her earlobes, this was Grace Ainsley at around eleven or twelve years old — fresh-faced and beautiful, not yet scarred by the lightning bolt that would change the entire Ainsley family's trajectory. Hot on her heels was a black-haired boy around the same age, clad in short pants and a white shirt. It didn't take young Benedict Faust long to find Grace's hiding spot. She jumped up and he chased her out of the room, both still laughing.

Vision: Katherine Faust, brown hair styled in sleek waves and wearing a basic knee-length belted dress, stood alone in the middle of the solarium. Both of her eyes were encircled by dark bruises. She slowly pulled a .22 caliber revolver with a mother-of-pearl grip from her dress pocket and examined it closely for a minute before walking out.

Vision: Elaine Faust, wearing a simple gray babydoll dress and her brown hair in a long ponytail, listlessly watered her plants. Her face was a mess of bruises, and she favored her left arm. A much younger Edison, his hair longer and the hems of his pants wider, stormed in. Elaine flinched as he screamed in her face. Then he grabbed her by the ponytail and dragged her out of the room through the door that led to the backyard — and the Bourbon River. Edison forced Elaine to her knees at the river's edge next to the old boathouse and held her head under the water until she stopped struggling. Then he pushed her body into the water and stalked across the backyard to the house, dripping wet from head to toe, madness swirling deep in his black eyes.

Vision: A thirty-something Morgan Faust, wearing a bloody t-shirt and jeans, sat on a weather-worn wooden chair holding a blood-soaked towel to his face. Blood from a long, deep gash down the right side of his face dripped and pooled on the clay tiles. Edison staggered in, clearly inebriated, straight razor in hand, and chased him out.

Vision: Simone Faust flitted about the solarium in a long maxi skirt and blue tunic top, watering and grooming an astonishing collection of riotous green plants. A forty-something Edison walked into the room and slipped an arm around her waist. She briefly stiffened before allowing him to dance her around the room.

∞

Danielle's stomach did backflips as she put her glove back on. There was so much to unpack and no time to do it. She left the solarium, closing the door behind her, and walked quickly back to her room. She made sure the doorknob was locked before pulling her door completely closed, then she made her way to the rocking chair and sat. Her room was fairly warm, but she pulled the blanket up around her shoulders to ward off bone-deep chills.

Edison killed his first wife. Drowned her in the river right behind the house, she thought, completely distraught. *My god, he sliced his own son's face with a razor. He's even more diabolical than I realized.* For the first time since she arrived at the Fortress, Danielle was truly afraid. She realized now she was playing a dangerous game with a card-carrying psychopath, and suddenly she wasn't so sure she could win it. *He might actually kill me.* She'd known this, but she'd been flippant about it, as if daring Edison to follow through on his threats. Now, though…now she truly *understood* it. The thought brought tears to her eyes and she shivered.

The Fausts arrived home, and Danielle's heart jumped in her chest. She could hear in their voices that they were running out of patience with searching the caves. She wasn't a God-fearing woman – no loving God would allow a family to go through as much hell as hers had – but she sent a prayer up to whoever might be listening. *Just one more day,* she thought. *Please.*

Danielle sat by the window and rocked until a knock pulled her from her near-catatonic state. Nicholas stepped into the room carrying her dinner: tomato soup from a can and a glass of milk. She glanced at him briefly as he set the tray on the table, then turned her head to gaze out the window.

"We're almost out of caves to search, Dani."

She didn't respond, just kept rocking.

"Edison told me to remind you that if we come home from Grotto Park empty-handed tomorrow, it won't be good for you."

Danielle turned her head and stared at Nicholas. He must have seen something in her eyes, because he blinked and took a step back.

"Are you all right?" he asked.

"I'm fine." She turned her face back toward the window. The gently rustling leaves on the oaks and maples outside failed to soothe her. "Tell him not to worry, he'll find the gold." Her anxious stomach twisted at the lie, but she had no choice. She was in way too deep now. She had to cling to the slim chance that she would find something tomorrow that would help make this entire nightmare end.

"Okay, well, I hope so. For your sake." He left, locking the door behind him.

Danielle just rocked, staring out the window, until darkness fell. Eventually, finally, fatigue overtook the awful memory of younger Edison's evil black eyes after he drowned his wife in the Bourbon River.

She crawled into bed and slept.

Saturday, July 24, 2021

CHAPTER 26

Danielle slept soundly and dreamlessly despite her anxieties and awoke later than usual. She stretched and sat up, and discovered her breakfast – a peanut butter and jelly sandwich, of all things, and coffee – sitting on the bedside table with a note. She expected the nearly unreadable scribble to be from Nicholas' hand, but the note was signed by Edison. A shudder wracked her spine as she read: Enjoy your breakfast, I suspect it will be your last.

Danielle's mouth went dry. *Well. That doesn't do much for the appetite, does it?* She got out of bed and went to the dresser, ignoring the food. She dug in the drawers and pulled out a clean pair of sweatpants and a faded gray t-shirt with HIPPIE CHICK emblazoned on it in a breezy, rainbow-colored font. She dressed and pulled her coarse white curls back in a ponytail, then made her way to the rocking chair. At the last minute she decided she wanted the coffee after all and went back for it. Then she sat, sipped, and waited to hear the Suburban start up, preparing to take the Fausts to their final day of spelunking at Grotto Park.

After twenty minutes Danielle's mug was empty and she'd heard no noises inside or outside the house. *Did I sleep through the ruckus of them leaving too?* she wondered. She waited ten more minutes to be sure; then, feeling bolder, she let herself out of the room and went straight to Edison's office. *No time to dilly-dally today*, she thought as she opened the safe and picked up the old pocket watch with her bare fingers. Numerous visions of varying age and intensity arose, each demanding to be seen. The first one Danielle chose would rock her world.

∞

At first Danielle thought she might be on a boat; she was gently swaying back and forth like a boat would on water. Then she realized she was actually in a car as it rolled down a moderately crowded city street. Central Avenue, in fact, on the far northeast side of Minneapolis. Edison had hung his grandfather's pocket watch from the rearview mirror of his 1970 Chrysler 300 like an ornament on a Christmas tree. The car's hood was cream-colored and massive, the interior upholstered in a caramel brown vinyl. Edison himself, somewhere in his mid- to late-thirties, wore a t-shirt, jeans, and smoky plastic-framed sunglasses as he cruised south toward downtown. Wind blowing in through the open window mussed his thinning black hair. She couldn't see his eyes, but the set of his jaw told her he was looking for something.

Something or someone caught his eye as he passed through the intersection with Fifth Street. He pulled over and stopped at the curb. He lit a cigarette and just sat there, watching a woman with a curly brown ponytail walk purposefully across Central and turn south, following the sidewalk toward the Mississippi River. She wore a white t-shirt and blue shorts with white trim, white sneakers on her feet. Danielle knew immediately who the woman was; her heart twisted in her chest and for a moment she lost all ability to breathe.

Aunt Pearl.

From the back she was nearly indistinguishable from her older sister Emily. They both had the same stick-straight posture and determined gait, although Pearl was an inch or two taller than Emily. Danielle knew that Emily was supposed to be walking with Pearl on this beautiful September day in 1978. But teenaged Danielle was on the tail end of a nasty case of mononucleosis, and Emily decided to stay home with her. It was a decision that Emily would regret for the rest of her life.

When Pearl was about a block away, Edison pulled away from the curb and followed her, then stopped along the curb again and continued to watch. Danielle's heart pounded in her throat.

Pearl continued her walk along the busy city street, past banks and bars and parking lots, unaware that she was being followed. Edison kept his distance for two more blocks, until Pearl passed the Coca-Cola bottling plant and stopped to wait on the light at the intersection of Second Street. Central Avenue was closed ahead as crews began work on a two-year rehabilitation of the Third Avenue Bridge that connected the northeast side of Minneapolis to downtown.

Edison pulled up next to her as she waited for her signal to cross Second and then head east to make her way to the riverfront, then he leaned over the passenger seat and shouted something through the open passenger window.

Pearl bent over to get a better look at the driver, and she immediately recognized him. Eyes wide, she backed away and took off running. She slipped through a gap between the temporary fences blocking access to the closed bridge and sprinted down the middle of the bridge deck. It was still intact, but construction crews had already removed the barriers that protected the sidewalks.

Oh, no, Pearl, Danielle thought sadly. You should have turned around and run back the way you came. You would probably be alive today if you had.

Edison yanked his sunglasses off and tossed them on the passenger seat. That deep, swirling madness had returned to his black eyes, and his teeth were clenched so tight his jaw muscles bulged. He stomped on the gas. The Chrysler blasted through the temporary fence and two ROAD CLOSED signs and barreled toward Pearl's receding back.

Pearl was a fairly fast runner, but she was no match for the 375 horses under the Chrysler's hood. The distance between them closed quickly. The bridge curved northward about a hundred yards out, and by that point Edison had almost caught up to Pearl. Rather than following the curve, Pearl desperately ran straight ahead toward an overlook on the other side of the bridge deck, where regular pedestrians could stop and enjoy a commanding view of the Mississippi River and downtown Minneapolis. She caught herself on the ornamental iron railing and risked a look behind her.

Danielle could see perfectly clearly in Pearl's eyes that she knew she'd made a fatal mistake. She had only two choices now: jump off the bridge and hope for the best, or allow Edison to crush her with his enormous car. She made the choice that had a slightly better chance of survival. She scrambled over the iron railing and was gone.

No! Danielle cried.

Edison slammed the brakes and the Chrysler lurched to a stop just inches from the railing where Pearl had been standing only second before. He got out of the car and looked over the railing for a few seconds, then trudged back.

The satisfaction in his eyes was more than Danielle could bear.

∞

The pocket watch landed on the floor with a clatter, and Danielle realized her cheeks were wet. *Oh god, I had no idea.*

She remembered the days after her aunt's body was found near the Franklin Avenue Bridge, two days after she'd gone missing. Emily had a pretty good idea of where Pearl had been and where she was going; she was supposed to walk with her sister that day and knew the route she would take. She had tried desperately to convince the MPD to broaden their search for witnesses three miles further upriver, closer to the Third Avenue Bridge. Her pleas fell on deaf ears. And then the detective called with the news that the coroner had declared Pearl's death a suicide and there would be no further investigation. Emily was inconsolable.

"Mom, let me go there and use my touch to see what happened," Danielle, seventeen years old at the time, had begged. "The police will have to do something once they know the truth!"

Emily had shaken her head. "Not based on our visions alone." Her voice cracked with the effort of controlling her emotions. "They'll refer us to the nearest looneybin. We know in our hearts what happened, and that's good enough." Her tears would not be controlled and cascaded down her face. "We'll get that bastard. Someday."

"But—"

"Dani, promise me you'll stay away from that bridge."

"But, Mom —"

"Danielle." Emily's tone could have shaved granite.

Danielle had caved with a huff. "All right. I promise."

It was a promise she'd faithfully kept, although at first the curiosity was almost more than she could handle. She never understood why Emily wouldn't want to know exactly how her sister died, and whether or not Edison Faust was involved. *Grief does strange things to people.*

She stared at the pocket watch lying on the floor, unsure if she wanted to see any more of the visions it held. Sunlight streamed through the office window and glinted off the surface of the silver watch, as if beckoning her. *Come on,* it seemed to say. Just one more try. *Whatever else you see can't be as bad as that, right?*

Yeah, right, Danielle thought. Her skin crawled with near-constant gooseflesh. She bent and reached for the watch.

∞

Gnarled oak and graceful ash trees towered over sun-drenched gravestones as far as the eye could see. In the distance a handful of people dressed in black huddled around a simple casket that had been suspended over a rectangular hole in the ground. This was Aunt Pearl's graveside funeral service at Lakewood Cemetery in Minneapolis. Danielle recognized her own pale and somber face first. She stood next to her mother, who stood stick-straight in a black belted shirtdress and heels and dabbed her eyes with a tissue. Pearl's husband Tom Christensen stood on the other side of Emily in a black suit and tie. He didn't bother with a tissue, just periodically wiped his face with his hands. His back and shoulders, already hunched from a long career as a plumber, bowed under the weight of his absolute grief. A few other people stood behind them; Pearl's friends and coworkers, perhaps. A minister in a flowing black robe finished his remarks, then closed his Bible and led the group in a prayer.

That done, attendees began milling amongst each other, offering hugs and comfort. Danielle watched herself step away from the group, sadness and discomfort obvious on her face. She wandered down the paved path, away from her family, lost in thought.

She started moving toward herself, and quickly. Older Danielle realized that the pocket watch was hanging around Edison's neck like a cheap piece of costume jewelry. It took only a few seconds to catch up, and there was her younger self, right in front of her, lost in thought and not paying attention.

A pair of arms reached out and grabbed younger Danielle in a bear hug. After a second of stunned confusion, the girl began to thrash and scream as the arms lifted her off her feet and turned, intending to run back. Edison Faust's cream-colored Chrysler 300 stood idling on a nearby path, its rear passenger door open.

Younger Danielle, despite being weakened from two bedridden weeks battling mono, fought ferociously. Edison tried to hang on, but it soon became apparent that he could not control the flailing girl. Younger Danielle's fingers hooked into the watch's chain and pulled hard. It snapped, and suddenly the watch was in her clenched fist.

Stunned, Edison let go of her and she took off running back toward her family. Older Danielle's stomach did a motion sickness flip as younger Danielle's arms pumped. Wide-eyed family members stood ready to catch her.

Instead younger Danielle stopped just short of her panicked mother and turned to face Edison, who was running after her full bore. Surprised, he skidded to a halt and stared at her, chest heaving and eyes full of rage. He shouted something. Then he frowned, confused, and shouted something else.

Motion sickness gripped older Danielle again as the watch sailed through the air toward Edison. It landed and bounced, then Edison picked it up and slipped it into the pocket of his faded Wranglers.

∞

Danielle remembered this encounter like it had happened yesterday. When she'd yanked the watch from around Edison's neck with her bare hand, she'd seen a brief vision of a gun pointed at a middle-aged man with black sideburns. The man stood in front of a door with the word BANK, among others, etched into the glass. He wore a baby blue leisure suit and his basset hound eyes were scared but determined.

This vision wasn't like others Danielle had had before. It was bright and very brief, and with it came an absolute certainty: Edison Faust was robbing a bank, and the man in blue, the bank manager, was going to die at his hand. There was no question about it. And that's what Danielle told Edison before she threw his watch at him: *If you don't change your ways, the bank manager will die. And it will be your fault.*

Danielle and her family didn't live in River Junction, so she never saw the news a month later about the robbery of the First State Bank of River Junction and the subsequent death of Frank Barnale. What she did experience was a steady increase in Faust encounters over the following decade, which finally culminated in her decision to go into hiding.

Danielle sighed. *I've seen enough.* She placed the watch back where she'd found it in the safe, then shut the door and swung the Stefan Faust portrait closed. *That's it. I'm done in here.*

Danielle left Edison's office, her gut roiling and her thoughts all in a jumble. She headed for the solarium, where generations of Faust women had gone to soothe their souls and find peace. Maybe she could find some there too.

Late July heat buffeted her when she stepped through the door, helping to calm the gooseflesh and the turmoil in her gut. *Mom was right the entire time,* she thought. *Edison had everything to do with Pearl's death. She just couldn't prove it.* This was followed in short order by *I wonder how Tom is doing. I should stop in and say hi now that I'm home.*

Assuming, of course, that she got out of the Fortress alive.

She moved absentmindedly around the room, running her gloved fingers gently over planters and gardening tools and a rusty watering can on a rickety old wooden chair. When she reached the enormous urn planter, she stared at it thoughtfully for a few moments. *Grace Ainsley hid behind this planter as a child, so it's been here a really long time,* she thought. *Do I dare touch it?*

She hesitated, remembering the vision of Edison dragging his first wife out of this very room by her ponytail and prematurely ending her life in the river. The thought of it made her stomach turn. What if there were other traumatic visions out here? She wasn't sure she could stand it. But. She also couldn't shake the feeling that she was missing something. That the one magic *thing* she needed to take the Fausts down for good was within her reach.

Danielle took a deep breath, then removed her glove and laid her fingers on the concrete surface of the planter. She chose the most recent vision she could find.

∞

Edison, the same Edison who had locked the upstairs door tight and walked away with the key, had a trowel in hand and was digging in the dirt underneath Simone's massive rosebush. His cheeks were wet with tears, and bits of potting soil stuck to his face as he dug. He placed something in the hole and covered it with dirt. Then he turned, tossed the trowel in a corner, and left.

∞

Danielle slid the glove back on her hand and looked around the room for the trowel. There it was, still lying in the corner where Edison had tossed it all those years ago, rusty and covered in spiderwebs. She picked it up, brushed it off, and went back to the planter. Then she started digging in roughly the same spot Edison had been.

It didn't take her long to find what he'd buried. It was a key.

And it looked to be just the one she needed to finally open the mysterious locked door.

CHAPTER 27

Danielle rushed back through the house and ran up the second staircase. The key fit perfectly into the lock, and with a twist the heavy wooden door was open. She stepped through the door and into a veritable time capsule.

This was the Fortress' turret room: high-ceilinged and round, with floor-to-ceiling windows covered with thick drapes. Danielle could see well enough to understand that this had been Simone's room: the brightly patterned canopy on the four-poster bed, the multicolored scarves that served as window valances, the patchwork quilt, and floral rugs scattered across the wood floor gave it her trademark bohemian style.

She pinged Raegan. *She'll want to see this*, Danielle thought. Raegan immediately opened the connection.

It was clear that nobody had been inside this room in a very long time. It smelled like dry paper, and a layer of dust – along with an occasional dead fly – had settled on every surface. Danielle removed a glove and touched a bedpost; visions in this long-neglected room were as scarce as they had been in the solarium. She decided to grab the three brightest visions.

∞

Vision: Simone, wearing a pair of sweatpants and the same Hippie Chick t-shirt Danielle currently wore, her long black hair tied up in a bun, entered the room struggling with something covered with a white sheet. It seemed to be quite heavy. Simone tried to set it on the bed and nearly collapsed with it. She didn't look well; she was pale and gaunt, her eyes sunken and ringed with dark circles. She took a deep breath to gather herself, and tried picking the object up again. She was too weak; she managed to take one or two steps before the object fell from her arms and landed on the floor next to the bed, just barely missing her toes. She muttered something and dropped to her knees, having decided to just push the object under the bed.

Vision: Simone, clearly very ill, lay in her bed, propped up with colorful pillows. Sunlight streamed through the windows. Pill bottles, tissues, and various sundries covered both bedside tables. She was writing in a leather-covered book, possibly a diary. She hid the book under the covers when Edison entered the room carrying a steaming bowl of soup on the same black floral tray Nicholas would use to deliver meals to captive Danielle two decades later.

Vision: The bed is empty. The curtains are drawn. And fifty-something Edison, pure anguish deepening the lines on his hawkish face, leaves the room, closing the door firmly behind him.

∞

Danielle stood next to the bed, momentarily paralyzed with indecision. The visions had given her two things to look for, and she could not for the life of her decide where to start. *Do I look under the bed? Or do I look in drawers for that diary?*

She started with looking for the diary. She found it in the first drawer of the nightstand farthest from the door. She was tempted to look at it, but decided to wait until later, when she had more time. *Maybe I'll try connecting with both Mom and Raegan and we can all read it together,* she thought. She stuck the book in the waistband of her pants at the small of her back and pulled her t-shirt over it.

She rummaged through the rest of the drawers in case they contained anything interesting. Seeing nothing, she dropped to her knees and checked under the bed: the sheet-covered object that Simone had struggled with so mightily was still there. She couldn't believe her luck.

She reached under the bed with both hands to pull it a little way out. Then she pushed herself back to her knees and removed the sheet, exposing a very old wooden beam. It was pitted and cracked and covered with a dark dried substance. She instinctively reached out and almost touched it – but stopped herself just in time. *That's Jack Hughes' blood,* she thought, her heart galloping in her chest. *This is the wooden beam from Ainsley Mill.*

She was so absorbed in her discovery that she didn't hear the heavy footsteps tromping up the stairs.

"What the *fuck* are you doing?" Edison snarled, his voice tight and raspy. Danielle abruptly stood, heart in her throat, to find him and Morgan and Nicholas all standing in the turret room's doorway with varying degrees of shock and anger on their faces. They were sweaty and dirty from today's cave excursion. Nicholas' expression looked a bit more like fear. Fear for her life.

Danielle immediately disconnected from Raegan. "I–"

"Grab her," Edison instructed Morgan. "Bring her to my office."

"Let's just –" Nicholas began.

"You?" Edison whirled to face his grandson. "You just *shut up.* This bitch has been sending us on a wild goose chase for *days* so she can snoop around my house. Now I think I know why you always had to be the one to bring her food." He turned to make his way back down the stairs. "All of you in my office. *Now.*"

Nicholas threw Danielle a regretful look and reluctantly followed his grandfather. "I told you to use a deadbolt on her door, didn't I?"

"SHUT. UP." Edison's voice cracked as they receded.

Morgan came around the bed toward her, his scarred and grizzled face unreadable. Danielle held up her hands and took a couple steps back. "I'll come with you, you don't need —"

He grabbed her upper arm and roughly dragged her out of the room, down the stairs, and into Edison's office. It was all she could do to stay on her feet. Once inside the office, he forced her to sit in a metal folding chair that had been set up between Edison's desk and the picture window. Then he sat next to Nicholas on the couch and they all waited. The room reeked of cigar smoke.

Raegan pinged her; she ignored the blue colors until they stopped.

Edison was in his desk chair, burning cigar jutting from between his yellow teeth and rummaging through desk drawers. She marveled at how old he was now compared to her visions. *This man has not aged gracefully,* she thought. *I suppose that will happen when you choose to live a life of evil. It takes more out of you than choosing to be good.* And that's what he looked like: depleted. Run down. At the end of his useful life.

She glanced toward the couch. Morgan, whose sixtieth birthday was only a couple years away, was following right in Edison's footsteps — aging too fast, not taking care of himself, destined to be a patsy for the rest of his miserable life. *That poor guy never had a chance,* she thought.

Nicholas, though. At thirty-nine years old Nicholas had a brightness and vitality that neither of his elders ever had, even in their youth. The brightness came from a light his mother had instilled in him – and his father and grandfather were trying hard to extinguish. *Don't let them win, Nicholas,* she thought. *Don't do it. You have a bright and shiny future ahead of you – even if it's a future without Raegan. You'll learn to carry on without her. You'll be okay, I just know it.*

"Aha!" Edison exclaimed triumphantly. "Found it." He slammed the drawers closed and turned in his chair to face Danielle. Her heart dropped when she saw what he held in his hand: a silver revolver with a wood grip. And it was loaded; she could see the tips of the bullets in the chamber. Danielle, Morgan and Nicholas all sat at attention, ready to scramble if Edison decided to do more than make idle threats.

Edison's black eyes had a nasty gleam in them as he inspected Danielle's face. "You think you're so smart," he said. "All you Ainsleys think you're so smart. Well, I've got news for you. No Ainsley plays me for a fool."

Raegan tried to ping Danielle again, and again she ignored it.

"You know what happens when you play me for a fool?" Edison rambled. He held the gun against one leg, gnarled finger precariously close to the trigger. "Unfortunate things happen, that's what."

What on earth is he talking about? Danielle wondered.

"I will have the gold." Edison's voice went surprisingly calm, a real contrast to the turmoil in his eyes. "I know you know where it is."

"I keep telling you," Danielle said, keeping her voice steady despite her pounding heart. "It's in the caves. If you can't find it there, I –"

"I said SHUT UP," he snarled, then cocked the hammer and pointed the gun directly at Danielle's face. Her heart jackrabbited in her chest, and she couldn't stop staring into the gun's sinister black eye. "I'm done listening to your whore's mouth."

Then Nicholas did something so brave it qualified as stupid: he jumped up from the couch and snatched the gun from his grandfather's hand. Then he opened the chamber and let the bullets fall to the floor.

"You ungrateful fucking brat!" Edison screeched. But that was all he did. His brittle old body had spent the last four days climbing rocks and exploring caves, far more activity than it was used to, and it was done. He collapsed in his chair and closed his eyes. The wrinkles in his face smoothed a bit as his jaw went slack. Morgan didn't move at all; he'd abandoned all pretense of caring.

Nicholas tucked the gun into the waistband of his dirty jeans and held his hand out to Danielle. "Come on, I'll take you back to your room."

Danielle gratefully took his hand and allowed him to pull her up to standing. Simone's diary shifted a bit against her lower back, but not much. Her sweat helped keep it in place.

Nicholas didn't say anything during the short walk to Danielle's room and locked her door behind him without a word. Danielle pulled Simone's diary from her waistband and tossed it on the bed, then fell into the rocker, wrapped the blanket around herself, and trembled uncontrollably for several minutes. She couldn't stop seeing the tip of the bullet deep in the barrel of the gun, just waiting for the hammer to launch it and rip her life from her. It was the closest she'd ever come to dying.

Finally the tremors subsided. She showered in an effort to wash herself clean of the fear and Edison's ickiness. After dressing in a well-worn and surprisingly comfy tracksuit that had probably belonged to Simone, she spied the diary on her bed. She took the diary back to her rocker, got comfy, and closed her eyes. *I hope this works,* she thought. *I'm sure they're worried sick.* She concentrated on her mother and her daughter, and she was surprised by how much mental energy she needed to send psychic signals to both of them at the same time. But she kept at it, and it wasn't long until they both connected. She opened her eyes and looked at the leather cover of Simone's book; she noticed for the first time that the word DIARY had been stamped into it.

I got them. They're okay. They know I'm okay. Danielle blinked back tears and opened the book. There was an inscription written on the inside front cover in blue ink: *I, Simone Rich Faust, am of sound mind as I write in this journal. My body? Not so sound.*

Danielle remembered her final vision of Simone and knew this was true. Nicholas had mentioned she'd had cancer, and it had ravaged her once vibrant body. She turned to the first page and began to read.

January 4, 2002

The doctors say there's nothing more they can do for me now. They referred me to hospice care two weeks ago. I guess that means I don't have much time left.

My biggest regret? Well, I suppose it's that I won't be able to do what I should have done a long time ago. So I'm writing it all down here in hopes that someone will find it and help set the Universe right.

First, I want to make it clear that I love my husband. Edison has loved me without condition for nearly eleven years. I'm very sorry to leave him.

But Edison has done some terrible things, things that weigh heavy on my conscience. I've kept his secrets, possibly to my own detriment. Would I be lying here, dying of pancreatic cancer, if I'd simply acknowledged the truth and turned him in for what he's done?

It's impossible to know. But I'm going to use what little time I have left to help the Universe make things right.

So tired now. Must rest.

January 5, 2002

Someone asked me once what I'm most proud of. I've been thinking about that a lot as I lie here waiting patiently for the cancer to take me. If I had to choose one thing, it would be my store. Hippie Chick, River Junction's first "spiritual healing center" and headshop, has been a source of irritation for River Junction's conservative establishment since the day I opened the doors. That's a fact I'm terribly proud of.

A hippie like me had no business in River Junction when I landed here in mid-1989, after my divorce from Stuart was finalized. I took my half from that fat bastard, threw a dart at a map, and got the hell out of Chicago. River Junction seemed like a nice place, close to the Twin Cities but not too close, perfect for a newly-single woman to take another shot at life on her terms.

It turns out that divorcing a multimillionaire is a winning proposition. My settlement with Stuart was so substantial that I didn't need to work ever again if I didn't want to. But I needed something to keep me busy – and Hippie Chick opened in downtown River Junction in January 1990. Every town needs a good headshop. My store was the only one in thirty miles that sold marijuana paraphernalia. I also offered crystals, incense and essential oils, bohemian clothing, and jewelry.

The kids loved me. Their parents, not so much.

When I wasn't working, I was bored and lonely. So I started spending much of my free time at the Majestic Saloon. That shithole bar became my entire social life. I spent nearly all of my free time there, drinking, smoking, playing bingo, pulling tabs, and bullshitting with friends. We could smoke inside back then.

That's where I met Edison Faust in May 1990. He started pursuing me on day 1, but I was not interested. He – really, his whole family – had a terrible reputation in town. I was lonely, but I wasn't that lonely.

When Edison realized his slimy pickup lines and outlandish lies – a CIA agent? Really? Give me a break – weren't working on me, he finally dropped the act. And I grew to sort of like this brash, sarcastic, brutally honest, hard-drinking man. We had a lot in common. And being with him made me feel less lonely.

He had anger issues, still does, and he kept making the mistake of trying to isolate and control me. That might have worked on a weaker woman, but I did not – and still don't – have time for that kind of bullshit. If he hit me, I hit back twice as hard.

I got tired of the games and kicked his ass straight to the curb. He came crawling back within days. We had to do that dance several times before Edison finally learned his lesson: if you want to be with me, you will behave. Eventually we came to an understanding. Sometimes he still hits when he's pissed off, and I still hit back.

We were married on Valentine's Day 1991, and for the most part life with him has been pretty good. We've built a mutual respect and he loves me in his own way. That's good enough for me.

I'm certainly not lonely anymore.

January 6, 2002

Edison tells me all the time that I am nothing like his first wife Elaine. I don't take his shit and I will not be controlled. He says he likes the challenge. He also hasn't been shy about his love for my money.

But he lives in a constant state of resentment and anger, and I fear my strength may have pushed him to take that anger out on others.

Laura, for example. She raised her boy Nicholas away from the shadow of the Fausts, and she raised him well. Nicholas is a fine boy. But Edison wants him in his fold and under his thumb. So, nearly two years ago now, he had Morgan kill Laura to finally get her out of the way. They did it sneaky too. They used the sux. Laura had type 1 diabetes and Edison knew nobody would think twice about a needle mark. He also knew heart problems are common in people with diabetes so everyone would assume she had a heart attack. Even if he hadn't had Wint Steele in his pocket, this was damn near the perfect murder.

I still feel awful about it. Laura was just doing her job and protecting her boy – and she paid the price.

I worry about Nicholas now.

January 7, 2002

My belly feels like it's on fire all the time now. The only thing that helps is the morphine the hospice nurse gives me. I write while the pain is less, and then I sleep. I sleep a lot now. My body is so damn tired.

But I'm not done yet. There's one other awful thing Edison did that I cannot abide. He killed an old high school classmate. Why? Because Jack Hughes supposedly had a stash of gold and Edison wanted it. He was – still is – obsessed with it. Which I don't really understand. Thanks to my divorce settlement, we have more than enough money.

Well...maybe I do understand: Jack Hughes stole Edison's girl back in high school. And Edison doesn't forgive a transgression like that. Not ever.

I don't believe Edison showed up at Jack's house that day planning to kill him. I think he only meant to scare him into giving up where he was hiding that damn gold. But I'll tell you what: thirty-seven years is a long time to carry that kind of anger. At some point it's going to boil over. I think Edison lost control. Instead of making Jack bleed a little bit, he didn't stop hitting him until he was good and dead. Morgan told me Jack's head didn't even look like a head by the time Edison was done.

I found the piece of wood they used to kill Jack in the basement. It still has his blood all over it. One of the last things I did while I could still walk was drag that beam upstairs. I hid it under my bed. You'll find it there if you look. (Edison knows better than to mess with anything in my room, even after I'm gone.)

You know what I find most appalling about this whole thing, besides what happened to poor Jack? After Edison beat Jack to death, he stole Arlene's heirloom scarab pin. It's a beautiful piece, looks like multicolored beetles standing tip-to-toe in a perfect circle. Something like that would fetch a pretty penny in my store. But it belongs to Arlene's family. Instead it's locked inside Edison's safe — the one thing in this entire house I cannot access.

January 9, 2002

Dear Universe, I hope you will do what I couldn't muster up the courage or the strength to do myself. I hope you will hold Edison accountable for these terrible things he's done.

Tears streaming down her face, Danielle closed the book and laid it on her lap. She disconnected from Raegan and Emily and leaned her head against the back of her chair. A sob loaded with emotion and exhaustion escaped her. *She knew.*

She knew exactly who Edison was.

CHAPTER 28

Danielle rocked in her chair and stared out the window at the darkening sky for a long time. Shades of blue started pulsing behind her eyes, and for the briefest moment she considered not responding. She was so *tired*. But she didn't want to worry her family any more, so she closed her eyes and opened the connection.

Raegan was holding a note in front of her face: GOLD IS IN OLD WATERWHEEL ROOM UNDER AINSLEY MILL. WE WILL BE THERE 10:30AM TOMORROW READY TO ARREST ALL 3 FAUSTS. CAN YOU HELP GET THEM THERE?

Danielle sat up straight despite her bone-deep fatigue. *Holy moly,* she thought. *They actually found it. This is really going to happen.* Her heart fluttered in her chest.

As soon as Raegan disconnected Danielle realized there was one vital piece of information Officer Jesse and the River Junction Police Department would need. She stood and looked helplessly around the room for a writing instrument. Frustrated, she ran her hands through her hair and blew air out between her lips. Then inspiration struck: Nicholas had left a ballpoint pen in her room the other day.

She retrieved it from the bedside table, tore a blank piece of paper from the back of Simone's diary, and wrote her own note: SAFE COMBINATION IS 98-47-13-62 She thought for a moment, then added one very important detail: TURN WHEEL 4 TIMES BEFORE COMBO

She pinged Raegan back and gave her enough time to read the note. Then she tore the paper into tiny pieces and flushed it down the toilet before hiding Simone's diary in the bedside table drawer.

Danielle had just gotten situated in the rocking chair again when Nicholas arrived with her dinner: another peanut butter and jelly sandwich and a glass of milk. She watched him set the tray on the table, then said, "Thank you."

He looked at her. "For what?"

"For saving my life." Tears effervesced behind her eyes again.

Nicholas sat on the end of the bed and leaned his elbows on his knees. "You're welcome."

"I would ask if Edison is okay, but it turns out I don't care," she said with a yawn.

Nicholas chuckled. "He ranted some more about how pissed he is that you got out of your room, and then he passed out. He's in bed now." He eyed her warily. "What were you doing out of your room anyway?"

"Boredom," Danielle said with a shrug. "And curiosity. I always wondered what the inside of this house looked like." A complete lie, but it served.

He gestured at her gloved hands. "Did you see anything...interesting?"

"Not really." Danielle yawned again. "That solarium off the kitchen is really neat."

"That was Simone's favorite room in the whole house," Nicholas said. "Edison never goes out there since she died."

"That's obvious." That was enough small talk. "Listen, I have something to tell you."

He sat up, concern clouding his eyes. "Is Raegan okay?"

Danielle held up a hand. "Raegan is fine. They found the gold."

Nicholas lifted his chin, unsure if he'd heard her correctly. "What do you mean?"

"Jack Hughes' gold. It's real, and Raegan knows where it is."

Understanding dawned on Nicholas' face. "Oh, my god. Where is it?"

"It's hidden at the old Ainsley Mill."

Nicholas frowned. "They tore the old Ainsley Mill down years and years ago. There's a big General Mills facility there now."

"Apparently a waterwheel room from the old mill still exists, and that's where Jack hid his gold."

Nicholas didn't say anything for a long time.

"You have a choice to make. You know that, don't you?" Danielle asked gently.

Nicholas, head bowed, nodded. A tear fell off the end of his nose and landed on the floor.

"This is your chance to do right by Raegan. Show her how sorry you are for hurting her."

He swallowed hard.

"You have the power to give her something she's never had. A normal life."

He covered his face with his hands and cried.

Danielle felt for Nicholas, but she was reasonably confident that his love for Raegan was much stronger than his loyalty to his family. She wasn't so sure he'd be willing to give up his chance at some of the gold, however. Or end up in jail as an accomplice to some of Edison's crimes.

He wiped his face with his black t-shirt, then took a deep breath. "All right. What's the plan?"

"All you have to do is convince Edison that I told you where the gold really is."

"I'm not sure he'd believe it," Nicholas said. "Not after you sent us to Grotto Park for four days of fruitless cave searching."

Danielle chuckled. "Come on. Is anyone really surprised I would do that? He forcibly takes me from my family and holds me hostage in his house, and he thinks I'm going to willingly help him?"

Nicholas nodded as he considered this. "Good point. Okay. Yeah, I can spin this. Lean hard on the fact that he wants this gold more than he's ever wanted anything in his life. The fact that it's at the old Ainsley Mill helps; Jack worked there for a long time. It makes sense that he would hide his gold there."

"Raegan says they'll be there around ten-thirty tomorrow morning."

Nicholas stood. "Then you should make sure you're ready for a field trip. I'll let you know the final plan when I bring your breakfast."

"I'll be ready," she said.

Nicholas made his way toward the door.

"Nicholas?"

He turned back. "Yeah?"

"You understand that you will probably be arrested, don't you?"

He nodded, eyes brimming with sadness. "I'll deserve everything I get. The people he's hurt over the years didn't deserve what they got. It's time to end this." He sighed. "I just wish I'd had the courage to do something sooner."

Simone had said something very similar in her diary. *Just two more bugs stuck in Edison's massive web,* Danielle thought. *Two of many. Of course they couldn't go against him. He made sure of it. Like a cult leader would.*

Nicholas left, locking the door behind him. Danielle changed out of Simone's tracksuit, brushed her teeth, and crawled into bed. Her last thought before unconsciousness took her: *Don't worry, Simone.*

We're going to get him.

PART 3:
RAEGAN
(THE AINSLEYS & THE FAUSTS)

Sunday, July 25, 2021

CHAPTER 29

"God, why am I so nervous?" I asked as I paced around and around Hendricks' kitchen. I couldn't sit still.

Hendricks watched me passively from behind the kitchen counter, wearing a black RJPD polo shirt, khaki-colored denim pants, black belt, and his gun in its belt holster. He sipped coffee from an RJPD mug. "Because your entire life is about to change."

I stopped. "Do you think so? Are we really going to get him?"

He nodded and held up a yellow envelope. "Goddamn straight. Captain Bailey has been working with Minneapolis on your mom's kidnapping. These are their arrest warrants, we're just going to execute them." He sipped his coffee again. "Rather unconventionally, I might add."

"Makes sense. Okay." I resumed pacing and shook my gloved hands at my sides as if they were wet. "Okay, okay."

"Hey." Hendricks reached across the countertop as I passed by and grabbed my arm. "Stop."

"I literally can't," I said plaintively, bouncing on the balls of my feet.

He let go and poured fresh coffee into another RJPD mug. He handed it to me and said, "Here. Take this. Sit down. We'll go through the plan again."

The plan. Yes. That sounded like a great idea. More caffeine, not so much. I did as he asked and sat at the kitchen table. The warm mug in my hands and the bitter aroma of Beananza dark roast helped soothe my frazzled nerves, although I found myself wishing the mug contained wine instead of coffee. I pushed the thought away.

Hendricks took the chair next to me. "Better?"

"A little," I admitted and ventured a sip. Beananza perfection.

"All right. It is nine-thirty right now. In ten minutes we're going to go next door and fetch your family, then drive over to the mill."

I nodded. "Check."

"Our friend Teddy Campbell has secured all necessary permissions from General Mills management for access to the turbine room. He will meet us there and guide us down to the pit."

"Got it."

"Captain Rooney will have a team stationed discreetly at key places around the mill: at all external doors, at the elevator that runs down to the old pit, and at the headrace and tailrace where they join with the Bourbon River. Those tunnels were closed back in sixty-nine, but they can be accessed if someone tries hard enough."

I nodded, loving the idea of having a police guard. A whole team of them.

"Carter's team will be our eyes, and they'll radio me when they see the Fausts coming. I have an earpiece so the Fausts can't hear anything, and they'll stay out of sight so Edison doesn't know they're there. He will very likely be armed and may start shooting if he sees cops."

"Makes sense," I said. "The first person to get a bullet would probably be my mother."

Hendricks nodded. "I think so too. Carter and his team will stay in position, and they will wait for my signal to enter."

"And of course you'll be armed, too."

He smiled, and my heart melted a little. "Naturally. You think I'm going to let the Fausts hurt my girl and her family? Not on my watch."

I set my cup down and leaned over to rest my head against his muscular upper arm. I had to work to hold back exhausted tears.

"When I give the signal, RJPD will enter and Carter will take the Fausts into custody under these arrest warrants." He held the envelope up again. "Boom. Done."

"You make it sound so easy," I sighed.

He kissed the top of my head. "Come on. It's go time."
****

The General Mills facility that replaced the old Ainsley Mill was cutting-edge and modern when it opened in 1969. After fifty years of producing a million pounds of wheat flour every day, the plant was starting to show its age. The white paint on the enormous silos was chipping, the concrete walls of the buildings were stained black, and a few broken windows had been covered with plywood. But the place was abuzz with activity, and the Bourbon River sparkled behind it all.

As we got out of our cars, Teddy Campbell emerged from what looked to me like a lean-to storage shed with a garage door connected to the main building. Hendricks stepped forward and shook his hand. "Good to see you, Teddy. Thanks again for your help."

"Are you kidding? Anything for Jack." He gave me a brief wave, which I returned with a smile.

Hendricks handled introductions, and Teddy brushed off the fervent thank-yous from my family. Although he did allow Mimi to give him a quick hug. "Come on, come on, let's go in." he said. His demeanor was gruff, but I thought deep down he was tickled pink to be a part of finding Jack's gold.

The lean-to shed seemed to be the main entrance for the mill. The floor was concrete and a single fluorescent light fixture hung from the ceiling. A computer monitor sat on a dusty desk, surrounded by piles of paperwork. An assortment of white hardhats with the distinctive General Mills blue G logo on them and bright yellow reflective vests hung from hooks on one wall. A handwritten sign above the hooks reminded people to PLEASE RETURN HARDHATS AND VESTS BEFORE YOU LEAVE. A heavy-looking and securely locked steel door led to the innards of the mill, and on the wall next to it was a very modern badge scanner.

"Go ahead and grab a hardhat and a vest," Teddy advised. He had his own, both of which were blaze orange and had been personalized with his name. Then he handed out ID badges on clips. "Make sure these are visible at all times."

That done, he led us to the door and scanned his badge to open it. It unlocked with a clunk and we all piled through, finding ourselves in a hot and humid steel-lined hallway. The constant hum of machinery forced Teddy to shout. "When this facility was built, the bigwigs almost didn't include a way to get into the old turbine pit. They were gonna just seal it up and forget about it. It was Jack who asked the bosses what they would do if the river ever flooded and the turbine pit collapsed. Probably the whole north side of the mill would go down with it." Teddy chuckled. "So the bosses not only installed an elevator, but they had the pit reinforced with steel beams."

As much as I appreciated Jack Hughes' heroics and history of the mill, I was anxious to get down to the waterwheel. "Which way to the elevator?" I shouted.

Teddy gestured. "This way."

We followed him down the hallway and around a couple of corners to a solitary elevator. Sergeant Carter Rooney stood there wearing a black RJPD hat and tactical gear, looking at his phone. His sidearm hung conspicuously from his belt. Hendricks initiated another round of introductions, and Rooney, a tall, fit man in his mid-forties with close-cropped salt-and-pepper hair and goatee, shook everyone's hands. "Are you guys ready?" he asked, his deep voice bouncing off the blue painted steel walls.

"Ready as we're gonna be, boss," Kieran shouted. Red streaks glowed on his pale cheekbones.

Rooney glanced at the bulky military-style watch on his wrist and nodded. "All right, let's get you down there." He pressed the button, and the doors slid open within seconds.

Teddy led the way and we all stepped in. My heart pounded in my throat as the car descended and I wondered if we would all make the trip back up when this was over. Hendricks took my hand and squeezed it reassuringly. I gave him a grateful glance. His face was neutral, but I saw a touch of anxiety in his green eyes. I looked around the elevator car at the rest of my family and wondered if they were as terrified as I was.

Judging by the way they all stared at their feet, I thought maybe they were.

The elevator stopped and the door slid open on a small steel-walled room with another steel door and a badge scanner. On the door was a red and black sign that read DANGER NO ACCESS.

"How many people have access to this room, Teddy?" Hendricks asked. He still had to raise his voice; down here the constant loud hum of machinery had been replaced by the unmistakable sound of a roaring waterfall. We were deep in the bowels of the massive mill, dozens of feet underground.

"Just Don Smith, the facilities director. They gave me special access for today's excursion. The bosses don't want anybody down here exploring. Liability reasons." Teddy scanned his badge and opened the door, and we followed him into the turbine pit.

This was a massive room carved out of the sandstone banks of the Bourbon River. It was cold and damp and felt a little like a cave. The massive room was lit by a series of sodium lamps suspended from the ceiling. I saw the steel beams Teddy had mentioned; they had been placed at perpendicular angles to the original old-growth oak beams for maximum strength. *Nothing is collapsing in here, even if the river floods, I thought.*

The waterfall sound came from one end of the room. Water rushed through a canal about four feet wide and who knew how deep that had been dug into the dirt floor toward a twenty-foot-high wooden waterwheel. The wheel was attached to a thick steel shaft that poked through a hole in one wall; I guessed it connected to more machinery in another room. The bottom of the wheel was submerged in the canal, although the wheel did not move despite the strong current.

I feel like I'm standing right in Paul Hughes' photo of Jack, I thought. I could see exactly where Jack had stood to have his picture taken all those years ago. I could also see why he was so proud to work here; the engineering behind grinding wheat into flour was truly impressive. "Mimi, where did Jack hide those bank bags?" I asked.

Mimi beelined for the huge wheel. She stepped gingerly across a warped board that served as a makeshift bridge across the canal (my heart stopped for a second watching her), ducked under the wheel's shaft, then disappeared behind the wheel. "Back here," she called.

We followed her, all careful not to go tumbling into the canal as we traversed the rickety board bridge. We found Mimi standing next to a thick wooden door set into the sandstone wall behind the waterwheel. She pointed. "In there."

"Of course," Teddy said as he pulled a keyring out of his pants pocket. "This is the room where we stored tools back when this wheel was functional." He selected a key and used it to unlock the door. That was the easy part; both Hendricks and Kieran had to put their backs into getting the door open. Finally the rusty hinges gave and the door opened with a plaintive screech.

Hendricks turned on his flashlight and we all gathered around the open door. There they were: eight heavy-duty canvas bank bags piled in a corner of the tiny closet-like room and covered in mold.

"Holy shit," Kieran whispered.

"There it is." I matched my brother's tone.

"It actually exists," Hendricks said. "It's real. I can't —"

"And now it's mine." A new voice made us all jump and turn around. The beam of Hendricks' flashlight landed squarely on Edison, Morgan, and Nicholas Faust, along with my mother, standing on the far side of the room where the canal emptied into a tunnel that led back to the Bourbon River.

"What the hell, Jesse, I thought someone was supposed to let us know they were coming!" I hissed.

"They were," he replied through clenched teeth. He pressed a button on his shoulder walkie and told Sergeant Rooney in a low voice that the Fausts had arrived. He listened briefly and then said, "Tailrace." Another pause, and then: "Deal with Lawson later. The current situation is a bit more urgent. Over."

He glanced at me and nodded; Sergeant Rooney's team was in place. Edison didn't know it yet, but he was surrounded. *Assuming Lawson is paying attention at the tailrace,* I thought.

Edison, eyes wild, had an old wood-gripped silver revolver in his hand. Morgan, his scarred face indifferent, held my mother's upper arms tightly. Nicholas looked like he would rather be anywhere else. My mother's eyes were clear and triumphant, and she gave me a quick wink.

Hendricks held his flashlight steady with his left hand as he slowly unholstered his own gun with his right.

I didn't even think. I just acted — just like the old Raegan would do as she chased down the truth for readers of the Minneapolis News & Review. I walked away from my family, crossed the rickety bridge, and strode toward the Fausts.

"Raegan! What are you doing?" My brother called after me in a muted voice.

"Fuck," I heard Hendricks mutter, and his flashlight went dark.

I stopped a few feet from the Fausts and looked Edison dead in the eye. "You killed Jack Hughes."

Edison blinked and let the hand holding the gun fall to his side. "Prove it," he sneered.

I gave him my sweetest, most infuriating Irish girl smile. "Oh. I can."

His nostrils flared, making him look like some deranged, pointy-nosed horse. I had to bite my lip to suppress a giggle.

"You've been a busy man." I held up a hand and ticked off on my fingers as I talked. "Myrtle Conley, nineteen sixty-four. Started young, didn't you Edison? Lewis Porter, Junior, nineteen sixty-five. Elaine Faust, nineteen seventy-two."

My mother blinked at the mention of Elaine's name.

"Speaking of Elaine," Hendricks chimed in; he had moved up beside me and had his gun trained on Edison. "She had an aunt in North Dakota."

I fake gasped. "That's right, Jesse, she sure did."

Edison's eyes turned ugly.

"A very wealthy aunt she was very close to. Isn't that right, Jesse?"

"Sure is, Raegan."

"The aunt died under mysterious circumstances in nineteen seventy-one. And guess who inherited the aunt's money after Elaine passed away six months later," I said.

"It doesn't take a rocket scientist to figure it out," Hendricks said.

"You two jokers have no fucking idea what you're talking about," Edison sneered.

I ignored him and went on. "Frank Barnale, nineteen seventy-eight. Any of this ringing a bell?"

Edison gave me a look that suggested he was thinking of eleven different ways to torture me to death.

"Pearl Christensen, nineteen seventy-eight," my mother added.

I blinked. "What?"

"What?" Mimi echoed. I hadn't realized she and the rest of my family were standing right behind me until she spoke.

"Edison ran Pearl off the Third Avenue Bridge with his car," Danielle said. "You were right the entire time, Mom – her death was no suicide."

I was glad I wasn't on the receiving end of the look Mimi gave Edison. "You son of a bitch." Her voice was calm but tight with anger.

Edison said nothing.

"Where was I?" I asked. "Oh, right. Chester Lange, nineteen eighty-one. He put you in the hospital, and while you were there you tried to steal a little redheaded baby."

My mother blinked and looked at my dad, who nodded. Her eyes widened as she made the connection to Kieran's eventful birth.

"Pamela Lange, just a month or so later. You killed her father, then killed her and tossed her body in the Bourbon River like a piece of trash.

"Shortly after that you pretended to be an investments guy and stole a bunch of money from a bunch of people. You did some federal time, but that's cold comfort for the family of Robert Martin, isn't it? You took every penny that poor man had, and he killed himself. That was – when was that, Jesse?"

"Nineteen eighty-seven," Hendricks said, his gun still aimed at Edison's head.

Edison blinked, his face still passive.

"Right," I said. "You got out and managed not to kill anybody else after you met and married Simone Rich, millionaire divorcée and proprietor of local headshop Hippie Chick. That is, until Laura Faust needed to be dispatched because you wanted Nicholas and she was in the way. She was *always* in the way."

Nicholas' face changed at the mention of his mother. What I had to say next was going to rock his world.

"Nicholas, Morgan killed your mom at the street festival with succinylcholine." Simone had called it *sux* in her diary. "The same stuff you were supposed to kill me with the night we met. Your mom's diabetes was the perfect cover for the needle puncture mark on her arm."

All color drained from Nicholas' face, and for a panicky second I thought he was going to faint. Instead, bands of fire appeared on his cheekbones and he turned to Morgan. "You—you motherfucker."

Morgan didn't react at all; he simply held my mother by the upper arms and stared off into space. *Something is seriously wrong with that guy,* I thought.

Nicholas stepped around Morgan and went to his grandfather. "What the fuck!" he shouted. The fire had spread from his cheeks to his eyes. I recognized *this* Nicholas; this was the one who had nearly killed me at Ainsley Mansion a week ago.

"You didn't need *her*," Edison spat. "You needed *me*. You're going to be a rich man, and you have *me* to thank."

For a second I thought Nicholas was going to haul off and hit his grandfather. Normally I would not have advocated for physical violence against the elderly, but in this scenario it seemed perfectly appropriate. Instead he got right into Edison's face, nose to nose, and said, "The only thing I have to thank you for is a wasted fucking life." He planted his hands on Edison's bony chest and shoved, sending the old man teetering backward, arms pinwheeling. Nobody moved even an inch to help him. Edison kept his footing, but just barely.

Then Nicholas did something that truly did surprise me; he crossed the room and stood about a dozen feet away from Kieran. Not too close, but close enough to send his grandfather an unmistakable message: *I stand on the side of good now.*

I glanced at my mother. She was positively beaming, as if one of her own children had done something she was so proud of. It seemed they'd formed a friendship while she was held captive at the Fortress. He didn't have his own mother anymore, and I was strangely glad I could share mine with him for a little while. Even if the circumstances were beyond unbelievable.

Nicholas' defection clearly enraged Edison, but he kept his composure. For the time being.

"Now, where was I?" I pretended to think, then leveled my gaze on Morgan. "Oh, that's right. Before Laura there was Ray Schuster. Nineteen ninety-seven."

"Everyone loved him, you bastard," Kieran said, scowling. The Ray Schuster incident had deeply traumatized him and was the primary reason he'd left Minnesota as soon as he graduated from high school.

"Don't forget about the bank robberies," Hendricks reminded me, his gun still trained on Edison.

"Oh, that's right. There were a couple of those, weren't there? You know, they say that bank robbery is a victimless crime, but that wasn't the case for your first one, was it, Edison? Frank Barnale died as a result of that robbery."

"Just like I told you he would," my mother chimed in.

"Which was a very helpful thing, Danielle. That's how I knew your…ability…was different from your mother's," Edison said, smiling smugly. "I never did get the chance to properly thank you."

My mother rolled her eyes.

"I believe I've heard just about enough," Edison said. He stepped up next to my mother, cocked the hammer on his revolver, and pressed the barrel against her left temple. She winced.

My heart plummeted to my feet and I suddenly couldn't breathe.

"Don't do it, Edison," Hendricks warned. He took a step forward and retrained his service pistol on Edison's head.

"I will be taking that gold," Edison announced. "If anyone so much as lifts a finger to stop me, she dies. Make no mistake."

Does he even realize how heavy gold is? I wondered. *It's not like he can just walk out with eight big bank bags full of it. Especially without Nicholas to help.*

I glanced at Nicholas; his eyes were wide and panicked. Suddenly he turned and rushed toward Kieran. At first I thought he'd had another change of heart and was fixing to take my brother down. Instead he grabbed Kieran's hardhat right off his head, then wound up and threw it like a pro quarterback. He threw it hard and his aim was true; the white helmet with the blue General Mills logo on it shot through the air and hit Edison's forearm with a *smack*. The old man cried out in surprise (Or was it pain? Both, if I was lucky) and dropped the revolver.

Instinct took over. I went for the gun and scooped it up. While Morgan was distracted watching me do that, my dad went to my mom and pulled her away from Morgan and into the safety of our family group. I squared up and aimed the old silver revolver at Morgan. He blinked and held his hands up.

Hendricks kept his gun pointed at Edison as he pushed the button on his radio. Then he said, "It's over, Edison."

Edison sneered. "That's what you think."

"No, it really is over," I said. "You know, it takes a pretty smart person to leave a trail of destruction as long and wide as yours and somehow manage to avoid accountability for almost everything." I feigned intense interest. "How did you do it? You could teach a masterclass on how to commit crimes and get away with it."

Edison met my gaze. He was supremely confident that his safety net would be there for him, like it had been most of his life.

"Nobody's that lucky," I said. "You kept receipts. You had highly damaging information on key members of government and law enforcement, and you used it to keep them in their place. They formed a protective little bubble around you, didn't they? You were free to terrorize the people of River Junction and never had to worry about getting caught." I smiled. "Until now."

"It didn't take much to get Pat Erickson singing like a canary," Hendricks added.

The old man's wrinkled face went slack with shock. His lips moved as if he were trying to speak but couldn't find the right words.

"I would like to add that Officer Jesse here has the combination to your safe," my mother chimed in.

I grinned triumphantly at Edison. "So. Like I said. It's over for you."

Edison's face was so pale it was almost gray. Morgan still looked indifferent. That is, until Sergeant Rooney and three members of his team — all wearing black tactical gear — entered the room. Then his eyes widened with fear.

"Edison Faust, Morgan Faust, Nicholas Faust, you are under arrest for felony kidnapping," Rooney announced. He recited the Miranda warning as his officers placed all three Fausts in handcuffs. This was a highly satisfying sight — one I had been waiting my entire life to witness. My entire family seemed to be enjoying the spectacle.

Hendricks holstered his gun and handed a scrap of paper to Rooney. "Here's the safe combination," he said. "I know for a fact that there's evidence tying him to Jack Hughes' murder in that house."

"There's a lovely scarab pin in Edison's safe, and it proves he was in Jack's house," I added. "Her sister can testify that the pin belonged to Arlene and it disappeared when Jack died. And the murder weapon — with Jack's blood still all over it — is under the bed in the master bedroom."

"Check the bedside table drawer in the farthest bedroom," my mom added. "Edison's last wife kept a very helpful diary."

"Which corroborates everything," I finished.

Edison had recovered enough to find his voice. "This is an outrage!" he howled. "That was all obtained illegally by a woman who went through my stuff without permission! My lawyer will have the River Junction police for breakfast! I'll be out of jail within twenty-four hours!"

"I think you fail to realize how serious the kidnapping charges are," Hendricks said. "You took Danielle from Minneapolis and held her captive in your house in River Junction. That's more than enough for a search warrant."

Edison glowered.

"You're looking at twenty years just for the kidnapping," Hendricks continued. "That's a life sentence for a man of your advanced age."

"Let's go," Rooney said. His officers guided the Fausts toward the door.

Nicholas stopped. "Wait. I need to say something."

The officer assigned to him glanced at Rooney, who nodded.

Nicholas approached me. His hands were cuffed behind his back, but my heart jumped anyway and my hand involuntarily covered my throat. My mom moved next to me and wrapped an arm around my waist.

Nicholas' beautiful black eyes brimmed with sadness and regret. My own eyes welled up in response.

"Raegan, I just…" He stopped and took a deep breath. "I'm just so fucking sorry."

The tears overflowed and spilled down my cheeks.

"I'm sorry I let my grandfather come between us. I loved the hell out of you. I still do. I probably always will." He took a shaky breath. "I hope someday you can find it in your heart to forgive me."

I swallowed and nodded. "Thank you," I whispered.

"And Dani, thank you for being so kind to me. Having you around was almost like I had my mom back." His voice cracked.

My mom smiled through her tears and rubbed his upper arm with her gloved hand. "You did good, Nicholas. You did the right thing. I'm so proud of you."

"Let's go," the officer said impatiently.

Nicholas nodded and turned away. He threw a final defeated glance back at Hendricks and said, "Take care of her, man. She's special."

"I know," Hendricks replied, stone-faced.

And then Fausts disappeared from our lives forever.

CHAPTER 30

"So, ah, what happens to the gold?"

We had all forgotten that Teddy Campbell was still there. He had stayed back by the storage room behind the waterwheel, probably to make sure nothing would happen to Jack's gold during our tense confrontation with the Fausts.

Hendricks keyed into his radio and called for a crime scene team to come get the gold and process the turbine room and tool closet for any potential evidence. Then he said, "The gold is evidence in Jack's murder."

"And after that?" Teddy's eyes were hopeful.

"After everything is resolved the gold will be released to Jack's family. That would be his brother Paul."

Disappointment fell over Teddy's face like a curtain.

"I'm sorry, man. Especially after everything you've done to help us."

Teddy sighed. "A man can dream. When do you think Colleen will get her sister's scarab pin back?"

"If Edison and Morgan ever go to trial for killing Jack, Arlene's pin will be a key piece of evidence," Hendricks said. "Unfortunately that means we have to hang on to it until there's a resolution in Jack's case. I'm really sorry, Teddy."

Teddy sighed and nodded. "That's all right, I guess. Colleen will be happy to know it's safe. She wants to see that crazy old bastard held to account for what he did to Jack, so she'll be okay waiting a little longer to get the pin back if that's what it takes."

My dad wrapped his arms around my mom's shoulders and looked around at the rest of us. "Time to go back to the surface, folks," he said. "What do you say?"

We all thought that was a great idea.

∞

The short ride back to Hendricks' house was quiet. I stared out the window, preoccupied with the idea that I didn't have to look over my shoulder anymore. That my mom was home for good. That maybe it was time to get the help I needed to kick my alcohol habit once and for all.

The future looked brighter than it ever had, and it sort of terrified me.

Hendricks broke the silence. "You okay?"

I sighed. "Yeah. Just a little overwhelmed, I guess."

"I bet."

He didn't press me for more. I resumed staring out the window as he drove. *I can live anywhere I want now without fear. My condo downtown is trashed, and I really don't want to go back there, or to that life. I can't stay at my dad's forever, especially now that Mom's home. Where should I go?*

An idea struck. "Hey. Can you turn around?"

Hendricks glanced at me uncertainly. "Uh, sure. Why?"

"I want to see the Ainsley Mansion."

"Okay." Confused but willing to humor me, Hendricks made three left turns to circle a block and got back on Greenhaven

Road heading west. He turned onto Bridge Street, turned again onto River Street, and parked in front of the Ainsley Mansion's rusty old wrought iron gate. The sun winked through gaps in the leafy canopy formed by old oaks and maples.

I opened the passenger door and got out of the truck, then went to inspect the gate. The Fausts had broken the old padlock when they brought my dad here two weeks ago, and it hadn't been replaced. The chain was wrapped around the end picket of each gate to tie them together, and a stick pushed through some of the links held it closed.

"Now that's what I call security," Hendricks joked as he came up behind me.

I pulled the stick out and unwound the chain, then pushed the gate open and started walking down the long driveway.

Hendricks jogged to catch up to me. "What's going on here?" he asked.

"I have an idea," I said.

He didn't say any more, just followed me through the hole where the front door of my family's two-story Greek Revival mansion used to be. I stood in the soaring foyer and looked around. My great-great-grandfather Bernard Ainsley had been forced to uproot his family in the late 1930s and move to Minneapolis, leaving the mansion to sit empty for eighty years. It was nothing but a shell now.

I wondered if I could make this my home.

I must have wondered out loud, because Hendricks replied, "You are out of your mind. Do you have any idea how much it would cost to make this place livable?"

I went to a wall and ran my gloved hand over solid wood lath where the plaster had crumbled away. "It has good bones," I said.

"It also has old plumbing, old electrical, a bad boiler, a bad roof, no kitchen appliances, no air conditioning, no windows, no doors, and who knows what kind of shape the foundation and the fireplace are in. Don't waste your money."

The more he talked, the more convinced I became that I wanted – no, I *needed* – to breathe new life into the Ainsley Mansion. "This is where I'm supposed to be," I said.

Hendricks closed his eyes and pinched the bridge of his nose. Then he blinked and looked at me with wide eyes. "You could move in with me."

I frowned, surprised. "What?"

He took my hands. "I've never met anyone like you, Raegan. You're brilliant, you're kind, you're maddeningly stubborn…and you love harder than anyone I've ever known. When I wake up in the morning and you're there with me, I wonder what I did to deserve you."

My heart pounded and my tongue stuck to the roof of my mouth.

He held my gaze, his green eyes alight. "After Amanda died, I was sure I would never love again. But I do, Raegan. I love you. I knew I loved you the second you offered to help solve the Mia and Isabel Masterson case. These last two weeks have been crazy and awesome, and even though two weeks isn't a very long time, I already cannot imagine my life without you in it. I –" Emotion caught his voice; he breathed deep and tried again. "I would really like for us to do this life together."

My eyes took in every inch of his handsome face as he talked, and I finally realized: it was time to let Nicholas go and forgive myself for wasting all those years waiting for him. *No more looking back*, I thought. *Only looking ahead.* I had so many good years left, and I wanted to spend every single one of them with this wonderful human. More than anything. I stepped into him, wrapped my arms tight around his toned midsection, and laid the side of my head against his chest. "I love you too," I said, tears percolating behind my eyelids. His heart beat steady and strong in my ear.

He enveloped me in his warm arms, and we stood like that for a long time. When he pulled back and I turned my head to look at him, he cradled my face in his warm hands and kissed me. Visions of happy us bloomed behind my eyelids and fire coursed through my veins. When we separated he asked, "So, what do you say about moving in with me?"

I wiped my eyes and grinned. "Sure. I'll live with you while I'm rehabbing this place."

Hendricks chuckled and shook his head. "Like I said. Stubborn."

"And then, when it's finally fit for human habitation, you can move in with me."

"Deal."

∞

Hendricks and I got back to my family's rental just as Kieran was loading bags into the back of my dad's SUV.

"You coming back with us?" Kieran asked.

I shook my head. "I'm going to stay with Jesse tonight. We've got some things to wrap up."

Kieran extended his hand to Hendricks. "Thanks, man. For everything. I feel like we owe you big time."

Hendricks shook Kieran's hand. "You don't owe me anything. I'm glad it all worked out."

Mimi came out of the house carrying a paper grocery bag. "Let's not leave the food behind!" she said merrily. She walked as if an enormous weight had been lifted from her shoulders: spine straight, shoulders back, easy smile on her careworn face. I'd never seen this Mimi before. I liked her a lot.

She gave the bag to Kieran and turned to me, arms outstretched. "Well, kiddo, we did it."

I hugged her tight. "Yeah, we did. I'm so glad you get to experience life without the Fausts in it." Tears threatened again, so I changed the subject. "Can I ask you a question?"

Mimi stepped back. "Of course, love."

"Who owns the Ainsley Mansion?"

Mimi's white eyebrows shot up. "Well, I do. Before he died my grandfather Bernard set up a trust for my mother Grace, specifically for the abandoned house. I think he wanted to make sure it stayed in the family even if we couldn't live in it. My mother inherited it when he died. She turned around and did the same thing: put the house in a trust for me and Pearl. We inherited it when Mother died. Pearl is gone, so that makes me the owner."

"What are you going to do with it?" I asked.

Mimi tilted her head. "I haven't thought much about it, to be honest. Why do you ask?"

"Would you sell it to me?" I asked.

Mimi frowned. "Oh, Raegan, the place is a disaster. Abandoned for eighty years. Why on earth would you want to buy it?"

"That's what I said," Hendricks chimed in, earning himself a smack on the sternum.

"Because I believe it can be saved. And I like this little town. Now that the Fausts are gone, I want to live here. In my family's house."

Mimi studied my face for several excruciating seconds. Then: "Well, I can't say I see the wisdom in this plan, but if you want the house, it's yours."

Relieved, I smiled and hugged her again. "We'll figure out the details over the next couple of weeks," I said, giddily thinking about attorneys and real estate agents and loans and general contractors.

My parents emerged holding hands, and my dad gave Hendricks the house key. "Here you go, Jesse. Tell Mike we say thank you." Then he too extended his hand. "And I want to thank *you*. For everything."

Hendricks shook his hand and accepted hugs from my mom and Mimi. "Of course," he said. His entire head blushed a bright pink.

I hugged my family and told them I would see them the next day. Then Hendricks and I watched as they piled into my dad's SUV and waved as they drove away.

We spent the evening relaxing and talking about our future.

Maybe, with Hendricks by my side, it wasn't so terrifying after all.

Monday, July 26, 2021

CHAPTER 31

The day dawned cloudy and humid, the precursor to a few days of badly-needed rain. It made me want to burrow into Hendricks' bed and stay there all day.

Until I smelled Beananza dark roast. Only then did I roll out of bed, throw on a pair of capri leggings and my KISS ME I'M IRISH t-shirt, and make my way to the kitchen.

Hendricks already had a mug waiting for me on the table, where he sat scrolling through his phone. He wore a pair of chinos and a green polo that made his eyes even greener. "Good morning, sunshine."

I dropped into a chair and took my first glorious sip. "Mmmm. Good morning."

"Sleep all right?"

"Like the dead," I said. It was true; I couldn't remember when I'd last slept so soundly. "Knowing the Fausts are in custody probably helped. I didn't have to sleep with one eye open."

He downed the last bit of coffee in his cup and stood. "I'm going to the station. I'll call you with any updates."

"Okay," I said. "I'm going over to my dad's house for a while. Check in with the fam."

He leaned over and kissed me. "I love you."

My heart soared, and I smiled. "I love you more."

∞

I picked up a dark roast to go from Beananza on my way out of town and left the radio off as I drove. After the chaos of the last three weeks, it was nice to just sit in relative quiet and let my mind wander while the windshield wipers kept time.

I couldn't believe how much had happened. On the Fourth of July I was Raegan O'Rourke, rockstar investigative reporter for the Minneapolis News and Review newspaper. My job title and career suggested a much more fulfilling life than I actually had. When I wasn't working I lived like a hermit in my downtown Minneapolis condo. I had a serious drinking problem, I hadn't seen my mother in over thirty years, and Edison Faust was a very real and constant threat in my life. Not to mention I was in love with Edison's grandson and had convinced myself I was going to get the fairytale ending.

Looking back now, I realized I wasn't really living. I was just existing. Always waiting for something to happen to me, never inclined to make things happen for myself. My life was overdue for a shakeup, and it came in the form of my neighbors' elderly cocker spaniel, Baxter. It was his unfortunate demise that sent me up north to Wanderer's Resort on Catclaw Lake to see if I could use my touch to give my neighbors Aaron and Kellie the answers they weren't getting from law enforcement after their little cabin burned down. Little did I know that sweet Baxter would send my life down a new and exciting path.

After I helped Kabetogama County Sheriff Chad Overton finally bring the Catclaw Kids case to a resolution, I realized I had a knack and a passion for investigating cold cases and, for the first time in I didn't know how long, decided to make a change. I quit my job at the newspaper – much to the chagrin of my boss, editor Todd Waterman – and made plans to strike out on my own as a private investigator. I didn't expect my first case as an independent to come along so quickly, nor did I expect it would come as a result of an Edison Faust attack on my family. It was weird to think I had that crazy old man to thank for bringing Hendricks and me together.

We made quick work of solving the eleven-year-old disappearance of Mia Masterson and her newborn daughter Isabel, and along the way we realized we made a good team – both personally and professionally. He was there after Nicholas tried to kill me. When my mom came home and Edison attacked again, he was there for every step of the sordid journey that followed. I doubted we could have nailed the Fausts for Jack Hughes' murder and found the long-lost gold without him.

On the Fourth of July, the idea that anyone other than Nicholas Faust could possibly be the love of my life would have been absurd. Now, just three weeks later, the idea that it could be anybody other than Jesse Hendricks was unthinkable.

How quickly perspective can change when you let it, I thought. *Jesse's right, I am way too stubborn.*

I pulled into my dad's driveway and went inside. I heard laughter and conversation coming from the sunroom at the back of the house. The sound of unrestrained laughter was so foreign that for a second I thought I must have accidentally entered the wrong house. I followed the joyful sounds.

"Raegan!" Kieran called when he saw me. "We were wondering when you were going to show your face."

I grinned and sat in a cushioned chair. "I'm here now, aren't I?"

"What's the latest from Jesse?"

I shrugged. "Haven't heard from him yet. He said he'd call when he had an update."

We chatted about how different we felt knowing we were actually, really, truly free from the constant threat of the Fausts. "I hardly know what to do," Mimi said. "I can go to the supermarket without worrying that I might be run down in the parking lot!"

"I can drive to and from the office without constantly checking my mirrors to see if I'm being followed," Liam added.

"I can live in the same house as my husband!" Danielle quipped, and we all laughed. The relief in our voices was palpable, bordering on hysteria. We would all have to relearn how to live – and as great as it sounded, the task was daunting.

"Oh," Danielle said as she pulled the glove off her left hand. "Here's Grace's ring back, Mom." She slipped the ring off and set it in Mimi's palm. "I don't think we'll be needing them anymore."

I followed suit, and when Mimi had Grace's rings in her hand, she closed her gloved fingers over them protectively. "I knew she would come through for us," she said, her eyes shining. "I knew she wouldn't let Edison Faust have the last word."

We pondered this in silence while my mom and I pulled our gloves back on, and then I remembered something I'd been meaning to ask but hadn't had the chance to. "Mom, something's been bothering me."

"What's that, honey?"

"When the Fausts came here on Thursday to take you away, you didn't warn us they were coming. Wouldn't you have been able to see that with your future touch?"

My mom sighed. "I might have, once. I discovered during my time at the Fortress that my future touch doesn't work anymore."

Mimi frowned. "At all?"

"Not at all." Danielle shook her head. "I worked very hard to suppress my touch while I was in seclusion. I guess I was a little too successful."

"Your past touch still works, right?" I asked.

"Yes, that works fine."

Mimi thought about this for a moment, then said, "I think that just means that the past touch is innate in us Ainsley women now. Coded into our DNA. The future touch was an effect of mercury poisoning in utero, and it must not have been permanent. It went away when you stopped using it, like the side effects of a medication."

"I'm glad," my mom said. "My future touch caused so much trouble. I prefer the standard, run-of-the-mill past touch, thank you very much."

We all chuckled and my dad slipped an arm around her shoulders. I was so glad they would have the opportunity to live the rest of their lives together.

"I talked to Annie a bit ago," Kieran said. "She sends her love."

"You're probably dying to get home," I said.

He nodded. "I'll be on the first flight back to Eugene tomorrow morning." He paused, then: "You know, spending these last couple of weeks with my family has been really good for me, even if it has been under crazy and rather dangerous circumstances. I've felt almost…normal. I would —" His voice faltered, and he took a few seconds to compose himself. "I, ah, I would have missed a lot if I'd gone home with Annie."

My mom's eyes brimmed with tears.

"I think it might be time for us to come back to Minnesota. I feel a lot safer here now that the Fausts are out of the picture."

"That would be wonderful, Kieran," Mimi said.

My mom went to Kieran and hugged him fiercely. They were interrupted by the buzzing of Kieran's phone. My mom finally let him go so he could answer it.

"This is Kieran." A pause as he listened. "Hey Paul, how are —" Another pause, then: "Oh, he did? What did he —" He listened some more, and a huge grin lit his freckled face. "That's great news, Paul! I'm so glad. You deserve it." Naked horror filled his pale blue eyes. "Oh, no, we couldn't accept that. We're just glad it's going back where it belongs." He paused, listening. "All right, Paul, that sounds good. Thanks for calling." Kieran ended the call and looked at all of us with wide eyes. "That was Paul Hughes. Jesse called to tell him that Edison and Morgan Faust have been arrested and Jack's gold found. He was very emotional."

"I can only imagine," Mimi said.

"He wants to give some of the gold to us, to thank us for our help. I tried to tell him no, but he wouldn't hear it."

"Oh, my lord," Mimi gasped. "Absolutely not!"

"He insists. He even went so far as to tell me he would be very hurt if we didn't accept it. He'll be in touch after everything is resolved."

"Plenty of time to talk him out of it," my dad said with a wry smile.

We laughed and talked into the noon hour. My mom captivated us with stories of her adventures in the Fortress; they added context to the seemingly random things I'd seen through her eyes, and the visions she'd had corroborated the information in RJPD's case files.

Other details, like how easy it was to break out of her room thanks to an improperly installed doorknob, sent us into hysterics. My dad laughed until tears ran down his cheeks. "What a bunch of noobs" were the only words he could choke out between guffaws.

My phone buzzed. I stepped out of the sunroom and into the kitchen so I wouldn't interrupt Danielle's description of the Fortress' solarium. It was Hendricks. I sat at the kitchen table and accepted the call. "Hey."

"Hey, yourself." He sounded like he was in a good mood.

"How's it going?"

"There's been a lot of activity around here in the wake of the Fausts' arrest. Captain Bailey called a meeting of the brass first thing this morning. Sheriff Connelly, Chief Briggs, Captain Smalls, ands DA Lonergan were in there for hours."

I knew Greg Smalls was Sarah Bailey's counterpart on the investigations side, and Carter Rooney's boss.

"They're trying to decide how to handle the Fausts, given Edison's sordid history with the RJPD and GCSO," he went on. "My money's on they're going to turn the case over to the BCA."

This made sense to me. Nothing that came out of the River Junction Police Department or Greenhaven County Sheriff's

Office would ever make it into a trial; too many conflicts of interest. Handing Jack Hughes' murder, along with all of Edison's other crimes, over to the state Bureau of Criminal Apprehension was the right thing to do. The agency would be able to objectively investigate and build a case against him.

I made a mental note to call Todd Waterman and offer to cover the Edison Faust story for the Minneapolis News and Review. Freelance, of course. *Nobody else is going to have the inside scoop like I do,* I thought, seeing dollar signs.

"Bailey and her Minneapolis counterpart already punted your mom's kidnapping over to the BCA," Hendricks said. "Agents have been at the Fortress since six o'clock this morning executing that search warrant. So far I hear they've taken Edison's safe, the bloody beam, and his computer. I guess it's just a matter of time before all of these separate cases become one."

"Let's pretend this all goes the way we want it to," I said, knowing it all might not. This was an extremely complex case – or series of cases – and Edison had the money to hire a good defense team. "What kind of charges do you think they'll face?"

"We already have them on felony kidnapping. Beyond that, if I had a say I'd look at charging Edison and Morgan first degree and second degree murder going all the way back to Myrtle Conley in nineteen sixty-four. There's no statute of limitations on murder."

"If there's enough evidence," I said.

"Right, of course. I'm sure Minneapolis will want a piece of them for Ray Schuster and your aunt Pearl. I know McKenzie County, North Dakota is itching for a shot at Edison for Catherine Parkay. And I'm sure the FBI will be intensely interested to learn more about the two bank robberies in seventy-eight and eighty-three." He paused. "You should know that Nicholas Faust will likely see third degree assault charges for attacking you at the Ainsley Mansion. That's a max five year sentence."

My eyebrows drew together as I pondered this. Five years for hurting me on top of twenty for kidnapping my mom. What a tragedy. "I doubt he'll fight any of it," I said.

"So here's what it all comes down to, brass tacks. Edison Faust will likely be charged for the following murders." Hendricks sounded like he was reading from a script. "Myrtle Conley, Lewis Porter, Elaine Faust, Frank Barnale, Chester Lange, and Pamela Lange. Edison and Morgan will both certainly face charges for Jack Hughes' murder, and brass is talking about reopening the Laura Faust case as well.

"The BCA will investigate all and prosecutors – either from a different county or the state attorney general – will decide what charges to bring based on the evidence. Patrick Erickson will be a key witness, I'm sure. Edison already served federal time for that Ponzi scheme, so there won't be any further action on Robert Martin's death."

I breathed deep and blew the air out between pursed lips. "Wow."

"But it sort of doesn't matter what happens with all of that, because the Fausts fucked up when they came to your dad's house and took your mom. That was the stupidest thing they could have possibly done."

"And having her didn't end up helping them anyway," I said and told him the latest on Danielle's future touch. "She just sent them on a big pointless spelunking expedition while she snooped around their house."

This made Hendricks laugh, which in turn made me laugh. "What a bunch of noobs," Hendricks managed between giggles, echoing my dad exactly. I wanted to hug him through the phone.

"Oh, shit, I almost forgot," Hendricks said. "I can't believe I almost forgot!"

"What?" I asked, unsure if I should be excited or alarmed.

"After Captain Bailey's meeting with brass ended, she called me and Carter into her office. You'll never believe what she said."

My breath caught in my throat. "What did she say?"

"I've been promoted to detective."

I screeched. "Are you kidding me? Jesse! That's awesome!"

"It is, but that's not all."

My eyebrows shot up. I caught movement in my peripheral vision and glanced at the door to the sunroom. My entire family stood there, questions all over their faces. I held my pointer finger up in a *please hold* gesture.

"Chief Briggs is so impressed with our work that he made room in this year's budget to make me RJPD's first and only *cold case* detective. I report to Carter Rooney and officially start the new gig next Monday."

I screamed. I couldn't help it. Then I pulled the phone away from my ear and told my family the news. They cheered. I cried.

Hendricks heard it all and laughed. "Rae? You there?"

I shooed my family out of the kitchen and took a deep, shaky breath. "Yes. I'm here." I wiped my eyes with the bottom of my t-shirt. "And I'm so damn proud of you."

"Bailey also said if there's ever another opportunity for you to consult with RJPD, she would be honored to have you."

That meant a lot, and I said so. Now that I had my first repeat client, Icebox Investigations could become a real business venture.

"She thinks the world of you, Rae. You've really impressed her."

"I had a good teacher." We both broke into the kind of giggles that act as a release valve when emotions are high. Where everything's funny, no matter how mundane.

After our giggles dissipated, I said, "I still can't believe it's all over."

"How does it feel to be free?"

"Amazing. For the first time in my life I feel like I have a bright future. And I can't wait to take it on with you by my side."

Silence from the other end of the line.

I pulled my phone from my ear and looked at the screen. Still connected. "Jesse? You there?"

He cleared his throat. "Ah. Yes. I'm here." His voice wavered a bit.

Aw, I think he's crying. "Are you all right?"

"Better than I've ever been. I'll see you tonight. I love you."

"I love you too," I said, and ended the call. I sat and thought for a moment, then scrolled through my contacts looking for a number. I had one more call to make.

"Hey Todd, it's Raegan. Have I got a story for you."

THE END

ACKNOWLEDGMENTS

My undying gratitude goes out to all of my family, friends and colleagues who have offered kind and supportive words throughout my journey. And to my readers, without whom none of this would be possible.

Thank you.

ABOUT THE AUTHOR

Brenda Lyne is the pseudonym of author Jennifer DeVries. Jennifer lives just outside Minneapolis, Minnesota with her two busy kids, two cats, two fish, and probably a partridge in a pear tree. She is living, breathing proof that it is never too late to follow your dreams. *Fool's Gold* is her fifth novel.

ALSO AVAILABLE FROM BRENDA LYNE:

Raegan O'Rourke is a talented investigative reporter with a secret gift: she can touch things and see visions of past events.

Can Raegan use her ability to bring two lost teenagers home – and live to tell about it?

ORDER HERE!

ALSO AVAILABLE FROM BRENDA LYNE:

Raegan O'Rourke teams up with Jesse Hendricks, police officer and aspiring detective, to investigate the case of a missing mother and her baby.

But when her family's feud with the evil Fausts escalates, can she solve the case – **and** protect her family?